FAREWELL LEICESTER SQUARE

By Jon Kilkade

Published by Magic Rat Books

magic.rat.books@googlemail.com

All rights reserved 2015

Copyright: Jon Kilkade 2015

Also available as an e-book.

Chapter One
July 2005

The radio called it a power surge but the tightness in my gut told me different. Call it a journalist's sense of a story, an innate morbidity or just an unpleasant streak of voyeurism, but I knew instantly that something big and deeply horrific was developing.

Of course, I had to know more. I switched on the television set and watched the scene of a block of streets in London. The camera was shaking slightly as the helicopter pilot held the aircraft steady.

There was not a lot to see at first and not much to say: the news anchors were recapping what they had heard. That there had been a number of incidents on the London Underground. There were early reports of a collision or maybe a power surge, but a tremor in the voices which described the scene hinted at the true awfulness of what they were hearing.

I sat and watched. It was not something I would work on. I'd given up the role of staff reporter a year earlier. I was freelancing now and not in London. Maybe I'd write something on it later but my days of chasing ambulances had long since past.

I still had the urge to be the first to tell someone though – even if it had to be only my mum.

I rang her at work, turning the television down as I told her something dreadful had happened in London.

On the screen a London street trembled gently under the airborne lens. It was an area outside a station. King's Cross, I think. People were milling out onto the pavement, stumbling a few yards and then standing still.

One could not see their faces, but their demeanour even from this distance suggested these were people who had seen sights which they could not clear from their minds.

They looked around them, as if startled by the bright fluorescent stripes on the uniforms of the emergency workers who surrounded them.

Or as if they had just arrived in a city they did not recognise.

When the phone rang back it broke through the silence of my thoughts. I grabbed at it.

'Hello?'

I could hear nothing but the television. It was a moment before I realised no-one was speaking down the line.

'Yes, who is this?'

The television was discounting power surges now. It was terrorism, the police were preparing a statement. A government source was saying there were at least 20 dead, according to the banner running across the bottom of the screen.

'Is that Mr Kilkade?' It was an aging, breathless voice. I felt my patience return.

'Yes, it is.'

'It is about the bomber,' he said. I was watching the screen and didn't understand: I felt a shiver down my spine. 'I have heard about your search.'

I did not say anything. I knew his hesitancy was simply due to his drawing on his breath. But, although he sounded frail, there was a steadiness in his voice which suggested he knew exactly what he wanted to say.

'I wasn't going to call,' he said. 'But then I saw all this, on the television. It brought it all back. It should be told.'

I had finally caught up with him now. The bomber, yes. But what had my little pieces of writing got to do with all *this*?

'I'd very much like to know,' I said.

'That is good,' he said, as if finally letting down a huge weight. 'Because I really do have a story to tell you.'

About a decade earlier I had worked in Milford Haven, a town at the extreme south western corner of Wales. It was a busy little news area and I worked out of an office in the centre of town. Many of the shops around me were empty: Milford had seen better times. But the town sits on one of the largest natural waterways in the world and, since the 1960s, the oil industry has made it one of its main British bases. So news-wise, it was a good patch. There was always something happening at the refineries or in the marina or with the coastguard. I'd normally find something for the weekly front page and a few leads inside.

Even when I left I still had some contacts in the town. I still chatted with them from time to time, mostly by email but sometimes on the phone. My best contact was in his seventies and rang me occasionally for a chat. There wasn't anything I could do with most of the stuff he now passed my way but we both had habits that were hard to break: he liked to share information on something he knew and I liked to listen. One never knows when you are going to hear something very sweet, something saleable.

Tom not only knew most of Milford, having lived there all his life, he also kept an eye out for news by having a scanner which monitored the emergency frequencies.

It had been about two months before that July 7 morning that he had called me with his latest snippet.

'Some boys were doing some scanning over the seabed,' he told me in his strong Pembrokeshire accent and sounding conspiratorial as always. 'They were checking over some pipes or laying some cables or some such. They were going along with their cameras when through the mud and mist and silt they picked up something. Do you know what it was?'

There was normally a question around this point. The fact that I would have to admit I did not know added more weight to the information which followed.

'What?'

'A Second World War bomber.'

'Really? In good shape?'

'I took someone out and had a look myself.' Tom had worked on the tugs. He occasionally picked up extra cash by taking people out on his own boat. 'Very good shape. It's well out, quite deep. Too deep to have been picked at by souvenir hunters and the like.'

'They are like war graves, aren't they? I suppose it happens a lot, doesn't it?'

'Not like this, boy.'

Tom was holding the big stuff back.

I chugged on.

'Is she one of ours or one of theirs?'

'Well, that's a matter of opinion,' Tom stated, satisfied with the bait he was laying out for me. 'And that, boy, is just the start of the mystery.'

5

I was down in west Wales the following week. I'd been going anyway but Tom set me up to meet a friend named Charles.

Tom drove me down onto the docks and along the quayside. He was smoking heavily and even though the rain was lashing the window I was forced to open it a little. I was already feeling sick with the thought of having to head out to sea.

We got out on the quay and Tom pulled the fur-lined collars of his black coat up against the wind. He had been off the tugs for ten years but I noticed now that he was still more nimble on the cluttered deck of his boat, the *Mary-J*, than in the street.

The *Mary-J* was about eight metres long – a lot smaller than I'd expected – and its blue paint had flaked off its sides to reveal the weather-beaten wooden planks which would be carrying me out to sea.

A figure moved in the wheelhouse and came forward into the rain.

'This is Jon," Tom said.

'Hello.'

It was Charles, a London-born Jamaican, who had apparently come to Milford Haven a year ago to study currents and marine life. After chatting in a pub overlooking the docks, he had decided on asking Tom for his help. Charles – as tall and athletic as Tom was short and thickset - was staying with Tom and his wife in their terraced house on the outskirts of town.

Tom pulled on a black fisherman's hat, leaving wisps of white hair poking out at its sides. The skin on his face had been beaten red-raw by years of exposure to the elements.

'We'll get out of this now,' he said, gesturing at the rain. 'Go and see your dead seabird.'

There was a swell in the spring tide which I gradually got used to as we headed out past the oil jetties and into the wide expanse of the haven.

Tom had had the *Mary-J* for 35 years and they had grown alike. They were not only small powerhouses, stronger than their appearance suggested, but they both produced a lot of smoke.

But as Tom sang the same verse of a song for the fourteenth time, we passed St Ann's Head to our starboard and reached the mouth of the haven. It was here in the shadow of the lighthouse that I had stood a decade earlier to report on the grounding of the Sea Empress oil tanker.

The huge ship had proved an eerie sight in the ghostly arc lights of the salvagers: lain across the rocks, helpless, its thick black cargo seeping into the sea, it had seemed like a gigantic beast, floored, beaten, but still dangerous.

I shivered against the cold and picked a little anxiously at a piece of the *Mary-J*'s peeling paintwork. The sea felt huge and heavy and frightening. I began to wonder just how far we were going in our little boat and exactly what it held for me.

Apart from Tom's occasional shout to me - 'You excited, boy?' - which was followed by a deep laugh, we were a quiet bunch on the *Mary-J*.

I was sat behind the wheelhouse, facing forward, my coat wrapped around me, and concentrating on not throwing up. The heavy rain had stopped but there was a fine drizzle on the grey sea which had seeped right through to my skin.

Tom was at the wheel. It was broad in his hands but as he took us out into the ocean he seemed to have become an extension of the *Mary-J* itself. There was no swearing or cursing as a swell took us too much to port or as a wave splashed over the glass: he was in complete control and watching him eased my nerves and my stomach.

Occasionally, he would step back, unlit cigarette in mouth, duck his head down and push his right hand up underneath his coat. There would be a flick of his lighter and then the cigarette would reappear, its end glowing orange.

Charles barely spoke at all. He was entirely preoccupied with the equipment he had stashed just inside the wheelhouse in brown canvas bags and two heavy boxes. He sat close enough to keep his hands on them and the only time he showed much acknowledgement that we were at sea at all was when the waves shifted violently beneath us and he moved his thick legs and huge feet just a few inches.

'Not too keen on this swell, Tom,' he stated after our skipper announced we were coming a-starboard to avoid the mid-channel rocks.

'It's better out in the channel,' the seaman responded without turning from the wheel. 'You mark my words.'

I had my eyes straight ahead, watching Tom working at the wheel and throttle. I looked up and could see clearing skies, not blue but a kind of creamy-white.

'Aye, you'll be alright for your gismos, boy,' Tom stated.

It was another hour before Charles began to undo the straps on some of his bags. I was intrigued to see what he had brought along but the first thing I caught sight of was a simple television screen.

It had stopped drizzling and, steadying myself on the side of wheelhouse, I took a couple of steps forward. Tom had a chart folded at his side. We seemed to be somewhere almost at a midpoint between the Isles of Scilly to the south-east and Cork to the north-west.

'You use the charts,' Tom winked. 'I use the GPS.'

He turned away and Charles joined us in the cabin setting up a 22-inch TV monitor at my side.

'Gismos at the ready, boy,' Tom muttered.

Charles gave me a smile. He was a changed man now. Literally in his element.

'You seen *Titanic*, Jon?'

I nodded, unsure if a response was necessary, then I followed him to the back of the boat. He now had a stainless steel tube in his hand. He held it briefly towards me and a lens flashed in the pale sunshine.

'A drop camera,' he said by way of explanation. 'Lightweight, colour images.'

I could see a cable mounting on top. He attached the camera and checked with Tom before lowering it over the side.

We seemed to be stopped now but I was still disorientated by the swell. The engine was still turning over like an old tractor. I looked around and could see nothing but water; it gave me a sudden sense of panic. I fell back on the old calming method. 'What happens now?' I asked, trying to concentrate on conversation.

'What should happen now is that the camera finds our seabird,' said Charles. 'The camera is connected to that monitor, basically like a security system. I'll show you.'

Charles led me back to the wheelhouse. I could smell Tom's nicotine breath at my shoulder.

The monitor clicked on.

'We have four screens in one, four quarters, see?' said Charles.

I nodded.

'Here, in the top left we will eventually have the sea bed. Top right shows the position of the *Mary-J* as shown by a mapping program. Bottom right: the bow of the *Mary-J*, just to help with the search. Bottom right, depth info. What you are interested in is this quarter.' He indicated the top left. 'This is where we should see our seabird.'

I stood back and let Charles get on.

'Interesting, isn't it, boy?' Tom said.

'So have you seen this?'

Tom nodded slowly, earnestly, although there was a smile behind his eyes.

I gave him a sceptical look.

'Don't listen to what old wives' tales tell you about fishermen and seamen. We deal in facts – charts, weather, weight, displacement.' I smiled but for once he did not smile back. 'And when I say Charles has something, you better listen.'

For a long while I stood there watching Charles and Tom as they debated, argued, speculated and searched the seabed. Twice they thought they had found the shape in the gloom, twice they were disappointed.

Then I heard Tom laugh and cough nosily, his eyes on the screen.

I moved in close to the wheelhouse. I put my hand above my head onto the frame of the door to steady myself. I could see the screens clearly, the shape of the *Mary-J*, the depth figures of the camera, but I could see nothing in the top left-hand screen.

'Ah-ha!' cried Charles. 'See it?'

He turned excitedly. I could still see only a strange infrared world of spiked plants and what I took to be a grey mass of sand and seabed.

I stepped forward.

And then something looked at me from the screen – a large dark eye.

I felt Charles grinning broadly at my side.

The camera moved over another eye and I realised they were the two front widescreen panes of a plane.

'Christ,' I said.

'Christ, indeed, boy,' added Tom.

The camera moved along the side of the fuselage to the wing. I caught a glimpse of an engine.

'It seems so intact,' I said.

'It's two hundred feet down,' stated Charles. 'It's cold, dark, calm. It decays very slowly.' He shrugged his shoulders. 'And, of course, there appears to be very little crash damage.'

'But it is a warplane, right?'

'Hmmm,' Charles said flatly.

'World War Two?'

'Bring it round again for him, Charles,' Tom said.

I watched the camera lose the plane and then find it again.

'I want to check this again,' Charles said to no-one in particular. 'It is remarkable.'

The camera moved back over the aircraft three times as Charles tried to find what he was looking for and when he saw it I saw it too: what appeared to be markings on the side of the tail fin. Six numbers. I tried to read them but couldn't. Charles was close to the screen, scribbling on a pad in front of him.

'Can you make it out?' I said. He didn't answer. I waited and could see some of the markings now myself. The first two letters were certainly 42.

There was a long pause.

'You can identify it?'

'Uh-hu,' Charles replied. 'We have, Jon. But I had to double-check.'

Charles took a folder from one of his bags and laid a clump of papers on the small table space left at the side of the wheelhouse. On the top sheet I could see a photograph of a man with receding dark hair, parted severely at one side. His eyes were dark but pleasant, staring just past the camera; his nose was straight, only a little too long, his lips thin. It was the pose of a man proud of the uniform which was just visible – the black tunic with bright shoulder and lapel flashes. Proud, in particular, of the Knight's Cross medal at his throat. Below the picture were the words *Egon Mayer, Oberstleutnant.*

'One of the Nazi's deadliest fighter pilots of the Second World War,' Charles explained. 'One hundred and two kills. Half of them Spitfires. A brave man: he developed the technique of attacking our bombers head on.' Charles made a gesture of two planes with his hands. 'He shot down 26 four-engine bombers that way.' Charles ruffled through the papers. 'Our seabird is a B-17F, an American Flying Fortress. One hundred and three feet from wing tip to wing tip. Seventy-three feet long. Crew of ten. Ten men who apparently, according to the numbering which can only be made out here, on the tail, were victims of Herr Mayer.'

I looked at the screen, thought about the men who had flown it. *My God, were their bodies still in there, trapped forever in this awful, lonely place?*

Charles was nodding his head gently, thinking about what he was going to say next.

'The records show, and you can find these anywhere, that Mayer shot this particular Flying Fortress down on November 23, 1942.'

He moved through the papers and pursed his lips.

'What I don't understand is that all the records state that this aircraft – this *exact* aircraft – came down in wheat fields on the western coast of France, eighty miles north-east of Bordeaux.'

I looked at Charles, knowing I had a rather foolish look on my face. I felt Tom smiling in my direction, pleased with my response: he had me this time.

There was a moment as I processed what I had heard, making sure what I was about to say was not too stupid.

'Then what is it doing here?' I asked.

'That, my boy,' said Tom, the end of his cigarette a red blaze, 'is a bloody good question.'

I looked at the records myself. Charles was right.

Ego Mayer, *Luftwaffe* ace. Killed in action in March 1944. But before that he had shot down 102 Allied aircraft over western Europe.

I found the November 1942 records too. They tallied with what Charles was saying. But not with the evidence of my own eyes: the aircraft lying at the bottom of the sea in St George's Channel. It had clearly been brought down over France.

I thought there was probably a simple explanation. I was no expert on the tail markers of a B-17 bomber for a start. If one crashed, could another take on the same number?

What about the official records themselves? Were they accurate? I mean they were posted on the internet and everyone knows how untrustworthy that can be.

I made a couple of calls to the Ministry of Defence and then to a United States airforce magazine I also found on the net. The MoD said they would get back to me. The magazine put me in touch with a historian whom I emailed. He checked his records and confirmed this aircraft went down over France. I asked tentatively whether two aircraft could have the same markings on the tail? No, was the answer.

I contacted a monthly military magazine I had written some articles for and explained what I was doing. They said I could do a 4,000-word feature but it would not be published for six or seven months. I did not want to wait.

I wrote a piece for my blog and then for my old local paper. It went in under the headline, *Blogger's web of wartime intrigue.*

No-one came forward with any ideas or information.

I drew a line under it. Figured I would never get an answer, and that the whole thing was just a fuss over nothing anyway.

And then I got the call on July 7.

A few days later I found myself heading down the M4 back into Wales. This time I stopped short of Milford Haven, coming south off the road after Carmarthen and driving down into Laugharne.

I stopped at a shop and asked about the address I had been given by the caller. The house was down on the front, under the castle. I would have spotted it easily if I had driven on.

I parked the car facing out towards the reed covered banks between the town and the muddy flats of the estuary, and walked up to the heavy black front door. There was an old-fashioned bronze knocker.

I waited. There was a small spy-hole in the door. From the outside you could not see anything clearly, but could just make out movement.

Someone came close and then opened the door.

The man looked out into the brightness, nodded his head and smiled.

"Mr Mortain?' I said. 'Jon Kilkade.'

'Mr Kilkade.' His voice was stronger now but was still unmistakeably that of the caller. He took my hand in his. His grip was bony but firm. 'Come in, please.'

He turned, leaning heavily on a walking stick, and moved back down the narrow hallway until we came out into the back garden.

There was a small lawn, a coal shed, some overgrown rose bushes and a hard-standing on which he had laid out two rather tatty-looking green and white striped deckchairs and a fold-down table.

He was a slim man, about my height, just under six feet, and he had a slight stoop. He wore silver-framed spectacles and had wisps of silver-grey hair at the side of his head.

He gestured me to a seat and then he eased himself back into his chair. An overweight King Charles spaniel sat at his feet. It lifted its head briefly in my direction but then shut its eyes again.

From there we could see over the wall to the stone of the castle.

'Did you have a good journey down?' he said. He was being pleasant, but his thoughts were on the old shoebox on the table at his side. 'Yes, thank you. Fine.'

He folded his hands for a moment and looked hard into my eyes.

'You would like to know about the aircraft?'

I nodded. 'Yes.'

He took the box and lifted it into his lap. He handled it as if it were a Ming vase. He took off the lid. I could see black and white photographs, bits of paper and newspaper.

He picked through them, his fingers a little clumsy. I realised his eyes were watering.

He took off his spectacles, rubbed his eyes with his fingers and then looked up into the sky.

I tilted my head slightly, followed his stare.

It was a beautiful July day. The sky was a rich blue, dotted only with the most ethereal wisps of white cloud. It was clean, peaceful, a poet's or an artist's sky.

There was nothing moving in it, although Mortain appeared to be studying something deep in the blue expanse.

It was then that he started to tell me his tale.

Chapter Two
Jersey 1940

No-one really believed their eyes as they watched the first war plane dip its wing, the metal glinting in the sunshine. But there it was: a clear black cross. It stood out, even at five or six hundred feet.

Philip Mortain thought the craft droned like bees in the purple heather across the island at Les Landes. But it was the patterns left by the exhaust which intrigued James, as the monsters – they'd all been taught to think of them as such –contaminated the clear blue sky. The air was filled with the drone of the aircraft coming one way and then the other, clinging to the coast, moving inland. Unchallenged.

James had stopped at the side of the road, his legs either side of the bicycle. The damp palms of his hands clung tightly to the handlebars as he watched two of the aircraft turn south-east in perfect formation and fly back towards the French coast. He wondered if the pilots could see him from there and thought of the times he had stood outside the airport at St Peter's and waved at pilots of De Havilland Rapide's stopping over between Britain and mainland Europe. These, though, were not them and he had read enough of his monthly war magazines to know about the machine guns in their wings.

He started to speak, but his throat was dry.

'Why aren't they shooting at us?' he said at last.

His brother replied without turning to face him. 'They are a reconnaissance flight. Dornier 17s. Just checking us out.'

Philip had his right hand cupped over his eyes, following the two aircraft as they became specks in the distance. Then he lost them. He stared for a little longer but then slowly stepped back off the grass to where he'd thrown down his bike when the aircraft first appeared.

'Do you think they'll come back?'

Philip laughed, pushing James' shoulder playfully. 'I don't suppose we frightened them off, do you, soldier? Not with the way they cut through Holland, Belgium and France. Like a hot knife through butter.'

The heat of the day clung to the land and shimmered on top of the sea. Across to the west Philip could see some tiny boats moving towards the port of St Helier. What had they been thinking when the German aircraft first came over? They must have felt the fear rise up. Everyone was more tense than ever now. There was no more hope that the British would be back to save them. This was it. The Nazis were as good as here. He already knew the consequences for himself, and he prayed for little Jim and his mother. He felt a pain rise inside him, which quickly turned to anger.

He couldn't bring himself to look around at James again. He felt tears in his eyes. *I'll have the Germans for this,* he thought. *This is just the beginning.*

He did not know he was speaking out loud. And that James was at his side, hearing every word.

For a build-up to war, it had seemed painfully slow.

Philip saw it affect the islanders as a series of small shocks. He was just 22 and considered himself the man of the family. But his mother spoke little of the fighting and she wouldn't let him in the pubs in town. However, if he occasionally managed a small drink he would hear chatter, and some other farmers were happy to give him their view. The old men said the war would mean nothing to the island. Millions had died in the battlefields of France and Belgium only 20-odd years ago, they said, and our lives were not disturbed. The only killing on Jersey, they joked, was what the traders – and farmers, they keenly pointed out to Philip – made on inflated prices. They thought the joke was very funny.

So September 1939 slipped past and the island went on as normal. The mail steamers even made their trips from Weymouth and Southampton, filled with holidaymakers from Britain. The tourist boards were saying it was good for the war effort if they took holidays as they returned to work refreshed.

Then, the little shocks began.

Holland and Belgium fell. That hit the drinkers as a surprise. The Belgians had held out so strongly in 1914-18. Very strange.

Then Dunkirk. Now the newspapers were not so comforting and unease crept into daily conversation. Could the French hold out? was the question in the stores, in the square and at every farm gate he stopped to chat or make a delivery. There was still no real concern though. Everyone thought the French would remain strong, at least until the British army was reorganised and ready to drive the Hun right back where it had come from. Wasn't the French army the largest in the world? Didn't they love their country with a patriotism worth an extra division? Two extra divisions!

And then, of course, as 'Dan Fish', who had three stools in three different bars in the narrow streets of the town, always reminded Philip, there was the Maginot. Philip was young and excitable, over concerned about the clown Hitler. 'So the Belgians have gone, there is still the Maginot Line,' he told Philip Mortain and a few regulars at The Mary Ann. 'The greatest defensive plan in modern warfare, young 'un. That'll hold Jerry up.'

But, of course, it did not. With the Belgians defeated, the main defences of the Maginot Line were by-passed by the Germans. Word went around of a bulge in the French line. Then of people being removed from French command. It was not going right.

Picnicking couples could listen to the gunfire and explosions from the French coast. Sometimes the guns drummed like a heartbeat as the Germans continued their relentless assault. James had dragged Philip to the clifftop at Col de la Rocque one night to watch the flashes and flames. It seemed so unreal to be a spectator on a war and it was hard to believe the fighting could come here some day soon.

Then the whispers went around that the Germans were in Paris, that the French had asked for terms of surrender.

Philip was cycling through town from one person to the next asking for the latest news. He could hear BBC voices behind each open door. The French had capitulated. Germany was now just across the water.

Dan Fish was smoking a cigarette on a bench near the Government offices on Mount Bingham. He didn't look up from the red ridges on the backs of his hands when Philip pushed his bike up alongside him.

'Just the Brits now, young 'un,' he said. 'It's up to us.'

Philip Mortain had not said a word. He was a Jerseyman. It was his island. He had never left in 22 years. His brother James was the same, and their mother too – at least not since before they were born. Their father's work with a merchant bank had taken him around Europe and, when he could, he had taken her with him. He had been a proud Frenchman; the family name he said could be traced to a town in Normandy. How would he have felt to know that today his country had rolled over and died? That it no longer existed?

A small flotilla of boats set sail for St Malo and brought back a grubby bunch of dishevelled and bloodied British and French troops. There were rumours that this ragged army which trudged along Albert Pier was going to help defend the island but no-one who saw them believed that and, within days, they were on the ferry boats back to Britain.

Others were forced to go. When Philip made his daily delivery of eggs to one restaurant, he found his friend, Paolo, who was Italian but had lived above the establishment's bright white kitchen for the last eight months and kicked a football with Philip whenever they both had an hour spare, had gone. The *restaurateur*, Guillame, was distraught, taking Philip in the back away from his few customers when Philip asked where the youngster from Milan had gone. 'He had to report as an enemy alien,' Guillame whispered, using a phrase which had been whispered a lot recently. 'I tried to pretend he was a nephew. No good.'

Philip cycled home, thinking of Paolo, already presumably on a boat to the UK and an internment camp. How long would he be there? He'd been brave to come all the way from Milan and had loved working with Guillame, who knew so many people and introduced him to everyone, proudly, as his trained Italian waiter. Now Guillame had no-one. And, Paolo, Philip tried to get this in his head, was the enemy.

On Wednesday, June 19, 1940, the island's Lieutenant-General, Major General JHR Harrison revealed His Majesty's Government's decision to demilitarise Jersey. No-one was surprised.

All those, he added, who wanted to leave, could do so. Women and children should have priority, along with men aged between 20 and 33 who could go to England and join up to fight.

Philip had not hesitated. He had been out in the town when he heard people were already queuing at the town hall to register. There was a long silent line of people. Many looked ashamed to be leaving. Even people he knew kept their eyes down to avoid greeting him. He stood for hours, watching people scurry out with their registration coupons and disappear to their homes to pack.

Grace Mortain was in the kitchen when he returned. She was sitting at the table. It was empty and she had been sitting in the dark.

He opened the door and had not expected her to still be up. She usually went to bed early for her five o'clock start. Her arms were folded and she wore a blue apron over a dark brown dress. She was just 43 and a widow without bitterness. Her face was youthful and smiling, despite the fact that her husband Gaston had insisted on retiring to this farm – and then of dying and leaving it to her to run. It was only really a small-holding but she worked hard at everything she did. She was a worker. She had not married Gaston for the money. And she loved to work the Jersey soil.

The only physical signs that this was a woman who had, not only spent 18 months caring for a husband as he was slowly ravaged by cancer, but had worked from before first light until bedtime to care for her home and family, was a slight greying of the hair at the temples and a slowly developing stoop that exaggerated her shortness. Both Philip and James got their height from their father, little Jim already being a couple of inches taller than his mother.

Her husband had been a handsome man, intensely serious about his work, but with a intense affection for his family which Philip did not always sense in the serious and frightening fathers of his friends. His early death would have left her life empty but for the kids and the farm. There were many other men on the island attracted by her good looks and the land she owned but she did not look at them twice. She was there now just for her sons.

There had been no smile when Philip had stepped inside the door.

They had looked at each other and she knew where he had been. 'Have you eaten?' she had said. He had shaken his head and silently eaten a plate of beef stew.

There was a great deal of disgust when it was found that thousands had demanded to leave. Not against people like Philip. They were going to fight. But even Mrs Mortain had something against the old Norman families who should be staying to tend to the island. 'Are they just going to leave their homes to ruin?' she asked Philip once, then quickly fell silent again. However, when James repeated something he had heard, calling those who were scrambling to leave 'rabbits and rats', she turned on him and told him they were only doing what they thought best.

On Friday, June 21, Philip cycled around town watching the growing panic. Lines of people waited at every bank to withdraw their savings and there was such demand that police officers guarded some of the doors. Many shops were doing a good trade with people picking up some last minute stores for their journey while other storekeepers had given in and the businesses they had kept for ten, fifteen, twenty years were boarded up.

The streets of St Helier were busier than he had ever seen them. There were crowds around the harbour, begging to speak to people in the shipping offices. Everyone was saying the Germans were almost here. And the fear was growing with each passing hour. Young, old. Men, women. Some who could hardly walk were looking for a way off the island. There seemed to be a baby crying in every frightened group, making everyone around even more tense. He cycled round and round, but none of the queues appeared to be getting any smaller.

'They are all going,' Dan Fish muttered, rolling a cigarette in one hand. 'Look at that,' he nodded at a crowd outside the Pomme D'Or Hotel, 'if Jerry sends his bombers over now he could have the island with a single stick. Boom!'

They watched together as the crowds moved towards the barricades at the head of a jetty. Hands flashed; permits for all the family clutched in the mother's fingers. They were leaving. No-one was celebrating. It was rushed, panicked but sombre. Then they were through the barricade and onto the jetty and walked gangplanks to packed passenger decks. It was a lovely sunny day on the holiday island of Jersey and here they were, screaming to get away. On the boats now, the crowds huddled together in the heat. Each ship filled to overflow. Most did not even look clean or particularly sea-worthy, but they were a life-line and people clung to them. Philip's eyes ran over the crowds. He saw people he knew but they looked different now. They weren't quite sure what they were escaping – although they had heard stories of Nazi soldiers bayoneting nuns in Poland and raping schoolgirls in Belgium - or what they would find when they left. But they had to go. He saw old people fainting; young children being sick.

The ships moved off one by one. They were sluggish, lumbering and overflowing with a desperate human cargo. They weren't even passenger vessels, but potato and coal boats. Would they make it across the Channel? *It was going to be some journey*, Philip thought.

The Germans were not even here yet but a look across the jetties made the onlookers think the islanders were being forced aboard ship at gunpoint. There were cars abandoned, their doors open; discarded bicycles; even suitcases thrown aside at the last moment, left open as someone scrambled for one particular valuable or keep-sake they could not do without. A horse stood sweating in the sun, left harnessed to an empty cart.

And after all the anger all Philip could feel was sadness and pity. These were his friends, his people. Like him they did not even really know what was beyond the island. Now here they were reduced to this. Refugees.

It was June 27 when Philip and James watched the *Luftwaffe* make its first pass over Jersey.

The aircraft had been the talk of the island. No-one knew how many had flown over or what they were really doing, but everyone feared for tomorrow.

Grace Mortain sat down at seven o'clock as usual to feed her sons.

All three sat in silence.

The Mortain farm was one of the smallest in the area. Just a house of pinkish Jersey granite with two bedrooms, a kitchen and a cluttered living room dominated by the heavy ticking of their father's clock. In the dead of night, when Philip could not sleep, he could hear the occasional far-off barking of a dog and the steady beat of that clock. That gift their father had bought at some junk shop on the front at St Valery-sur-Somme as he prepared to set up home with Grace, still provided the heartbeat of the house.

They had a cobbled farmyard and a gate onto a road which threaded from St Helier across the south-eastern corner of the island towards the harbour village of Gorey. There were pigs in the sty and fowl free in the yard. In the corner was an iron field rake, about eight feet across on two narrow wheels and a shaft so it could be pulled behind horses. It was older than Grace Mortain but still one of their most important pieces of equipment.

Behind the house was an outdoor toilet and brick cowshed. The farm's main field then stretched more than half a mile southwards, dipping at its farthest point so one could not see the neighbour's hedge from the Mortain's farm. There were two other farms to the west. Philip would cycle down into the port in minutes; sometimes, if there was no work to do on the farm, James would be struggling to keep up behind. They shared duties on the farm; always striving not to leave their mother alone for too long.

James scraped his spoon on his plate.

His mother looked at him for a moment, hesitated, and then turned to Philip. 'You promise me you will eat well,' she said.

And now the silence was broken and James told them what they had seen as they returned from the St Clement's road after watching the German planes.

They had come across the house where three of James' friends lived with their parents, the Maughans. Two were twins with whom he was at school. The third was a girl called Trudi, a year younger than her brothers. James blushed when he was around her. Her brothers, James' only real friends, teased him about it.

'Their gate was open,' he explained hurriedly, running a last piece of bread around the remains of his stew and popping it into his mouth. 'And we could see the door at the side of the house was open too. It doesn't make sense. Their car had gone but Annie was running around.'

Grace Mortain did not say anything. She was still halfway through her food and gave James no sign she was listening. He continued anyway.

'Annie's a sheepdog,' he went on. 'We went to the door and shouted. It was quiet. So Phil and I went inside...'

Grace looked up at her eldest son.

'You went in their house?'

Philip didn't have the chance to respond before James carried on. It was his story.

'I went inside too,' he said. 'It was really strange. The cupboards were all open. There were clothes and some toys. There were open suitcases on the bed.'

'You went upstairs, did you?' She was more interested than angry now.

'It was a total mess,' James added, picking up his spoon.

'They left in a hurry,' Philip said flatly, looking at his mother. There was a sympathy in his eyes which she picked up on: he was not thinking of the Maughans. He thought, *Please God, let you be all right when I go*.

James was talking again. This time he wasn't looking up from his dish and it was all more of a mumble.

'Anyway,' he said, 'we fed Annie and tied her up but she can't stay there. Most people have shot their dogs, you know, mother? Phil said he would go and get her with me before he left tomorrow and she can stay here with us.'

There was no change in the weather on Friday, June 28. It was a beautiful day, courtesy of the Gulf Stream air that had brought the crowds flocking to the Channel Islands throughout the 1930s. The British had loved the sunshine, the unspoilt countryside and – sometimes above all - saving money on the duty free cigarettes and alcohol; while the Italians and Spanish had come for seasonal work and to chase the occasional local lass between the palm trees on the shore.

Grace awoke and dressed, taking her clothes off the chair under the window. They were the clothes of a farmer's wife, a million miles away from some of the things Gaston had bought for her in the fashionable shops around Place Vendome in Paris when they were courting. Before the children. When there were two of them.

There would be two of them again now. James. Little teenage Jimmy would be head of the family.

Philip was a man now, she knew. He towered above her. He was six feet tall, like his father had been before the cancer had taken hold of him. He had broad shoulders and strong muscles from the farm. But his dark hair was longish and shaggy, like a boy's. It seemed like only a short time since Gaston had taken him for his first day at Hawthorn School, where his father had known a teacher and entrusted him with his education. It was a private school but Gaston had plenty of money put away and wanted his children to have the best. He wanted both to go to live in France one day and to travel the world. He'd always spoken French at home with them; Grace had spoken English. It was a game for a long time; then a bore.

Grace sat in front of the dressing table with the large mirror shaped like an upside down teardrop. Gaston had bought it for her but it was much too large for the low ceiling of this room. She brushed her hair and then picked a small clump of brown and grey hair out of the brush.

The sun was coming up outside and fanning a golden glow across the bed. She could hear the hens in the yard; she never normally noticed them.

She stood and walked to the door, and for some reason she found herself tiptoeing. She supposed she did not want to wake the boys, although she was sure at least one of them was already up: she'd heard him. Philip, she guessed, would not have been able to sleep. James would have tried to stay awake as long as he could with his big brother, would have lasted maybe to midnight and then dropped off. Philip probably woke him again as he put the last few things in his bag. She lifted the little metal latch on the door and stepped out onto the small landing.

'Tea, mother?' It was Philip.

His voice stopped her in her tracks. She felt the tears well up inside her and put her hand to her mouth. She stood there, sobbing quietly, unable to reply.

She came downstairs and stood in the kitchen doorway. Philip was watching the kettle boil on the family's large porcelain stove. He did not turn. He was wearing his black trousers; the ones he wore to church, to his father's funeral. She could see the collar of a white shirt above his black waistcoat. He was looking his best for his going away. Grace turned her eyes to the ground. When she looked up again, he was facing her, a smile on his lips. She had her hand on the doorframe, steadying herself, but she did not want him to see she was upset. She quickly moved into the room and busied herself.

The kettle whistled and Philip poured three cups. The latch crashed on the door and James appeared. He was smiling broadly and banging his dirty boots on the ground.

'There are more planes,' he said, leaning out and looking up at the sky. 'I think one of those Jerry blighters waved to me.'

He immediately checked himself and looked at his mother. 'Sorry, mother.'

Grace looked at him sternly. But that was all she could manage today.

'Here you are, Jimmy,' Philip said brightly, passing him his tea. 'And I hope you waved back at that Jerry too.' He winked at his brother and made a two-fingered gesture out of sight of their mother.

James laughed: 'Oh yeah!' he said. 'Certainly did.'

The boys sat at the table as Grace cracked two eggs into a pan. James smiled broadly at Philip. He was excited about him going and looking forward to his chance of getting off the island, putting on the uniform of the Royal Air Force and fighting the Germans. He'd talked for an hour about it with Philip last night, his older brother barely getting a word in. He had not seemed to have thought about how he would be able to leave Jersey once the Germans came.

Philip looked at his mother out of the corner of his eye. She was sipping her tea, looking thoughtfully at the brown case, propped against the cupboard. It had been her husband's and he had travelled so far with it. But never to war. It was packed now with Philip's things. *It's 20 years old*, she thought, *I hope the catch will hold.*

The time came quickly for Philip to leave as the mail steamer left early to call in Guernsey before heading on to England. And James was in a hurry for his brother to get a move on.

Grace pulled and smoothed the arms of his jacket down at the sides and brushed a mark off the chest pocket.

She looked at him full in face. He wasn't used to that. His mother had a way of keeping her eyes to the ground. It had got worse since their father had died, unless she was dealing with orders of eggs or chickens or potatoes. Then she played the businesslike farmer's wife.

She studied Philip's face. He had her deep brown eyes and high cheek bones. But the tight straight lines of his mouth reminded her of her husband. Those lips could keep his face looking stern and serious even though his eyes wanted to laugh. Like his father, he was a joker, able to tease someone while appearing angry. He shouldn't tease now.

Philip gave her a short, sad smile, and she reached up and put her arms around him.

He held her, staring over her shoulder at the stool in the corner. It had been his French grandfather's, he had been told. He'd made it himself and it was still as strong as when he had knocked it together, despite the fact that Philip had brought it crashing to the floor a few times when clambering on it as a kid. It had been his favourite. He had sat on it, his feet barely able to reach the rung, watching his mother baking, for hours when he was little. Or so it seemed.

Grace moved her head away from his shoulder, gave him a gentle push away and turned. Still she did not say anything about his departure.

Philip picked up his case, stepped quickly to the door and went into the yard.

James was leaning on his bike. Behind him stretched the big field. It looked like freedom to him now, but yesterday and all the days before it had just represented endless hours of work, fetching vraic – seaweed – from the western corner of the island to spread on the land as fertiliser as they tried desperately to bring on the potatoes. The Mortains had never had anything near the number of animals to produce enough manure for their crops. Vraic had been the Jerseyman's solution to that problem for centuries. Coating the field with it allowed the seaweed's rich nutrients to enrich the soil. It was hard work but good work.

There was an edge to the morning, although the summer sunshine bathed the yard. Philip pulled his cap down hard onto his head and stepped on his bike, balancing his case across his handlebars. James was going to walk their bikes back later.

Together, like a dozen times before, they cycled through the yard, their wheels grinding over the rough cobbles. Philip only looked back once. His mother was standing very still, one hand on the gate.

As they freewheeled down the lane, James quickly reminded Philip why he had been in a hurry himself.

'You'll still come quickly to Trudi's farm to check Annie's okay?' he shouted after his brother.

'Yes.'

'Yes?'

'Of course.' Philip's knees were up tight to the case as they swung into Trudi's farm.

The restless cattle had come in close to the fence. They were calling out, their bellies swollen with milk.

'Someone will have to see to them,' Philip said sadly, putting a foot down and looking around. The grey doors of the long, low-roofed cowshed were flung wide open. Philip had developed a farmer's instinct that his father never had. 'It's not right.'

James had cycled ahead. He could see Annie tied against a wall to the side of the house. Annie leapt to her feet and started barking as he approached. James put down his bike and produced a length of rope from his pocket. Philip watched as he tied it to Annie's collar and got back on his bike.

'You are bringing her now?' Philip said, taking off his cap and brushing his hair off his forehead. But James was already cycling slowly out of the yard, Annie panting along a couple of feet from his pedal. Philip didn't say anymore: he knew they were shooting abandoned dogs all over the island; Jimmy knew that too. He also knew exactly how James was feeling behind his teenage bravado: he did not want to come back to the empty farm on his own.

Philip cycled a distance behind his brother now, both going painfully slow, partly for the dog, but also, it seemed to Philip, because neither now really wanted to get where they were going. Philip listened to the low hum of insects in the tiny hedgerows.

There was virtually nothing in the harbour, apart from a few old vessels which had made their final voyage sometime ago – probably when the world was at war last time. On the quayside the cranes stood silent on their four iron legs.

Philip got off the bike and stood looking at the mail boat. It was already busy with passengers. He felt the bulge in his pocket from the sandwiches his mum had given him. It was cuts of roast lamb – his favourite – but he imagined they were slowly beginning to sweat in the sun.

James was kneeling down, tutting at Annie.

'Don't worry about us,' the youngster said, not looking at his brother. He tousled the sheepdog's ears busily. 'I've been listening in town and they reckon the British fleet's moored somewhere outside St Aubin's Bay.'

Philip turned to him. 'Remember you're the man of the house now,' he smiled, embarrassed at his own words. 'You are fifteen next week. You must look after mum.'

James stood, the length of rope hanging free at his side allowing Annie to wander around, sniffing the litter at their feet.

'We will be fine,' James said and held out his hand.

Philip laughed and pulled him close. 'Be careful, Jimmy,' he said quickly, and turned and walked away.

James desperately wanted to say something to leave his brother on the right note. He hesitated.

Philip was already down the steps, his case banging against his leg.

'Kill some Jerries for me, Phil,' he shouted. 'Get some for me!'

Philip turned once and waved his arm to tell James to get going. He couldn't bear to have him standing there.

His boots thudded on the wooden gangplank as he left Jersey soil. This was it. He felt an uncomfortable lump in his throat. How long would it be until his return?

Chapter Three

The sky was busy. Standing on the side of the ship, Philip could see trails from a dozen aircraft thousands of feet above him. Some over Brest, some St Malo, he guessed. Black smoke belched from the funnel above his head as he leaned against the rail looking over at the French coast. He imagined he could see German army vehicles moving slowly up a road and suddenly wondered whether the Nazis were already on Guernsey, lying in wait for them.

He felt a tug at his side and looked down. A small boy of no more than three or four years of age was holding on to his trousers. The boy was looking at him and staring earnestly. He had a runny nose.

'Hello,' Philip said but the boy just stared. His eyes seemed to be asking a question Philip could not understand.

'Charlie!' A woman came pushing through the group of passengers to Philip's right. 'What are you doing?'

If she was Charlie's mother she was incredibly young, not much older than Philip. She scolded Charlie and took a handkerchief to his nose and held him to her side, and made it obvious this was her little problem. 'I'm so sorry,' she said. She had startlingly green eyes and tufts of brown hair poked out from her headscarf and flickered in the wind. She pulled her coat tight across her chest and smiled.

'Do I know you?' she asked.

Philip was surprised by how forward she was. Girls had been something to whisper and scoff about at school and working on the farm did not leave much time for running around with the teenage tourists. There had been one English girl called Meryl, who had come over from Yorkshire with her family. They had walked together on the beach. Her father had been a headmaster and very frightening.

She had had green eyes too.

'I'm sorry. I don't think so,' he stuttered, feeling the child's stare.

'Aren't you Grace Mortain's boy?' God, that made him sound like a child.

'Yes. I am. Philip.'

'I've seen her at our house. She visited Dr Pembridge. She's very pleasant.'

The girl had a sharp, English accent, which he did not recognise.

'I've seen you there too,' she added.

'You're one of Dr Pembridge's daughters?' he said.

'No silly,' she giggled. 'I was a housemaid. I saw you and your mother bringing potatoes and eggs to the kitchens.'

He smiled: 'White cap, white apron, blue dress.'

'That was my morning uniform. It's sad no one sees our face.'

'I'm not like that,' he said. 'I'm sorry.'

He looked away and saw that they were passing a small fishing vessel crammed with more than a dozen passengers. A little boy waved but the others sat silently, watching the steamer slowly move past.

'It's alright,' she said, pulling at a small strand of hair which had blown into her mouth. 'I don't mind. This is Charlie, by the way. I'm meant to call him Charles.'

Philip nodded.

'He's not mine,' she said quickly. 'I'm Alice, by the way. I'm looking after him.'

'What's happened to the doctor and his wife?'

'Hang on,' Alice looked down at Charlie. He was planning another tour of the ship. 'Stand still, Charlie, or I'll put you overboard.'

She let go of him for a moment and brought a packet of cigarettes out of her pocket.

'Have you got a light?' she said.

'Sorry. I don't smoke.'

Alice stopped, a cigarette half out of the light blue packet.

'Where are you going?'

He felt a moment of pride. 'To England. To join up.'

'To join up? And you are too afraid to smoke,' she teased. 'Perhaps you're afraid of Charlie too?'

Philip did not respond.

'Are you going to join the army?'

He wasn't used to being teased. He thought about not getting into conversation at all.

At last, he said: 'The air force. I want to fly.'

'That's good. I think the air force is wonderful, very romantic. Those boys are real men,' she smiled as Philip turned to face her. He smiled back, a little embarrassed. 'I'd like to fly one day.'

He hesitated. She was pretty and chatty but she frightened him too. 'So where are you going?'

'To England too. Well, Wales, actually. Mrs Pembridge is there looking after her sick mother. Dr Pembridge is not well and didn't want to make the journey. He never intended leaving the house – loves it too much. But he wanted Charlie out and safe. So here I am.'

'You have relatives in Wales?'

'No. I'll be staying with Mrs Pembridge. But I might even have some time to myself.'

Philip said: 'That's good', and then realised she was making an invitation.

'So if you are nearby…' She was leaning back on the rail now, and Philip noticed the curves of her body.

He looked away.

'Weymouth seems a long way away,' he said at last, biting his lower lip. 'Wales even further. And it is not where the war is.'

Philip had eaten his mother's sandwiches as soon as the steamer had left its berth. He had sat astern and watched St Aubin's Bay disappear.

Now he was hungry again.

'Are you all right, Philip?'

'Yes, yes, I'm fine,' he said quickly, feeling himself put out by the question but also strangely affected by the sound of his name on her tongue. 'Just a little hungry, that's all.'

Alice reached into her pocket and brought out a bag. 'We girls are always prepared,' she said. 'Have some.'

He reached in and took out a piece of cake. It crumbled in his hand and was warm and sweet.

'Thanks,' he said.

'We'll be there soon,' Alice stated, popping a piece into her mouth. 'Won't we, Charlie-boy?'

St Peter Port harbour was busy with small groups of people, all huddled together despite the afternoon sun. But, like them, they were not day-trippers or tourists, they had their most important possessions in suitcases at their feet. The main organised evacuation was over but there were still last-minute refugees.

'I hear they're really panicked here,' Alice said calmly, drawing on a cigarette. 'Dr Pembridge said it is much worse than Jersey.'

Philip looked back ashore and caught the eye of a middle-aged woman standing with a brown shawl wrapped tightly on her shoulders. She looked terrified – even of him.

'I just want to be on my way,' he murmured.

As the paddle steamer docked, the stronger figures ashore moved quickly forward; the others drifted like ghosts. The islanders had initially been told there might be a complete evacuation of Guernsey and those left were terrified to still be within earshot of the German planes. Time was running out.

Philip watched the middle-aged woman with the brown shawl move slowly in the line coming to join the ship. They were nearly all aboard, their shoes slowly tramping the gangplank, kicking the backs of the feet of the person in front of them. There was a distant sound, like wildlife baking in the grass, like the mumbling of the people's voices. Philip didn't even register it really. It was as if every one of them coming on board was murmuring to the next.

And then they were screaming.

The explosion hit a huge pile of crates somewhere to Philip's left. It came like a huge fist, crashing down with a white flash and sending pieces of splinter and shrapnel flying in a thousand directions. Then in the same instance the fist uncurled, picked Philip's body up and hurled him against the bulkhead. The air rushed out of his lungs and he lay on the floor his body gasping for air and wracking with an empty dry cough.

For what seemed like an age, he could not hear a thing, except something far off in the distance, like an echo in a shell. Then sound built up slowly inside his head, first a piercing ringing and then an almost continuous screaming.

He lifted his head and saw people trying to run up and down the gangplank at the same time. They pushed and clawed at each other.

A young man in a black shirt and waist coat sprinted along the dockside at incredible speed, the concrete disintegrating behind him under cannon fire. The material across his back ripped and shredded like paper but his legs carried him a few paces further before he fell face forward on the ground.

Philip struggled to his feet and stood with his back against the cold bulkhead. Another explosion went off somewhere in front of the ship and he turned his head quickly to see a spray of water rear up over the bow like a wild, mythical seahorse. He found himself wiping salt water away from his mouth. There was blood on his hand too.

'Charlie!' It was Alice. She was crouched down at the rail, her hand clinging to the boy's sweater. He was straining, pulling to get away from her grip.

She was losing him and falling forward on the deck. The headscarf had come loose and her hair was blowing into her face.

There was a roar of an engine and another explosion. Charlie ripped free and began to run at the gangplank.

Rat-tat-tat. Machine gun sprayed the dockside again. Philip saw two people come together in a clinch and then fall like puppets when the master lets go of the strings. He was only 20 feet from them but he could not even tell if they were male or female.

Charlie stumbled at the gangplank. Philip could suddenly hear his wailing above the aircraft. He ran forward and plucked the boy up in his arms. *Rat-tat-tat.* People were running back and forth between the sheds and warehouses on the wharf. Philip clutched Charlie between him and the wall. Alice was at their side and saying, 'It's all right, Charlie, they'll be gone soon.'

Philip could suddenly feel a terrible heat on his face. He crumpled against Charlie, banging heads with Alice. They lay there in a huddle, each intimately aware of the other's laboured breathing. Everything seemed to be burning all along the dockside. The acrid air seemed to be choking them. Philip looked up and saw that a shed close to them, where he had seen so many run for cover, had been partly demolished by an explosion and was now a tangled cloud of red, orange and black flame. The air around him crackled.

A tiny child called out and an adult sobbed. A man with wisps of grey hair on the side of his head was sitting against the rail. His hair was standing as if waxed to point upwards in two tufts for a joke. Tears ran in trails through the ash on his face. The bottom-half of his trouser leg was blown away and there was a deep red gash down his left leg.

But the planes, it seemed, had gone. And Philip had not even seen them.

He turned to Alice. She let out a deep sigh and looked at the scene of twisted bodies around her. Some people were starting to stand, tottering as if they had never been upright before. Others were lying face down, their bodies shaking.

'I'm fine,' she said, but she noticed her fingers were gripped hard into Charlie's hair and the child's eyes were screwed tight shut. Philip rubbed his hand over hers and she released her grip.

She leaned forward quickly and put her arms around his neck.

Philip hesitated for a moment, unsure what to do. His heart was still rushing from the air attack and he suddenly feared he might faint. So he put his arms around her and held her tight, burying his face in the softness of her hair, trying to block out the awful smell.

His head on her shoulder, he felt his strength come back and his jaw tighten. He thought how the time would come when he would fall out of the sun on those bastards and chase them out of the sky.

His eyes flickered to the wharfside. Two legs lay twisted awkwardly under a pile of clothes. Dancing from it in the breeze of the fires was a brown shawl.

When the German bombers arrived over Jersey, James felt their every twist and turn in his aching stomach.

There was no way he was not going to see a German plane that day. He had to see them. The excitement rose in his heart. It was only when he saw the fire they rained that the emotion turned to revulsion and he felt sick.

He had watched Philip's steamer until it was right out of sight. As long as it was physically possible to see his brother moving, walking, lifting his cap, he stared. He'd moved away from the quay so as not to embarrass Philip but he wanted to watch until he could see him no more. He didn't cry but as he wiped his hand over his face he felt his eyes sting.

Then Annie and he had turned away off Pier Road and made their way back to the farm. The streets were quiet and, although Annie sniffed at doorways, there was no-one at any of them. A few curtains flickered, that was all. Those that were left were waiting for the invasion.

The afternoon was warm and windless. As he cycled he felt a thin sweat on his brow. The skin on his arm prickled in the heat.

James' attention was shared between Annie and the sky. Every few hundred yards or so he stopped cycling and looked up, turning right around, cupping his hands over his eyes. He longed to see another aeroplane. A few times on the journey home he thought he heard one but saw nothing. He knew it couldn't be long though and he quickened his pace. He wanted to be there to protect his mother when the Germans came. Perhaps troops would land today?

Grace watched her son and the dog come down the lane. James clicked the gate shut behind him and tied Annie, tired and disciplined, by the barn. He walked passed his mother and went into the pantry to get Annie some scraps of food. He had not talked about losing his friends, the Maughan twins or the daughter, Trudi, despite the fact that the mere mention of her name had once made him blush from forehead to neck. He had transferred his complete affection to Annie. Grace left him to it and went to feed the three pigs they were fattening up in a sty behind the house.

There was no sign of James when the first explosions rocked Jersey that evening. The brilliant afternoon had faded and the Germans had arrived as a sleepy Friday evening fell softly on the island. It was the cruellest blow to those gentle hours of a summer day. Grace felt her blood run cold in her veins when the first boom shook the ground under her feet. It was followed quickly by another and another and the heavy rattle of machine gun fire. *My God, they are here.* There had been all that talk: from some, that the Germans would take the island without a shot being fired because of the demilitarisation; from others, that the demilitarisation of the island had been a British sham to lull the Nazis. The first theory had been wrong, she thought, as she ran around the side of the house. Now they would find out if there was any truth in the second. *There were so many windbags. No-one knew anything.*

Then she saw James. He was standing against the eastern hedgerow of the farm. He was quite still, facing St Helier. Beyond him the sky was pitted with puffs of smoke like little tricks from a magician's wand. Grace looked up and could make out a tight formation of thin black aircraft. She could see others banking towards the town. As she watched, she heard the rattle of machine gun fire again and imagined she could hear screaming.

'*James!*'

The teenager was transfixed by the diving aircraft, swooping like hawks on the stricken port as if picking off the fish from the islanders' trawlers.

He turned quickly and saw his mother's distress.

He ran back to her and said: 'They are shooting up the town. Those aircraft, there!' he said, pointing at the pencil-thin dark devils coming back across the town. 'They are Dornier bombers...'

'I don't want to know, James,' his mother told him.

Clouds of dust and debris filled the air. They could smell it on the breeze which an hour earlier had brought them the soft scent of the sea.

'Maybe I should ride down. See where I can help out.'

As James spoke fresh explosions rang out from the south west and the sky above their heads filled with the heavy drone of aircraft. Grace shivered and James put his arm around her shoulders. Another wave of explosions hit St Helier, deep thuds of sound moving through the air towards them. The flames lit their skin and Grace suddenly felt as if the pilots would see the orange glow of their shocked faces. James' arm tightened around his mother as she turned quickly. There was the deep rumble of an engine behind them. Their eyes swept quickly skywards. Then James saw that it was a motorcyclist pulling up at their gate. Normally they would have laughed; not now, with the burning St Helier as a backdrop. Neither recognised the visitor, even when he lifted his goggles off his face. He was out of breath and blew through his thick moustache before he spoke. 'They're hitting the port,' he called. 'There are cars on fires. And houses too.'

He stared at them, shook his head and then roared off.

'There is nothing you can do tonight,' Grace said to James. 'The soldiers will be here tomorrow. It is then we will need our strength.'

Chapter Four

Despite the shock raid on St Helier it was still a surprise to see the first German soldier at the door.

But they did not come the next day. In fact, the weekend passed peacefully. A few airplanes circled overhead but their pilots just looked around and headed back to Cherbourg or wherever they had come from.

Grace and James worked as normal although James had not been able to resist cycling in to town first thing on Saturday morning. He rode around the harbour and saw windows blown out of buildings. Some people were still brushing up the glass. There was a crushed fishing boat and a number of small rowing boats turned back to splintered timber on the sand. They looked like toys crushed under the boots of a giant as he strode across the island.

James looked to see where the giant's next footprint lay and turned slowly into Mulcaster Street. There were hundreds of holes punched in the concrete walls, some as big as a man's fist. Windows were cracked open so that the estate agents and shops that had looked like new yesterday now looked like they had been abandoned years ago. He stopped to reach down and pick up a piece of jagged metal. It was about the size of a cricket ball. It was black and twisted. He had no idea what it was. Then his eyes fell to the floor again. About two paces away was a thick pool of dried blood. There was no blood on his find though so he tucked it guiltily into his pocket. It was heavy and banged against his thigh as he rode. It hurt like hell but it was the first souvenir of this war and he wasn't going to let it go. Even if he found something better.

He cycled up to where he had been to wave Philip off the day before and looked back over the harbour. The town was already beaten. It had seen so many of its citizens flee. It was defenceless. It seemed to ring out still with last night's screaming. It did not understand why it was under attack. It had nothing to give back. An ambulance bell burst through James' thoughts and he watched it weave between the houses. He wondered who was inside and it made him cold.

He remembered Philip's words when they spotted their first German planes – just two days ago! – 'This is just the beginning.' *Yes, and where did it go from here?* These were the Germans he had read so much about. The Germans of the Somme who had ran through brave Tommies with their bayonets. The pilots who had shot at his heroes in Wizard and Skipper. Now they were here and he hated them. All that he read was really true. But those were comic books. He needed to know his enemy. He turned and rushed home. As he cycled the air-raid siren sounded behind him but this time no bombs came.

Late in the afternoon he went out again, this time at Grace's behest. He was sent to stock up on more food. The shops were busy, some closing early. The shelves were pretty bare. He used Grace's bike, which had a pannier but was slow and clunky. The seat was too low for him, but he didn't care because the ride gave him another chance to look over Jersey's war.

He was standing near St Helier Church. The building, like the town, took the name of a missionary who was, according to legend, murdered by pirates. They took axes to poor Helier. Now the pirates came in murder machines, twisting up buildings and people.

'What are you doing, young Mortain?' A man was hurrying across the street. James didn't recognise him until he was right up close and he adjusted the unsteady white helmet on his head. It was George Dibney, a burly Londoner who had been a teacher at Hawthorn. 'You shouldn't be here. Those bombers could come back at any moment.' Mr Dibney was proud of the W for warden on his helmet; doing his bit again.

'I'm here for mother,' James lifted the grocery bag in the basket at the handlebars.

'All the same, this is a dangerous area to be hanging about. The war is on, Mortain.' Mr Dibney had served in France during the Great War. The boys had always talked about it because he looked very different from the heroes in the books. He was, James supposed, a disappointment. 'The Hun's already given this place a pasting and Guernsey too. They hit it last night and killed a great many people. Now get along.'

'Our Philip's boat was calling in Guernsey, Mr Dibney, on the way to Weymouth,' said James, not used to talking back to the teacher.

Mr Dibney hesitated and almost smiled. 'He's gone to fight the Hun, has he? He's a brave lad. Now, I am sure he is fine. So get along home and look after your mother.'

Sunday passed slowly. Grace had been given a small herd of cattle left behind by fleeing neighbours and James spent the day preparing feed and fixing fencing at the far end of the lower field. Twice as he laboured in the heat he heard aircraft. He never saw them but he assumed they were German. They had to be: no-one knew where in the hell were the blasted RAF.

Late on Monday morning James saw Grace in deep conversation with Mr Reid, who owned a hotel and restaurant in town and was one of the farm's best customers. They were standing at the back of his van which was parked in the centre of the yard, its rear doors flung open. Both Grace and Mr Reid were frowning and James' mother had her arms folded.

'What is it, mother? Is it news about Philip?' James had not mentioned Mr Dibney's news about the bombing at Guernsey to his mother.

'The bloody Germans,' Mr Reid said, before adding aside: 'Pardon my language, Mrs Mortain.'

'What's happening, Mr Reid?'

'I was talking to a mate of mine up at the States,' said the hotelier, referring to the politicians running the island. He slowly moved his hat in a circle through his hands as he spoke. 'Word is they've sent a message to them. Made a list of demands, the bloody Germans. Pardon me, Mrs Mortain.'

Grace Mortain ignored the apology as her son asked: 'What do they want?'

'It's a bloody list – excuse me. They want a large white cross painted at the airport, Fort Regent and at the Weighbridge in the port,' he said, marking the demands off as a list with his fingers. 'Let me see...they want white flags flying just about all over - churches, houses even my bleeding place. Pardon me.

'And, now, what was it he said? That's it, "All hostile action will be followed by bombardment", or something like that. They want full surrender. That's the only way to guarantee our safety.'

Grace said quietly: "There is nothing we can do."

'More's the sodding pity, Mrs Mortain,' replied Mr Reid, putting his hat firmly back on his head and knocking it down with one swift pat. 'If you'll pardon my language.'

James went back to work but couldn't stop thinking about the German demands. *It would be like that for good now*, he thought.

The Germans will be our first thought in the morning, our last at night. As if to rub it in two lumbering Junkers 52 transport planes flew in low from the coast and headed in land. The troops were arriving. The planes were so low he could see the peak of the pilot's cap as he turned his head and the sun glinted off the cockpit window. James hated that man's guts. He threw down his shovel and walked swiftly back to the house.

Then he saw it. It was fluttering gently in the afternoon breeze which swept in from the sea and could be felt at the first floor window but not in the yard. He stood looking up at it, sensing his mother come to the door.

He lowered his face to hers. She stared back at him strongly, although he sensed she wished to turn away.

'Don't say anything, James,' she said at last.

'It's a white flag, mother.'

'A white towel. A tatty, old white towel. It means nothing,' she replied, looking away at last, over his shoulder.

'It means surrender,' he said slowly. 'Mother, it means we are cowards. We have given in.'

'We have surrendered,' Grace said. 'This changes nothing. There are white flags all over the island. And do you know why? Because when the soldiers come up the road there is nothing we can do but let them pass.'

'And what if they won't go on their way? What if they want the farm?'

James suddenly sounded like Philip to her. This wasn't the shy boy with friends you could easily count on the fingers of one hand, the boy too afraid to sing in the church choir. This was his older brother. His father even.

Grace's hands were shaking. 'Don't talk to me like that,' she said, her voice wavering. 'I am not having this discussion.'

But the sudden change in her son struck at her heart as hard as her own fear of the occupation. She knew she had lost the little boy. Little Jimmy had gone as the Germans were arriving on the island; and there was a strong adult coming in his place. Part of her wanted to weep for the lost child; but she also glad because deep down she was the one who was now very afraid.

They sat down to vegetable soup at about seven. Grace had made it with large cubes of potato the way James liked it. But they barely spoke during the meal. The soup was hot and sweat broke out on James' brow as he ate. He wiped a curl of hair off his forehead. The kitchen door was open behind him and occasionally a tiny gust of sea breeze lifted the white towel and slapped it on the wall. They both ignored it although the third time it flapped hard, determined to be acknowledged, and James pushed his food away. But it was almost finished anyway.

Grace took his dish. She had not eaten much of hers and she scraped what was left back into the pot. She began to wash the plates. "Will you put away for me?" she asked, her back now to her son.

James did not answer. He had taken an envelope from the dresser and pulled out a red bordered publication with the words The War in bold letters on the front. A friend of their father's who now lived in England sent the threepenny publication to Philip and James whenever he could. And James loved it. It wasn't a kid's funny. It had real articles on the war.

This edition, dated May 24, 1940, had a drawing of a German parachutist on the front and the headline: *Human bombs dropped from the skies by the Nazis.* It described the German parachutists who had taken the Low Countries. Everyone was terrified of these troops. James flicked through the descriptions of the first big battle of the war. *"We see now that if Germany can gain bases in Holland and Belgium she will be ready for her attack against Great Britain,"* one writer noted. A photograph showed Belgian refugees, old and young, wrapped in blankets and huddled together on the back of a lorry. A few pages on, six or seven RAF pilots stood around a map in an operations room. They were all wearing flying gear. James wondered if his brother would soon be among them. A panel below described the new British war cabinet put together by Churchill: Chamberlain, Attlee, Halifax and Greenwood.

James devoured it all. He could hear the throaty mechanised sounds of war. The screaming aircraft.

He looked up at his mother. She had stopped wiping the dishes. She was standing at the sink, leaning against the wooden worktop. Her shoulders seemed to have dropped.

A motorbike revved loudly and there was a screech of brakes. James turned and looked straight out the kitchen door to the gates of the farm. He could see two soldiers sitting astride motorcycles. One got off and walked to the gate. He had a machine gun across his chest. His uniform, like the others, was grey. He looked just like the parachutist on the front of The War.

He reached over a thick arm and clicked the gate open. He pushed it and it swung back.

The two motorcyclists turned their bikes into the yard and James could now see they were not alone. A staff car followed them in, its tyres rough on the cobbles.

A door opened and a man stepped out. He was tall with shining black boots. James noticed the immaculate tunic, which he pulled down smartly as he stood straight. There were badges or medals on the tunic and a large black holster strapped to his side.

James was at his mother's side now. They were both staring through the window at this man. Even under the cap they could see his face - the sharp, pointed nose, and more noticeably the grin. His teeth shone. He was enjoying his war.

James felt an awful coldness run through his veins, as if he were standing on the top of a cliff, about to topple forward.

One of the motorcyclists rapped on the open door and took one step inside the kitchen. His machine gun clicked against the buttons on his jacket, his boots were heavy on the stone floor. He saluted and then said something which James missed. It meant only one thing.

They were here.

Chapter Five
Britain

The first glimpse of Howell Grove greeted the visitor as they turned into the last dip of the narrow valley. The gentle green slopes were giving way here to the foothills of the Cambrian mountains. This was not one of the dark industrial valleys of south Wales but a quieter, smaller, western neighbour. It was barely half a mile long and there was little to break up the lines of oaks and clusters of brown and white cattle: only Howell Grove and the narrow road which wound its way to its gate.

From the corner of the hill that turned in on the estate, Howell Grove did not even look real at all: it could easily have been a doll's house. Although, with its large white stone and turreted roof, it really wanted to be a castle.

It was surrounded by a drive of small yellow stones and there was a black motor car parked at its side. That too, from this distance, looked like a toy.

Two horses had come to a fence near the house and were nodding their heads together. They looked like they were kissing.

Philip Mortain turned up the collar on his coat and looked at the withered fields of the valley. There was a shallow, fast running stream. The water, even from the road, looked like it might freeze solid if it did not keep running as fast it could over the bed of sharp stones. Although it was now well into spring, here in the hills there was still a cutting mid-day chill and the watery midday sun was doing little to heat up the air.

It was some time and a considerable walk since he had stepped off the train and his hands were sweating now inside his gloves. He was warm too inside his greatcoat but his face and ears were still cold and the breath broke like steam from the Cardiff train in front of him.

He turned his head up from the withered fields of the valley, only slowly recovering from the winter, to the grey slate sky, and started down towards Howell Grove.

This was his first leave since Christmas 1940 and his first trip to see Alice at work. It had not been allowed before with the pair having to meet up in Cardiff or Swansea on the rare occasion they were both free.

At first, it had been easier for them to meet. Philip had not been in uniform then, at least not in the blue of the Royal Air Force.

Now as he walked through this quiet countryside which seemed a million miles from the war, his mind turned back to St Clement, Gorey, home. He could not imagine what their life was like with the Nazis at their door, in their homes, and when he feared the worst, he pushed every thought of that war to the back of his mind. He liked to imagine he had gone away but Mum and James were going along just the same. But sometimes, when he least expected it, the dark thoughts would return. He would see the same terrifying image of James, younger than he was when Philip left, playing in the yard of the farm. His mother would come to the window and look out to see her boy, blissfully unaware of the group of grey-uniformed German soldiers stood around him, their rifles poised. Grace Mortain then weeps and Philip has to screw his eyes tight and think of Alice, or air speed, or the sound of the air-raid sirens blasting across London. That always cleared his mind.

That was not real anyway. Grace and James were just working the fields, making the deliveries, he told himself.

They would not know him now either. Or his life.

It was a matter of months, not much over half a year, but everything had been picked up and turned upside down.

In the train on the way down he had caught his reflection in the window. It still sometimes made him draw breath. His black hair was short now and combed tightly back. The jacket of his uniform was smartly pressed and brushed. He still felt restricted by it, but it was a constant reminder of the pride he felt too.

Especially when others noted it. Although soldiers, airmen and sailors were everywhere, he had been the only serviceman in the carriage.

He'd smiled then at his own vanity. One of the women in the carriage had noticed and, embarrassed, his hand had shook: the paper in his hand had given that away.

He'd been holding a small white envelope and a single sheet of writing paper. Both the envelope and letter were well-thumbed. It was Alice's latest and Philip had read it a thousand times. He loved her letters. They were as full of fun and cheer as Alice herself. And there was a great degree of affection too.

When her letters were first handed to him back at the air station, he always felt a burst of guilty excitement. He would tuck the letter quickly inside his jacket and head off somewhere quiet to read it. If there was work to be done first, then so much the better: the delay made reading her words all the more pleasurable.

He was, he realised, falling in love with Alice. And how strange that as he trained for war, tried desperately to prove he was now a man – stranded as he now was a sea away from his homeland – that he should find such tenderness with someone who, but for the war, would have always remained a stranger.

When he and Alice had arrived at Weymouth with young Charlie they had already felt a great deal older. It didn't help that they were so tired they could barely walk and they had nowhere to stay. Or that English customs officers insisted on searching them for cigarettes.

Alice had missed the Cardiff train so they sat in the station. Every now and then something familiar flashed by: a Jersey school cap on a little child with a bag tied on string across his stomach, a woman's face he remembered from…where? A schoolroom, a café, a busy Jersey street bathed in sunshine? His eyes were so tired.

Alice had rested her head on his shoulder and Charlie finally slept, his head in Alice's lap and a spare blanket she produced from her case wrapped around his shoulders. 'We girls are always prepared,' she had joked again. They must have looked like a very young family.

Although, as he had sat there, her head heavy on his shoulder, he began to realise what had aged them – or him certainly – during that long day. Surprisingly, he thought, it was not the sights of Guernsey dock, horrible though they were. Yes, the images remained, drifted back like ghosts inside a tired mind, but it was not them that truly haunted him in that cold railway station. It was the noises of war. God, how thunderous it had been. The screaming of people and machinery. The explosions, real explosions, which rocked the ground.

In the morning, as a few people began to drift in and out of the station, the young couple had shared a snack in a café but the town was busy and they had no time to themselves. When they tried to talk, Charlie, who had not been able to sleep on the six-hour leg of the journey from Guernsey and remained grumpy after his nap on Alice's lap, had pouted and become angry with them both. He knocked over a cup and red-faced they both had to leave and stand in the street.

Alice had held Charlie close to her side but, she looked so weary herself, Philip had suddenly become worried that she might faint. It had been the first time he felt stronger than her.

That was when he had put his hand against the side of her face, just to feel her skin, and they had kissed.

Her train was one of the first of the day. They parted and he was thankful when she suggested they meet again. He had had no idea how to broach the subject. She gave him Mrs Pembridge's address and then she and Charlie were gone.

He wondered what to do now. He walked about Weymouth for the day, reading the Daily Express, thinking about home, feeling like not only a stranger but a foreigner. He saw some other islanders who were heading off hundreds of miles to the north of England. They looked so frightened they might as well have been told they were to be driven straight into the machine-gunned clutches of the Nazis.

His first thoughts for Britain, strangely, were that he hated it. No one seemed to want to talk to him. When he went for something to eat the waitress avoided his gaze – but then chatted elaborately with a man on another table.

Late in the afternoon, he found himself back at the railway station. He stood looking at a map of the rail networks. Looking back it was as if he had been sleepwalking. He went over to the ticket office, bought a one-way and got on a Bristol train.

He would be in Cardiff for nightfall. He would be near Alice and he would be able to join up. Anyhow, it looked closer than London on the map and if he felt like a stranger in Weymouth how would he cope in London?

He managed to get digs in an area of the Welsh city called Roath and, after a couple of days, a poorly paid job in a café. It would keep him going until he got into uniform.

On the second day he wandered into a recruiting office in the city centre and got application forms for the Royal Air Force. As he filled them in, he daydreamed about chasing Stukas around the sky and seeing them tumble and spin to earth in flames. He knew it had to be the RAF. James had always loved planes, getting so excited when they visited the airfield on their bikes. And, as the war had approached, that had actually rubbed off on his older brother. Anyway, Philip reckoned he wouldn't like the navy - and he'd already had a miserable time at sea - and photographs from France had convinced him that he didn't want to be an infantryman firing off rounds at screaming German dive-bombers.

He had prayed he would get accepted and, to help it along, he took the advice of a customer at work whose brother had been taken on and said he wanted to be a wireless operator/air gunner. Of course, he really wanted to be a pilot but he reckoned so did everyone who filled in this form – and he'd been told that as he didn't have a university education he'd be lucky to be aircrew at all.

The most important thing was to get in the air.

The form handed in, he worried about everything else. In fact the one thing he wasn't concerned about was his physical fitness: he'd spent so long working on the farm and had clocked up hundreds of miles of bicycling that he reckoned he'd have the edge on most other recruits.

But apart from comic book stories and dreams he did not know much about flying itself. In fact, he knew nothing. He had an idea of what it might feel like. He imagined it would be like taking his old bone-shaker bike, made from spare parts and without brakes, and hammering it down the hills and lanes; your face pushed forward into the wind, your heart beating madly.

He browsed books on aviation in local shops. There were some new ones on the Hurricane and Spitfire, German aircraft – many of which he had already committed to memory – and books on aircraft recognition which he took particular care on.

He preferred thinking about what he might shoot down to studying drag, stalling, lift, topics in some of the dustier volumes.

He cleaned tables and dished out plates of sausages and fried bread in the daytime and lay on his bed in his tiny room at night. All the while he waited for the call.

The city was becoming an increasingly frightened place. Many of the little signs of the coming war he had witnessed in Jersey were more developed here. Hundreds of windows were crossed with sticky tape to try to reduce the levels of flying glass in an explosion. Main roads had a thick white line up their centre to show the middle of the road in the blackout. As the nights began to draw in that autumn crossing the road at dusk had become precarious. There was some real grumbling when the August Bank Holiday was cancelled.

He got friendly with Bryn, a fireman who lived in the same boarding house and was in some sort of difficult relationship with a girl working in a local cartridge case factory who kept finding new ingenious ways of spending his money.

Bryn had a thick black moustache which covered any effort that his face made to smile and emphasised his dark, Welsh nature. His pessimism made Philip smile though and Bryn didn't take offence at being teased for it. He was almost 10 years older than Philip but was still half the age of the two other tenants in the house.

During August 1940, Bryn and hundreds of colleagues had fought a massive blaze 100-or-so miles away in the oil tanks at Pembroke Dock. He spent several days down there in two shifts as the inferno blazed for three weeks.

When he came back the last time he went to his room and slept for two days.

Philip heard that some of his friends had died fighting the fire and that firemen had been shot at by enemy planes returning to hit the coast, so it took time to pluck up the courage and find the right moment to ask Bryn how it was. Philip was desperate to know.

'It was not good,' Bryn said, still suffering a cough from the huge clouds of burning oil.

Bryn – and even his girlfriend Kitty - were a reminder that Philip was doing nothing towards the war. On top of that, he was mocked by little boys and old women collecting for the Spitfire fund to pay for aircraft production. They were only selling ceramic pots and flower displays but even they were doing more than him in that grotty little café.

The waiting went on and, through Bryn, Philip found himself volunteering to be an auxiliary fireman. He sat around the Fire Service headquarters in Westgate Street with a bunch of ragged volunteers, male and female, and was trained up on how to fight fires and store the Auxiliary Fire Service's limited equipment: a ladder, stirrup pump and some canvas buckets. His team of five would have a taxi to take them to emergency call-outs, although all they were doing at first was teaching people all around the city how to use stirrup pumps on small fires.

Bryn told him: 'Get this right, boy, and you could be a regular.'

But that's not what Philip wanted. Much as he respected Bryn, he wanted the beautiful blue uniform and the wings of a pilot.

Then one day he rushed in late from the café. He had to change quickly and get out to the Cathays AFS station. But Bryn grabbed him on the stairs. 'There's a letter for you, boy. Looks official,' he nodded back down to the small table behind the door. A single envelope was propped against the wall.

No letters had got through from home. He had received some from Alice and a couple from fellow Channel Islanders who had been seeking as much comfort as they could give (but it had been good to know they were at least safe in their new homes). But this was official. It was them.

He wanted to go to his room and open it but Bryn was waiting. He'd listened to Philip go on about this moment long enough; he had earned the right to be there.

Philip ripped the letter open with his finger, trying to be casual as if it didn't mean anything. He was being called back to the recruiting office. He told Bryn.

'Excellent, boy. Now go and play at fighting some fires.'

The day before his RAF interview was the first anniversary of the start of the war. It was to be his second brush with fear.

The bombs crashed down on Roath that night and in a nearby street three houses in a row crackled and blazed. Flames engulfed the furniture inside and the broken windows flashed like the eyes of the devil.

Together he and his team tried in vain to kill the fire but out of the corner of his eye he noticed a white figure moving in the orange-black shadows. Despite the heat of the flames on his face, he felt a shiver at his back. He realised it was a person, shuffling forward, feet stumbling on broken bricks and wood, only it wasn't just bricks and wood it was the walls of a house, pieces of favourite furniture.

Philip tapped a colleague on the back and pointed. When he got up close he realised the figure was a man, an old man he guessed but he could have been anything between 40 and 80. His clothes were shredded, and his arms and face bloodied, although the blood looked black. He was covered from head to toe in dust, and walked like a ghost that was afraid of its own shadow.

Philip put his hand on the man's arm but he didn't seem to notice. He was muttering something, his mouth moving as if he was in full conversation, but no sound came from his bloodless lips.

Philip's stomach was in knots but he'd waited for this meeting for weeks so, when he climbed the steps, he did so two at a time.

This was like the AFS again, but God how he really wanted this. There were a few people, ringing their hands in a mixture of excitement and nervous anticipation.

A heavy door opened and a woman in uniform stepped out, her shoes clicking loudly on the wooden floor.

She said his name and his heart leapt into his mouth. He followed her through a large oak door into an office which turned out to be much smaller than he expected.

Suddenly he was stood in front of a heavy desk. The squadron leader sitting behind it, looked up, smiled and said: 'Sit down.'

The officer talked in clipped, brief sentences, all straight to the point. They quickly discussed Philip's background and why he was in Cardiff, and then what he wanted to do.

Philip relaxed a little as he was asked about his family and his journey to Wales, but then, as the squadron leader hesitated to make notes, Philip found himself blurting out his hopes – even of being a pilot, one day.

The officer listened and then smiled.

'I have to be aircrew,' Philip heard himself saying. 'I want to be,' he paused, already embarrassed by what he was to say next, 'at the front end of the war.'

There were a number of crumpled pieces of paper in a wire wastepaper basket in the corner of the room. *Must be failed applications*, Philip thought.

The squadron leader leaned forward slightly, clasping his hands in front of him on the desk. The young man prepared himself for the worst. 'Well, why not be a pilot?' asked the officer.

Philip took a moment to take in that he wasn't kidding him.

There was no answer. Of course, he wanted to be a pilot!

It went down on a piece of paper and Philip was whisked through for a brief medical.

Afterwards he stood outside and felt the people brush past him. He could hardly believe it could be that easy.

He pulled his hat down firmly over his hair and began to run up the busy street, a smile fixed firmly across his lips.

In Cathays Park he could see a barrage balloon straining on its ropes about fifty feet above the ground. *Did the Nazis have them?* he wondered. By Christmas he could be machine gunning them out of the sky!

Later that night he heard Bryn going into his room. He waited in case the fireman was tired but the excitement got too much. He tapped the door and Bryn barely had time to say 'Yes?' before Philip was inside and leaning against the tatty chest of drawers at the foot of Bryn's bed. He told him his news. Bryn smiled briefly, stepped across the room and shook Philip's hand. The Jerseyman sensed a slight tremble in the older man's grip. It surprised him but he had quickly forgotten about it as he told Bryn how the squadron leader seemed to be encouraging him to be a pilot.

Bryn lit a cigarette. 'We must have a beer,' he said, going over to the window and drawing the heavy black-out curtains. 'It's getting colder.' Bryn rarely talked about work now or news from the war. He had developed a keen interest in the weather.

He went on talking, not looking at Phil. 'Last winter it was bitter,' he shivered, as if already feeling the chill. 'The Severn was blocked with ice. The power went. The docks shut down… Desperate.'

Mrs Annabel Pembridge's grandfather, a member of parliament, had built Howell Grove. Although the mansion looked rather grand to Philip with its turrets and single, bold tower, the stones laid on the land in the middle of the 19th Century had been placed on the site of an even larger building which had been destroyed in a fire.

Now Mrs Pembridge would inherit the MP's retreat and a large swathe of rolling countryside when her mother died. Her mother had lung cancer and had not been expected to live into 1941, but she was a stubborn old woman who, despite a life of almost uninterrupted luxury, still felt she was owed something. However, she could do little now other than sleep most of the day.

Alice Dearmont was pleased the old woman's regular maid was carrying out most of the nursing duties. A district nurse also called twice a week. Most of Alice's days now, thankfully, were spent with Charlie. Mrs Pembridge recognised that a bond had developed between the girl and her son, and she seemed happy to let Alice spend time with the child - when Charlie was playing, of course: there was no way she would let Alice have any role in his formal education.

Alice had followed her mother, Lillian, into domestic service. Lillian had left school at fourteen and found work through the Girls Friendly Society. She stopped work when she became pregnant with Alice towards the end of the first war. She now worked as a seamstress in her native Lancashire. Alice's father, a railwayman, had been killed in an accident when she was just three. She had always resisted finding out exactly what had happened, but her mother's face went grey after he died and people said a light went out inside her. Alice and Philip did not speak about this shared loss of a father, but it was there: the companionship caused by it comforted them.

Like her mother Alice had found herself working for the middle classes, rather than in the larger houses where a busy under-stairs staff worked to facilitate long days of hunting, politics and entertaining. She got the job with the Pembridges through Mr Brightman, a friend of Lillian's. He was a partner in the factory where Lillian worked and had started giving Lillian a lift home in his shiny black motor car. It had caused mirth, ridicule, then jealousy with some of Lillian's workmates. Then he mentioned his friends in Jersey and Alice was sent away. Alice resented him then and it was only recently she realised he had been deeply and genuinely in love with her tired but still pretty mother. Now it made her feel sad to think of his embarrassment and her mother's total unease with any thoughts of men other than her late husband.

At the Pembridges' Alice had started as third house maid and, although she was desperately homesick at first, she grew to adore living on an island, cherishing every opportunity she had to get away from the house. Not that there was anything especially wrong with her employers. Her mother said they were good people, a dream compared with some of the masters she'd had.

Alice managed to get out and about regularly, one of her jobs being walking the family's three dogs, Tot, Jill and Tessa. But one thing work kept her from was the opposite sex. Mrs Pembridge took it upon herself to ensure that Alice was allowed no time with men. It seemed like a promise to Alice's mother, or Mr Brightman at least.

Philip Mortain had slipped through the net, partly because they were no longer in Jersey now and Mrs Pembridge was running a strange household with new staff, but also because of the war. The rules were changing, even for people like Mrs Pembridge.

Mrs Pembridge's brother, Michael, travelled regularly to Cardiff and twice Alice had managed to go along to meet with Philip in a coffee shop in Cowbridge Road.

But time had passed since that gentle kiss at Weymouth and Philip was preparing for yet another departure: this time leaving Wales to begin his training to be an RAF pilot.

Despite her naturally cheerful disposition, Alice could not get rid of the nagging feeling that she would lose Philip before she even really got to know him.

The next official letter to arrive at Philip Mortain's Cardiff lodgings had been a call to report for duty.

One icy cold morning in early November he found himself standing on a platform at Cardiff railway station. He was dressed in dark trousers and a navy blue coat. He had put on a faded black and gold tie which Bryn had given him. He had said goodbye to his friend the night before and packed everything he owned into a medium-sized bag which he flung over his shoulder.

A train halted in the station and stood there hissing. The steam broke through the brittle morning as Philip stepped forward and opened a heavy door.

That journey had taken him to Devon, an RAF reception wing. He'd stepped off the carriage at the other end into a new world. He walked onto the RAF station to be given his kit.

He spent the next week being introduced to marching. It seemed, looking back, that was all they had done, although in fact he spent a lot more time waiting and queuing. He stood behind dozens of others to swear the oath, to get jabs, to get his flying kit, his uniform and his identity card. And at the end of it there was another queue: this time for a rail ticket to take him to an Initial Training Wing (ITW) at RAF Paignton.

For Philip, it was to be the winter of the physical training instructor, fearsome figures with muscles bulging under their white pullovers. There was PE, drill and class work for three months:

lessons on the theory of flight, engines, meteorology, arithmetic, aircraft and shop recognition, navigation and signals.

At night, with legs tired from drill, Philip and the others would get dressed in their bright new aircrew cadet uniform and go out to show themselves off to the public. The nights in the pub often turned into drunken bragging, placing chairs so that four or five of them appeared to be seated in an aircraft. Harry, a Scot, would normally lie across a chair on his belly, wink at a girl in the corner, and then stare down at the floor pretending to be a bomb aimer. For some reason, both girls and his colleagues responded to Philip – he was quiet and assured, with gentle good looks – and while his friends pushed him into the 'crew skipper' role in their charade, the local girls often had eyes only for him. After a couple of seconds over the "target", Harry would chop his hand down, shout 'Bombs away!' and then race to the bar to drink back whatever remained of his pint in one go. Philip and his co-pilot would salute the girls before joining Harry for another beer.

Philip passed his pilot selection course and found himself waiting for a place at a flying school. He looked at his reflection in the mirror – the uniform, the regulation haircut – wondering when he was going to get a chance to learn how to fly. Then the next posting. Leading Aircraftman Mortain was going to a base near Stoke-on-Trent.

Only five weeks earlier he had donned a 1918 flying helmet and goggles to climb into the open cockpit of a Miles Magister. As the instructor took the controls in front of him, he had felt a surge of excitement – and turned to look at the far off perimeter fence. He imagined James stood against it, counting all the aeroplanes. Eighteen days ago he had flown solo for the first time and since clocked up 65 hours at the controls. Then, just two days ago, he had flown the 'Maggie' for the last time, a chief instructor in the front cockpit. He had rolled and looped, and shown the instructor how he would recover from a spin. It had been the final test.

Now, as he approached Howell Grove, he longed to tell Alice how he had been fully recommended to train as a bomber pilot.

Chapter Six

A dark green ivy obscured much of Howell Grove, including the façade of the tower. It was so thick, Philip reckoned, he could easily climb the three-storeys to the roof turrets like Errol Flynn.

The door was built black and heavy as if to muffle the crunch visitors' feet made on the gravelled drive. Philip tugged a wire bell-pull that rang a brass bell in the inner hall and waited.

It was not until he heard someone fumble a latch inside that he began to consider whether perhaps he should have gone to the kitchen entrance of the house, as he would have while making deliveries to the grand places back home.

'Sir?' It was a maid in a white apron. She was very young but had a slight stoop and a local accent.

'Hello,' Philip said awkwardly, still aware that his Jersey accent was a curiosity here, 'I'm Philip Mortain. I'm here to see Alice. Miss Dearmont.'

'Mrs Pembridge is expecting you,' the maid said, opening the door to reveal a large wood-panelled hall. It was an empty space looked over by a staircase and three large portraits of well-dressed and stern Victorian men. The room did not welcome the visitor and Philip's eyes took a moment to adjust to the lack of light.

The maid opened another door and Philip was relieved to find himself in a well-lit drawing room.

The furniture seemed to have been collected over the last century and little matched. There were three heavy mahogany chairs under a large window looking out to the side of the house. There was a broad fireplace with a mantelpiece as high as a man's shoulders. A gold clock ticked loudly. In the centre of the room was a soft three-seater brown sofa and two odd armchairs, each with square pieces of lace thrown over the back.

Annabel Pembridge sat in one of the chairs. She had been reading when Philip walked in. She put the book down on a round walnut table at her side and stood.

'Mr Mortain,' she said. 'Welcome to my home.'

She was a striking-looking woman of middle-age who, Philip was to discover, had a deep interest in the war in the air. She asked him how he had enjoyed his training and, a follower of the fighter squadrons, she was only mildly disappointed when he told her his next posting would be to Flying Training School to train as a bomber pilot. The discovery phased her for only a moment and then she quickly went on to talk about recent bombing raids on Hamburg and the attacks on the German battle-cruiser *Scharnhorst* in Brest which she had been reading about.

All the time, Philip wondered when he would be free to see Alice.

It was an hour before Mrs Pembridge called the maid and told her to fetch Alice.

The door went and Charlie came in. He looked at Philip, thought he might recognise him, but then turned and climbed up on to one of the chairs by the window. He kneeled on the chair, facing out and making smudge marks on the glass with his hands.

But Philip was quickly ignoring him too: Alice had been right behind the little boy. He stood as she came into the room and then there was an awkward moment as they faced each other, unable to touch. Alice glanced at Mrs Pembridge and then sat on the sofa.

Philip no longer had his coat on now and he could see Alice running her eyes over his uniform. He pulled the tunic down smartly and sat back down.

'I expect you two have a lot to talk about,' Mrs Pembridge said and smiled kindly. 'I shall see to Charles for an hour. Perhaps you would like to show Mr Mortain the grounds?'

'Oh, yes, Madam,' Alice said, standing quickly.

'Thank you, Mrs Pembridge,' Philip added, making for the door.

'You will eat with us tonight, Mr Mortain,' the woman went on. 'It's rabbit. And I have a special guest whom I am sure would be very interested to meet you. He used to take his holidays in the Channel Islands. And he serves the Government as, we may say, do you.'

'I look forward to that,' Philip said, but all he really wanted was to stand somewhere quiet and take Alice in his arms.

At the rear of the house, in its shelter, was a large outhouse in which Michael Pembridge normally parked his Singer Le Mans. One of the doors was open as Philip and Alice past it and the airman could see old farming tools hanging from nails in the walls. There was a large stubble rake: fan-shaped with a handle at one end and a curve of sharp iron prongs at the other. They had one at home.

Alice led him past a wire cage full of yellow ducklings and stopped when they could no longer be seen from the house. The pair stood for a moment, the branches of a chestnut tree creaking in the gentle breeze above their heads.

Then Alice laughed, put her hands on the collar of his tunic and pulled his face towards hers.

The man at dinner that night was introduced only as Mr Bachelor. He never actually said what he did other than the fact that he had an office in London. Alice said she had heard Michael Pembridge and him talk about the War Office.

Bachelor was short, about five feet five inches, with a heavy round body and a slightly piggy face, so it surprised Philip when he said: 'You're a bit tall for a Frenchman, aren't you?'

They had been talking about Philip's life in Jersey and Mrs Pembridge had questioned him as strongly as Bachelor. She seemed to have forgotten she had ever lived there at all; although their lives had been very different.

'I am not French, Mr Bachelor,' said Philip, who was now wearing a second-hand black lounge suit. 'My father was a proud Frenchman and I am glad of that. But I am a Jerseyman.'

'What is your French like?'

Philip hesitated and shifted a little agitatedly. He was uncomfortable sitting in this quiet oak dining room discussing personal or military details with two strangers. Even if one was apparently from the War Office.

'I grew up speaking it,' he said flatly, composing himself, aware it appeared that he was being provoked. 'Around my father, so it is his French rather than Jèrriais. I suppose I speak it like a Frenchman. Although my slang is some years out of date.'

Bachelor made a 'humph' noise which could have been critical but might just have been an acknowledgement of the response.

'It is terrible what is happening out there,' Bachelor said. 'France. Are you a patriot, Mr Mortain?'

Philip had never been asked such a question and he hesitated, totally unaware of how to respond. To England? France? Jersey? What did this mean?

Both Mrs Pembridge and Bachelor had lain their spoons in their soup bowls and were watching him.

'I have never been prouder than now,' he said, "Within six months, sir, I will have my wings.' He touched his chest as he mentioned the badge that would confirm he was a fully trained pilot, and he felt like a child in that stuffy room.

He held Bachelor's stare.

'Here, here,' Mrs Pembridge said firmly and finished her soup.

Chapter Seven
Luxembourg, 1941

It was almost totally black dark with just a sliver of a moon.

It had been raining gently all day and, although it had stopped now, moisture still hung in the air. It clung to everything in Marc Rameau's limited field of vision.

Everything appeared to be covered in the thinnest of cobwebs.

He had become familiar with the shrubs and bushes that now appeared to have grown up around him. The dark stalks of the vegetation had taken on lives of their own. Each stem stood silent before twitching as if startled or communicating with its neighbour. Each leaf was covered with a thin damp sheen like a light sweat. He'd followed the lines of each curve and junction, each plant which stood black in the night.

He was freezing cold; the damp having simply and slowly seeped through him over a period of two, nearly three hours. Right down to his bones. His left arm had gone dead again under his body.

He had been doing a lot of thinking. There had been so much time and, the struggle to keep warm, the fear he had felt with every rustle or footstep, had concentrated his mind. *Why was he here?*

Rameau was lying at the foot of a low hill in the south-eastern corner of his homeland. Behind him stretched a wood that he had taken two hours to trek through as the night had fallen. To the east a second cluster of trees protected the lower slopes of another small valley – his back-up escape route. In front of him and only a short distance from the thick shrubbery stood a six-foot high wire fence.

This was where the Moselle Valley wound its way lazily across the pre-invasion frontier between Luxembourg and Germany. Here the south facing slopes had been creating wealth for winegrowers since before the birth of Christ. Rameau had no interest in either: the merchants or the Messiah.

Rameau had been born in the north of the country between Clervaux and the Belgian border. His Belgian father had given up teaching in the village school when his wife died. He had spent his meagre savings bringing up *petit* Marc and died just as the teenager was turning into a young man.

Rameau wanted to be a painter and travelled to Namur to study the views of the Meuse and Sambre rivers. He managed to make a living during one season selling sketches and watercolours of the *Citadelle*, the fortress that dominates the city, to tourists.

He made friends who described how his country had been a pawn in games played by financiers, royal households, generals and aristocrats for centuries. They described a world in which the working classes of every country could take power of what was rightfully theirs. It seemed right. The people who struggled to scrape a living in the forests of the Ardennes in his country surely had more in common with the Indians of Peru than with Grand Duchess Charlotte in her palace in Luxembourg. And how his father had railed against her sister Marie-Adelaide when she had welcomed the conquerors in 1914 and been forced to abdicate when the Germans lost the Great War.

Very soon Rameau was working for the small but growing band of Belgian communists. He travelled around the Netherlands in 1937 to see how the communists there ran a successful election campaign by building alliances with the socialists. He used every bus and train route within 200 miles of his attic home in Namur to talk to trade unionists and spent six months in Spain fighting with the International Brigades and dodging Hitler's terrifying new *Luftwaffe*.

His friends faltered when the party flipped its political somersault during the Nazi-Soviet pact but Rameau held firm. He knew that one leader was much like another. The revolution meant far more than any of them. While people scoffed and even threw back their membership cards, Rameau insisted they held firm. He argued his case in meetings from Spa, where from Roman times until his grandfather's generation the rich had come to take the waters, to the fishing bars of Ostend, which before the war had watched the fine ladies pass under parasols, imaging the fine days of Leopold II and the English Queen Victoria. The old targets were never far from his thoughts or his rhetoric.

Then on May 10, 1940, Heinz Guderian's 1 Panzer Division steamed through Luxembourg unchallenged.

Charlotte and her husband, Prince Felix of Bourbon-Parma, simply drove out of their palace and got clean away. Now she was apparently in Canada and the idiots who had been running the government before the invasion were pretending they were still in charge from some pokey office in London.

Luxembourg had exchanged its royal masters for a governor named Gustav Simon, after the Nazis swallowed up the tiny nation into their Gau of Moselland. The name of Luxembourg ceased to exist and Gauleiter Simon set about incorporating his new land into his beloved Third Reich. He quickly banned French, the language of government, and then had it taken off street signs. Then came a ban on the local dialect, Letzeburgesch.

Many of Rameau's countrymen accepted what seemed to be just another set of changes to their mongrel culture. After all, the Germans were not strangers.

But by the summer of 1941 Rameau, who was seeking to pull together a small group of men to take up arms against the invaders, began to sense a growing feeling of anger, aggravated by food shortages which saw some in the towns close to starvation.

Then in September, the Nuremberg Laws against the Jews, forbidding them to marry Germans, to sleep with Germans or to hold professional posts, were extended to Luxembourg. It added to a growing unease which revealed itself the following month when a census required every citizen to state their nationality and mother tongue. Simon, of course, expected the people to put down German but 97 per cent put down Luxembourger and Letzeburgesch instead. Everyone was talking in whispers about the census. Many thought they had done the bravest thing in the world. Not Rameau. It was not enough for him. He had learned something in Spain before, wounded and exhausted, he had dragged himself in retreat towards the River Ebro, and, if he would use it to protect his comrades hundreds of miles away on strange soil, he would certainly use it here. And now.

So here he was lying on the edge of a forest about 40 miles from his childhood home. He had returned there after the Germans came.

And last night he had set out from the northern corner of the forest to come here to lie in the dark and wait.

Slowly, he stretched out his legs, one at a time. He wiggled his toes and rubbed his gloved hands together.

He was wearing his old black hunting boots. Their leather had softened around him over the years but the sole was still strong. He had kept a black woollen hat down over his ears and had blackened his face with charcoal. As he had come through the forest he had also coated himself in mud. It was risky: he would have to get back to the north and looking so scruffy would certainly raise suspicions if he ran into a patrol. But his two previous visits to this site, seven and fourteen days earlier, had taught him that the sentries who patrolled the forest – although not the wire - always had dogs with them and he hoped the mud and dirt would cover his scent.

Rameau rubbed his right hand against his thigh and then reached inside his jacket. He slowly felt for the six-inch knife, one of the few things he had kept of his father's after his death. It still had its original brown leather scabbard. Rameau unclipped the clasp across the shoulder of the dagger and then, leaving the blade in its scabbard, put it back in his pocket.

He brought his hand out again, this time with a small set of wire cutters.

He could barely breathe now, such was the effort to keep his senses alive to any movement or sound around him.

He looked at his watch, slowly pulling back the cuff of his brown corduroy jacket. He was afraid that even the ticking of the watch might give him away.

It was two-and-a-half minutes since the sentry had moved away to his right, walking slowly inside the wire. He had more than twelve minutes until his return. He had timed the guards on his previous visits, first from right back in the woods and the previous week from the exact spot where he lay now.

He crawled forward, gently parting the plants in his way and letting them drop back behind him. He looked to the right and thought he could still see the sentry way out in the gloom where the two arc lights lighting the depot finally gave in to the night. He stared and realised all was still.

He looked left. Nothing.

He brought the cutters out in front of his face and settled them against the fence. *Cut!* The sound seemed to ring out. He held his breath. Nothing moved. He adjusted the cutters to another section. *Cut!* And again. *Cut!* Even the crumpling of his jacket seemed to break though the quiet night. The wire was broken enough to be pulled back now and for him to slip through. He pulled himself forward, his body half through. In front of him was a line of three-ton Opel trucks, all black squares with covered backs. Occasionally a piece of canvas snapped in the breeze. Slowly, Rameau raised himself to his feet and, stooping slow, walked briskly to the nearest vehicle and crawled underneath it. He took out the wire cutters and fumbled for a cable with his left hand. He found one, held it between his fingers and snipped. He crawled quickly back out, stood still, listening; and then unscrewed the cap on the fuel tank. For two months he had been collecting sugar. His trouser pockets were weighed down with it. He'd separated it out into six small bags. He untied one now, fumbling with his gloved fingers, and poured it into the tank. He put the cap back on and then went on to the next lorry. On the fourth truck, he undid his trousers and relieved himself in the fuel tank for good measure. He glanced at his watch and realised the sentry must be moments away. Swiftly but moving lightly on his feet he made his way back to the second truck.

It was now he started to panic. He should have got out before the sentry passed this way again. He had pulled the wire back together and the sentry had previously not been shining his light on the fence as he walked, but he still feared he might discover the hole.

He crouched under the cab of the second truck, the rear of the Opel facing back towards the wire. These three-tonners were high off the ground but the bulky rear axle obscured some of Rameau's view of the fencing.

The sentry's feet clipped on the concrete. Rameau lay still like a cat, his blood seemingly beating like a drum in his temple.

Chapter Eight

Rameau could tell by his walk that it was the same guy as before.

This man hated being a soldier. Believing there was no-one around he was slouched, weighed down his rifle, helmet and greatcoat. It looked faintly absurd.

But he was walking much closer to the wire now, or so it seemed. Rameau watched him disappear by the first rear tyre of his vehicle and shifted his gaze to watch him come through. But he did not.

Rameau suddenly felt sick and feared he was going to vomit with fear. He lifted his hand to his mouth and felt a warm liquid on his lips. It was oil or brake fluid and he almost gagged on it. He rubbed it off his lips frantically. The guard still had not appeared and Rameau inched forward.

Then the sentry came into view, he was walking towards the first lorry, bending and studying the ground. *Jesus, the fluid must be leaking right into his path.* Rameau took a breath. He wondered if the sentry would go under the truck to see if a cable were cut or would assume it was just a mechanical fault. The sentry stopped and his boots turned. He was heading back for the wire. As he took his second step, Rameau's right hand was in under his jacket and taking the knife out of the scabbard. At the same time he carefully scooped up some grit and dirt, and clutched it tightly into his left fist.

He edged backwards out from under the truck and shuffled forward on the blind side to the guard. He could see the sentry now. He was about ten feet away, moving nearer the fence. The beam of his torch set the shadow of the wire on the grass behind. It stopped where Rameau had come through.

It took two maybe three seconds for the German to realise there was a break in the wire. It took another for him to realise what that meant. As he did so, his feet shifted, his body becoming alert.

Rameau had flexed the knife in his grip, once, loosening the tendons of his hand.

As the sentry took an involuntary step back and began to turn, Rameau launched himself off his back foot and in two long strides he was at the man's back, his left arm going around his face, shoving the dirt into his mouth and causing the startled German to give out a muffled choke.

Even in his heavy boots the German was shorter than the six foot two inch Rameau and Rameau's oily glove slipped over the lower part of his face.

Rameau felt one of his fingers go between the sentry's teeth as his other arm swung up and drove the knife through the heavy coat and into his back to the right of his spine.

As the sentry struggled, Rameau's arm moved and the knife ripped upwards. The German was already collapsing backwards, forcing Rameau to fall too.

The soldier's helmet struck Rameau above the eye and then clinked on the ground and rolled away. Rameau still had his hand firmly over the man's mouth. He could feel the heat of the man's final breaths through the glove.

Rameau lay panting for a few seconds until the dead man became unbearable heavy on him.

He steered the body off him and looked swiftly around. Somehow he expected to hear sirens and shouts. But there was nothing.

It was as if there had been only him and the sentry in the world, and now there was only him.

He caught a glimpse of the German's face. He had young, blemish-free skin and soft fair hair which fell gently on his fringe. He looked like a schoolboy, except for that terrified and startled look in his eyes.

Rameau tried to steel himself, to think of the Stuka dive-bombers, the lethal shrapnel of the hard Spanish rock and mountainside.

He grabbed the shoulders of the man's great coat and pulled him back to the nearest lorry. He took the pistol from the sentry's holster and jammed it into his own waistband. He rolled the body under the lorry, collected his helmet and rifle, and then listened again. Still nothing, but he realised his breaths were coming quick now and he was afraid his hearing was less keen.

He stooped and walked over to the fence, slipped through the hole and disappeared into the trees.

Shortly after Rameau had arrived in Spain, Franco had launched a massive offensive on Valencia. The 27-year-old communist had found himself fighting in a strange city's streets in the summer sun. People had been maimed and killed around him, but in atmosphere of noise and confusion. He had not killed in such silence as this. Gripping that Nazi and driving the blade into him had felt strangely exhilarating, he had felt like a terrible force hurtling down a mountainside. As he moved through the wood he began to think how easy it had been. Holding the man right up close. The surprise. And then the other man's body had been still and feeling twice its weight.

Suddenly he stopped and crouched against the side of a tree. He had to take breaths. He realised the excitement - he had to accept that was what he felt - of the kill was making him careless: he was crashing through the undergrowth like an elephant. If he were challenged, he was dead; there was no talking himself out of anything. He'd been planning this for two weeks and, although he had to admit he was starting small, the dead German had not just been a bonus but the whole prize. The planning and execution had gone well but it was not a success until he was home, safe and free.

Rameau knew the guard was due to be relieved at four o'clock so he knew he had to come out of the wood a different way. He turned towards Remich not wanting to be trapped in the trees when the search began. Then he began to panic that there was another guard further around the depot that would miss his comrade. But it wasn't much of a target after all and there had been virtually no sabotage activity in the area. He was basically, he reckoned, on his own.

He crossed the Mondorf-les-Bains road as it was getting light. During his trips to check out the depot he had cleaned and simply made his way back home during the day, catching the train into Luxembourg city and then home. But by now the alarm would be raised and he had to rethink everything. This was the least well thought out section of his plan, simply because he had not expected to have to kill and thought he would have hours before his sabotage was discovered.

He had an old friend living in a small farm on the eastern outskirts of Remich. There was no doubt Bertrand Gillier could be trusted. He was an old communist whom Rameau had met when developing links with the rail workers union. Gillier had been an angry official, heavily-built with a red face from drinking too much of the local wine. Several times Rameau had seen him use his huge fists in brawls in the town and, though he knew Gillier's temper and mouth could be trouble when he had two or three bottles inside him, he reckoned he had to take a chance.

He had not seen Gillier since shortly before the Nazis arrived. Then the union man had been living alone. Rameau hoped that were still the case. He didn't think Gillier, who was well into his 40s and more interested in the grape than romance, would have found a wife, but he was worried as he approached the building.

It was a white-stoned house with a steep red roof. It was surrounded on three sides by an old stone wall which looked like it would collapse if anyone leant against it. The farm – Gillier had about an acre of land – appeared to have aged a decade since Rameau last visited. He began to wonder what had happened to Gillier. Dead? Worse, taken by the Germans?

Rameau thought about simply finding a stream, washing his hands and face and taking his chances on the railways. But, the light was coming up and he could see that it would take more than a swill in a stream to clean himself and his clothes. There was a short field between him and the house. Away to the left was a road, little more than a lane. Nothing had moved down it in the hour-or-so he had been watching the house. He ducked down and moved along a hedgerow so he could not be seen from the lane. The ditch along the hedge was sodden with the previous evening's rain and his boots squelched in the mud. As he got nearer he could see the side window of the house much clearer. There was a crack in the pain and an ugly, yellow curtain fluttered in a draft behind it. A cobweb as thick as lace danced in the draft. Rameau reached the wall, stopped and listened, and then lifted himself over it. A dog barked somewhere on the other side of the house. For a minute he expected it to come bounding around the corner but it kept barking and the noise came no nearer. It was straining against a leash.

Rameau walked quickly around the back of the house until he was shielded from the road. He stood with his back to the wall. There was no noise from the house at all.

He was pretty sure the Nazis weren't using the house: it looked too run down. But if Gillier was no longer there and someone else was, Rameau realised he was probably doomed.

The yard out the back, Rameau noted, stank of dog faeces and knee-high weeds had broken back the age-old cobbles. The corner was crammed with a ramshackle toilet and a loosely gathered woodpile which one had to study to tell apart.

Rameau ducked under a window and stood with his back against the wall. From here he was looking out through the wooden five-bar gate to the long grass of the meadow beyond. The morning was breaking and the watery October sun was doing its best to heat up the ground.

He needed to get inside. Slowly he pulled the German's pistol out of his trousers and held it at his side. He took a breath and started to lean towards the back door. He was trying to be careful but he knew he was clumsy through exhaustion.

Suddenly, he felt a blow to his ear and a huge fist grabbed his clothes, pulling his head towards the door frame. He heard a sickening crack as his head hit the wall.

His legs were tangled and they went from under him. He crashed onto the stone floor inside the house, feeling the gun fall from his grasp.

His head took another blow, this time on the cold floor, and it felt like his eyeball was racked loose. The air rushed out of his lungs. A knee pushed down onto his chest and a foot stamped heavily on his right hand, the killing hand.

Fingers, so thick and long that they covered his face, pushed his cheek into the floor. The stone cut his skin.

He was totally immobilised. He gasped for breath.

Then someone said in French: 'Good God, Marco the red.'

It was a light voice; it was almost impossible to believe it came from behind the force of that knee, that suffocating hand.

The grip lifted off Rameau's face and he suddenly realised something else: that smell. He had noticed it on the fingers, but the pressure on his nose meant that it hardly registered. Despite its pungency.

Now he had the full effect. From the skin, the clothes, the breath of Bertrand Gillier.

Gillier had not changed much, although Rameau reckoned he might have actually put on a few pounds. His face was red as a poppy and at first he thought it was from the exertion of the struggle – but it barely faded as they talked. He was wearing brown tweed trousers, which were so threadbare in places Rameau could see the grazed flabby flesh of his knee, and a white undershirt so loose at the neck it hung open so that Rameau could see down to his huge belly.

'Marco,' Gillier was saying and using the hands which had brought him down to help him back up. 'My friend, my friend.'

Rameau wiped a hand across his bloody mouth and sniffed, taking in the stench of drink, tobacco and body odour.

'My dear Bertrand,' panted Rameau, slowly regaining his breath. 'I hope I did not startle you...'

The men's eyes met for the first time. Gillier still had that wicked twinkle. The one that would tease and goad some fellow union official who the big man felt was too spineless to tackle the bosses. Now those laughing eyes moved from Rameau's ashen face down his crumpled body.

'Yes, yes, you startled me, Marco,' he said loudly and tipped his head back in a long, deep laugh. 'Sit down, my friend, sit down,' he spluttered, still chuckling and gesturing to a large armchair, as brown and threadbare as Gillier's trousers.

Rameau laughed quietly with Gillier; but his head hurt, he had a shooting pain in his elbow and his feet were aching. He was exhausted.

Gillier was holding the sentry's gun in front of him.

'This is a German pistol, my friend,' he said flatly. He'd stopped laughing and was rubbing his flabby chin with one of those shovel-sized hands. 'Have you joined the *Wehrmacht*?'

It was another good joke and the laugh returned.

'I need your help, Bertrand,' Rameau stated, this time without sharing the other man's good humour. 'Just a few hours. A place to wash and to rest for a few hours. Then I'll be on my way.'

'The Germans are after you?'

Both men, although they spoke French and German, had now slipped into forbidden *Letzebuergesch*.

Rameau hesitated. 'I'm sorry, Bertrand, no questions. It will be better for you.'

'I understand that, my friend, but I'd like to know whether I should expect them today. My house could do with a clean, you know...'

Rameau smiled. He was getting really comfortable in this dirty old chair with this ragged old friend who looked 20 years older than he remembered. It was dangerous.

'I don't see that they would necessarily come here,' Rameau said. 'I took a detour through a stream. That works with dogs, doesn't it? There's no reason without a scent that they would know I had come in this direction. They know nothing about me.'

Gillier nodded his head very slowly. 'If they cannot make trouble for you, Marco, then I am afraid they will make trouble for some other poor fool,' he frowned.

He was sitting back. He had the kind of belly which forced a man to sit with his legs apart.

'You have not changed, my friend,' he said at last, nodding in agreement with himself. 'Still in Spain.'

'The Germans came here,' Rameau replied.

'You are right, they did, and there's no denying that,' Gillier replied, his voice breathless in the act of heaving his huge frame out of the chair. 'And there is no denying what bastards they are.'

Gillier moved to a cluttered oak sideboard and fumbled with a piece of dark cloth.

'Now, my friend, I will put this gun into a bag and bury it under one of the very many loose cobbles which decorate my poorly tended yard! It may only be for a few hours but we cannot be too careful.'

'In that case,' Rameau reached inside his jacket, 'you had better take this also.' He held up the dagger and its scabbard.

Gillier studied it, saying nothing.

Then he quickly laughed, took the knife and disappeared out the back door.

Rameau straightened his back: it felt as though a knot had formed in every single muscle. He stretched his legs, stood and went to the window. Gillier was struggling down on one knee in the corner of the yard near the gate. One hand lifted a cobble as if it were a pebble and his podgy fingers scrabbled around in the dirt.

He pushed off the ground with two hands to get back up.

Rameau went back to the chair and felt his eyes begin to close as the back door clicked shut.

'You must wash and sleep now,' Gillier said, closing the back door. 'Come through.' When he saw Rameau, he laughed to himself, wandered off and brought back a blanket to cover his exhausted guest.

Chapter Nine

When Rameau woke he could hear Gillier moving around in the kitchen. The house smelled of smoke, burning meat.

Rameau stretched and wandered to the door to watch the big man moving slowly in front of a huge stove which, together with a stack of wood, dominated the room. A thin loose strip of wallpaper flickered at one corner of the stove, angered by the heat.

Gillier had fried small pieces of ham and two eggs for Rameau. He put a cracked plate on the table with black bread.

'I have not cooked for anyone since...I do not know when!' he said.

Rameau ate it all up greedily, wiping the bread in the egg yolk and washing it down with a glass of a sharp red wine.

He looked at the heavy brown clock on the mantelpiece.

'Is that the right time?'

Gillier looked at the clock. 'Yes.' It was after 2pm. 'You slept very heavily.'

'I'd better be going.'

'I will drive you home,' said his host, scratching his gut through his shirt.

'Don't worry about that,' Rameau stated, sipping the hot, black coffee Gillier had made him. 'But it would help if you could take me *en ville.*'

Gillier had a small green van which ran on gas. Rameau could see the back was littered with tools and boxes. Hammers, boxes of screws, screwdrivers.

'There are perks to a life working on the railway,' said Gillier. 'Such as never having to buy your own tools. Ha-ha!'

The van chugged into life and, as the dog started barking again, Gillier set off towards Luxembourg.

The big railwayman filled the driver's side of the vehicle. He'd pulled on a dark blue jerkin which bulged at the seams. He wore a red neckerchief which was covered in dark stains and had obviously regularly doubled as a rag. Soon after they set off he loosened the knot with one hand and used it to wipe his brow. He then hung it loosely back around his neck.

For a short distance they followed Gillier's beloved railway track. Rameau watched a long freight train come up behind them and travel alongside. There must have been a dozen carriages, maybe more.

'Bringing coke in from the Ruhr,' Gillier said. 'Still money in steel. Only now it goes to the German war effort.'

Rameau did not reply or even smile as Gillier enjoyed his black joke. He watched the last truck disappear into the distance.

'Are you still driving?'

'No, I'm not trusted,' Gillier replied proudly. 'Even my bosses did not trust me. The Germans certainly do not. Sometimes they let me travel as fireman. But they wouldn't let me on a troop train.' Gillier turned to his friend and winked.

His body rocking back and forth on the loose suspension of the van, Rameau watched a flat, hedgeless countryside move past him slowly. There was a knocking in the engine which got louder everytime Gillier crunched the gears. It seemed to even disturb the wildlife. But Rameau now paid no heed to it.

As they arrived in the city, he turned to Gillier and asked quietly as if in danger of being overheard: "Is there a set time table for the steel trains?"

Chapter Ten

Marc Rameau sat in the café off the Place D'Armes, a cigarette burning down between his fingers. He wore a thick brown sweater with a rolled neck and a darker corduroy jacket. It was a cold day and as he pushed his left hand back through his ragged mop of black hair he felt his body shiver.

Facing the door from his seat at the back of the café, he could see right into and across the street. A German officer stood outside the shop opposite. He was pointing and smiling at something in the window. The girl at his side was laughing and grabbing his arm. When the couple moved off, still giggling in each other's warmth, others soon replaced them. The city was busy with people looking for scraps for Christmas, wandering from one half-empty shop window to the next. Most though went to the black market now, for anything from food to lightbulbs.

Rameau took a heavy drag on the cigarette and stubbed it out in the ashtray on the table in front of him. He leaned forward on his elbows and felt the steam rising from his mug of black coffee. It was going to be a long winter. He felt it – every time he took the slow train down to the city; every time the north of the country felt the icy, dark touch of another power cut. He could see it too in the faces of the other customers in the small café: the pale, drawn skin of the mother in the corner, her reddish tweed coat pulled around her shoulders as she tried to cheer up a crying child; the old man puffing angrily on a pipe. These were the faces Rameau saw everywhere; he'd seen them before the war too. Tired, working people, now given in to a fresh defeat to an invader.

The door clicked open and Giles Wallis came in. Both the woman and the old man turned to look at him. He was different. He wasn't making do with three and four-year-old clothes. His suit was cut especially with smooth black cloth. He looked disdainfully at the wooden chairs and tables, and came to sit opposite Rameau, putting a neat grey trilby hat on the table. He called to the owner who was wiping glasses behind the counter and ordered a coffee. Rameau declined another mug.

'No milk again.' Wallis shook his head. He'd developed a taste for milky drinks during his travels in England before the war. Now he was doing well in the head office of one of the city banks. His work brought him into contact with many of the German officers administering the city and he had access to *ausweiss*, the travel passes everyone needed to move around the Reich. 'Why do we have to meet in dumps like this?' he went on in a whisper. 'It's okay for you, but I look... well... out of place.' He smiled broadly at Rameau, who noticed for the first time that he had perfect white teeth.

Rameau lit another cigarette.

'Have you got it for me?'

The men paused as the café owner delivered a large mug of coffee to the table. Wallis put his teaspoon into it and stirred once. He obviously did not like the look of it.

'Now our own people are trying to kill us,' he said, just loud enough for the owner to hear him.

Rameau looked uncomfortable: he really did not like to draw attention to himself and he hated to criticise people trying their best to live their lives.

Wallis realised his companion was not likely to make small talk. They had known each other for years for despite the visitor's job he had been a member of the Communist Party since before Rameau himself. Rameau did not think Wallis a good communist but he knew he had taken a beating from a squad of SS in Kiel in 1934 and, that under the wolfish grin, there was a deep burning hatred. Wallis' work and connections had been helpful to the Party before the war; they were essential now.

'Everything is in place,' he stated.

'Exactly what I asked for?'

'More than enough,' he replied. 'I suggest you keep some back.'

'*Ausweiss*?'

'Proving more difficult. I need the dates.'

'Anytime this month,' Rameau said.

Wallis moved the other man's hand: the cigarette smoke was in his face.

'Before Christmas?'

'Anytime,' Rameau said.

'Luck of the draw, eh? In that case, you shall have it. Like a festive gift.' Wallis tried another sip of his coffee, and then gave up. 'Don't tell me what you are going to do with any of it,' he said, standing and putting his hat on. 'I'm a respectable man.'

'I won't,' Rameau said. 'And you are.'
Wallis winked and walked briskly to the door.

The steel industry in the south-west corner of the grand duchy had been producing more than two million tons a year during the 1930s, relying on ore from Lorraine and coke from the Ruhr. With the steelworks, like the rest of Luxembourg, now incorporated into the Reich, Rameau knew the industry was forming a significant part of the German war machine: Gillier reckoned it was producing between five and ten per cent of Germany's steel. It was the kind of target which made Rameau's mouth water. He had taken as much information from Gillier without letting him in on the plan: while he trusted Gillier's heart, he feared his propensity to drink could lead him to be boastful and, besides, he was already known as a troublemaker. Safer for both of them to keep Gillier out of the plan.

His contacts were helpful though and Rameau knew from a man in the old steel unions that the plants themselves were heavily guarded.

But trains were trains. They could be derailed.

Wallis' contact was a man named Weber who worked as some sort of liaison between the police and the town hall. Rameau always met him at a small bar where Weber went every day at ten past one for his lunch.

Rameau rarely felt nervous. He was a loner. If he was to worry, it would be only about himself. And he did not worry about himself. He had been frightened in Spain, yes, everyone was, but with all the destruction around him, the fight against such overwhelming odds, he had never expected to get away from Spain. Once he had developed that kind of fatalism it had never left him. And it had freed him from real fear.

However, that did not mean he wanted to be captured or killed: he had a job to do.

So people like Weber still made him nervous, not just because they were usually meeting to trade money for a travel pass, but because Weber appeared completely untrustworthy. His head moved continually like a bird's, his gaze barely settling on Rameau. He drummed his fingers on the table, even as he ate, shovelling his food in with a fork in his right hand.

He was tearing apart a liver dumpling when Rameau sat down opposite him.

'Kurt Wilberg,' Weber hissed, a piece of brown meat settling on his low lip as he spoke.

His tongue flickered and chewed quickly before adding the name of a hotel which Rameau knew was near the railway station in Trier, the closest German city to the border. Finally, he wiped his face with a paper napkin, and added: 'Tuesday.'

A German newspaper was folded on the table and Rameau could see a story about a delivery of Christmas presents to soldiers in the east. Wrapped inside, as usual, would be the requested travel document.

Rameau picked up the newspaper and, without saying a word, walked out.

Chapter Eleven

Kurt Wilberg had once been a bear of a man.

Well over six feet four inches tall, he had been a miner in Cologne. But down the pit he slowly developed a hunch which forced his broad shoulders forward and left his huge hands dangling somewhere, it seemed, near the ground.

Now, still only forty-nine, the muscles around his shoulders had receded and his lungs were full of dust. He had also lost almost every hair on his head.

When the Nazis had come to power he had been a member of the Revolution Trade Union Opposition (RGO), a communist group trying to organise revolution among German workers. Hitler banned the unions and came down hard on the group. In 1934, Wilberg had been arrested, put on trial and sentenced to several years in jail. When he came out three years later, he had nowhere to live and no job to go back to. But he managed to find work through an old friend back in Cologne as a salesman for a firm selling ties. That was how this giant earned his living now, travelling across Germany trying to persuade boutiques across the Fatherland to invest in his neckwear. Spirits were high at the moment and sales were good.

Wilberg had seen through the Nazi slogans and grand gestures from the beginning. As a trade unionist, he felt, he recognised propaganda and as a communist he knew the Nazi's promises to create a better life were false. It was something the embittered and destitute fell for and not the politically-aware.

Getting around with two suitcases filled with samples, he saw so many of his old friends from the unions and the old Social Democratic Party (some of them were his best customers); many had lost the will to fight or simply wavered from the cause. Others were organising resistance, producing leaflets and even newspapers which Wilberg promoted or passed on where he could.

All those he met, whether they still stood alongside the former miner or not, liked him. For despite his convictions, he was a sunny figure with a smile as broad as his shadow.

The hotel owner at Trier liked Wilberg a lot. The salesman made a point of staying there every time he passed through the city, twice or three times a year, and was a good customer, although obviously not the best. The reason he really liked the huge salesman who would burst through the door with two suitcases under his arm was that Wilberg had convinced him he had been a stuntman and security guard at the UFA film studios in Berlin before the war. Wilberg would regale the wide-eyed hotelier with a few stories of Emil Jannings and Maly Delschaft every time he called as if he were selling the filmstars to him. Wilberg had struck on the ruse on his first visit when he had noticed a studio portrait of Brigitte Helm pasted to the wall behind the man's head. Helm, who stood in long trench coat and smoked a cigarette, had been many people's favourite until a few years ago.

Months spent recruiting for the district RGO office had taught Wilberg how to use someone's weakness, however slight, to his advantage. It started as fun but you never knew when it could be helpful.

Take this visit. He had received an exhilarating message that someone was coming to meet him and would ask for him at the hotel. That could be suspicious and so it helped that Wilberg's misty-eyed friend downstairs would be happy to send a message up to the room. For all the star-struck little man knew this was someone who could have acted opposite his heroine! Wilberg laughed at the thought. What if this contact was 70 and had one leg? Some matinee idol!

But now he was here. The messenger had come through from the foyer and brought the stranger. Wilberg shook his visitor's hand like an old friend, and then tipped the teenage boy whom he knew to be the owner's son. 'Thank you, young one,' he said, guiding him out the door. Then he stood back and looked at his visitor. *He could have been in films*, he thought. Late 20s or early 30s. Slim but strong. Six foot-ish. Dark eyes with a straight mouth. Good for close-ups: a youthful look but eyes that told a different story, of difficult deeds done and of experiences the tight lips would never share. His black hair was untidy mop though, thought Wilberg, he wouldn't get the girl looking like that.

Wilberg sat back on the bed and the mattress sunk beneath him.

'Good to meet you, comrade,' he said, smiling. His voice had a broken sound, like the breath was only travelling through half his windpipe and the rest was blocked. The words almost arrived on a gentle whistle.

Rameau knew nothing about his host. They had no friend in common. Just messages through a series of contacts organised through Wallis' friends in Germany. It seemed odd that they were about to embark on such a dangerous mission together. *Would I die next to this stranger?* Rameau asked himself. It was a question he posed several times when he had first arrived in Spain. No, others died; he survived.

Rameau took out a small crumpled packet of cigarettes and offered Wilberg one.

The man lifted a hand to decline.

'They are trying to draft me into the *Wehrmacht*!' he said, his shoulders beginning to shudder in a laugh. 'Me! I barely have the lungs to shout them on when they march past. The mines, the dust. My shoulders and arms are strong, oh yes, my friend, but my lungs are already an old man's.'

Rameau looked around at the anonymous items in the room: the small bedside table, the wooden chair, the green curtains that were so completely frayed at the bottoms they looked as if they had been designed with a frill. He did not want to know anything about his accomplice. If they were caught, the less they knew about each other the better. But he especially did not want to know that he was unfit and he certainly did not want to hear the wheezing that signalled the end of Wilberg's laughter.

Wilberg took a handkerchief from his pocket and wiped it across his mouth, spitting into it noisily. His face had moved from a bright pink to a darkening red.

'I see you are worrying about me,' he said, waving a finger. 'Don't. Everything is in order. I have everything ready. I may not be going into the *Wehrmacht* but I am still fighting the war.'

He struggled forward, opened one of the cases and rummaged through a stack of ties, each separated by thin white paper. He found a flap and pulled out a small block of plastic explosives.

'Besides,' he said, holding it in between them, 'the fresh air does me the world of good.'

Whatever his reservations about Wilberg's health, Rameau had to acknowledge he was a smart organiser.

After checking out of the hotel, the pair walked to the back of a building facing the *Liebfrauenkirche*. It seemed they were at the kitchens of a busy *gasthaus*. Rameau could hear plates clattering as he stood in the door looking up at the dark stone of the gothic church. Wilberg was inside for only a short time before reappearing with two bicycles. He had ditched one suitcase and placed the other across the handlebars of his bike. The seat was set too low for him and he settled on it as if it were a milking stool.

'Do you think we should reset the saddle?' Rameau was afraid the comical sight of Wilberg struggling through the countryside might arouse not only ridicule but suspicion. Rameau had reached Trier using the *ausweiss* from Weber but the lump of explosives in the case meant they were unlikely to survive a search.

'No time. Not if we are to be in position by dark. Any questions we are meeting an old tailor called Zorn in the next village. He's an old friend. Will vouch for us both. Come on, let's blow up a train.'

Wilberg let out a huge puff as he pushed off, wobbling away past the church. Rameau allowed himself the thinnest smile and then followed.

The strange pair were not challenged, despite attracting some strange looks from soldiers following local girls towards the market in the old town, and they were very quickly out in the countryside.

Rameau had ceased to be mesmerised by the sight of the wheezing ex-miner banging his knees on the suitcase as he propelled himself along. He was looking now at the railway that they were following as it wound its way along the valley back towards Luxembourg.

Had Marc Rameau's visit been to a similar nondescript hotel three hundred metres away on the other side of the railway station, he might have been surprised to see an old friend.

Bertrand Gillier was stood silently next to a German soldier. He studied the man who looked furtively around before undoing a button and scratching inside his tunic.

Gillier raised an eyebrow.

'I don't know what they are doing to our clothes,' said the army private. 'They turn your skin red raw.'

'It is a soldier's right to grumble,' Gillier responded, smiling to himself: this is not the way he had planned to spend his afternoon off, talking to some enemy soldier about his laundry. Besides it was freezing.

He had been called out that morning to meet a train which was stuck three miles outside the city with a sick fireman and an apparent blocked oil line. It still had not arrived. He cursed his luck: so many people off sick or on Christmas leave and he had to play engineer to a troublesome locomotive.

It had been four weeks since his meeting with Rameau. Their chat about the steel trains meant nothing to him now.

He just wanted this beast to roll into town so he could take it the short distance into Luxembourg and through to the steelworks. He was getting tired of stamping his feet and he desperately wanted a drink.

The railway tracks that crossed Luxembourg from north to south and east to west met in the capital. The steel trains arrived from the Ruhr on the railway crossing the old border from the east. Around the time Rameau killed the sentry at the vehicle pool in October, he became aware of a new decree from Hitler that there would be a reprisal for each act of terrorism. Now he had chosen to strike inside the old border: in Germany's Rhineland. He did not know how the Germans would react but he hoped it would lessen the chance of retaliation on his people. Many of his comrades did not care, feeling retaliation would only strengthen people's hatred of the Nazis.

The valleys here were not deep but each side was lined with dark trees which stood hunched together like green-jacketed football supporters on a terrace. Wilberg's network had identified a spot in the track where there was a slight gradient and curve as the line found its way towards a border village.

Just before they reached that spot, with darkness now falling, Wilberg dismounted and wheeled his bicycle off the road. He looked massive even as he stood against a tall oak, wiping his face.

'We are warm now, we will be cold soon,' he smiled grimly. 'Over there,' he said. 'That is the way you should go - afterwards. That is my way.' He pointed south. Rameau guessed he would be staying with his friend Zorn.

Despite being seemingly completely out of breath, Wilberg picked up his bike with one hand and stamped forward into the trees. Rameau took a look around and followed. He tried carrying the bicycle on his shoulder but it tangled in the branches.

'We will leave them here,' Wilberg told him. 'Far enough from the road not to be found; but near enough for you to hop on and get away. I suggest you stay well off the main road when you leave.'

They covered the bikes and went on into the wood. Every now and then Wilberg stopped and looked around, checking for markers or something in the thicket to guide him. Rameau followed. He was pleased not to be working alone.

When they had walked for about ten minutes, Wilberg held up his hand, looked quickly around and eased himself onto his knees next to an old tree trunk. They had stopped about a man's height from a dying tree which had fallen across into its neighbour and lay slowly perishing in the y-shape formed by the other's trunk and a large branch.

Wilberg panted as he used a stick to uncover a thick covering of shrub. Then he reached into the earth and brought out a muddle of old cloth which he laid at his side. He unwrapped it as it were a heavy slab of cheese and revealed the dark shape of a short barrelled sub-machine gun. It shone in the thin streams of moonlight which penetrated the trees and Rameau could see it was coated in Vaseline or jelly.

'It is a British Sten gun,' Wilberg said and Rameau nodded. 'Only use it if you get up close. It tends to jam which is not good, my friend. When you hear the empty click, I suggest you say goodbye to your mother.' He passed it to Rameau. 'Wipe it with the rags.'

Wilberg was already holding another Sten-shaped bundle of rags and scraping around further into the hole, taking out a similar sized bundle, a square lump and a smaller package. He laid them out as Rameau took the second Sten and began to wipe that down too.

Wilberg gave Rameau three magazines for the Sten and Rameau put them in the small haversack he carried over his shoulder.

Wilberg told him: 'The Sten breaks in to three sections, like so. You can take it with you, if you wish.'

The cold and damp of the ground soaked through their trousers as they worked.

Wilberg had opened his suitcase now and arranged paper across his collection of ties.

He opened the cloth packages. A long length of wire, a box-shape detonator with T-head plunger and a smaller tube-shaped item which

Rameau could not see clearly but which he knew was some kind of detonating fuse.

Within moments Wilberg had everything packed in the case and was arranging the leaves, branches and brambles back over the hiding place.

He struggled to his feet and they carried on through the shrub to the railway line.

They walked along until they were just at the start of the bend and then Rameau helped Wilberg up the stone ballast to the track.

Wilberg knelt and opened his case. He handed Rameau a block of the plastic explosive.

'You should have seen some of the explosions I produced at the coalface,' Wilberg whispered, busily unpacking his case and smiling in the darkness. 'Have you ever used this stuff?'

Rameau shook his head.

Wilberg had taken a lump of plastic in his podgy fingers. 'Two pounds,' he said, moving some of the stones next to the track and moulding the material to the outside of one of the rails. 'More than enough to break this rail right open.' He pressed it hard against the rail, gasping from exertion as he did so. Then he took a small tubular detonator and packed it hard into the mould. He took the wires from the end of the detonator and stood, his knees clicking. He stepped backwards and Rameau, who had sat with the Sten across on his knee as Wilberg worked, followed him, loosely pushing the wire down in amongst the stones.

Halfway down the ballast Wilberg sat briefly and twisted the wires from the detonator into the ends of the longer section of wire.

'Let's go,' he said.

They walked back about eighty yards to a small triangle of trees which jutted out from the wood and pushed aside some of the spiky branches.

Wilberg sat with the wind-up detonator at his feet.

He took a grubby hanky out of his top pocket and wiped it across his brow; then turned to Rameau, who caught a wink and a glint of teeth in the darkness.

Rameau leaned back against the boney bark of a tree and took a moment to catch his breath.

He knew from Gillier and his contacts that every minute lost on the delivery trains had a knock-on effect inside the steelworks and that the day's failed train at Trier would be creating havoc at the plant.

He knew the train had to come through.

And he was sure too that the message he had got through to the fireman from Remich had worked too and he hoped the ruse would have meant the Germans would have to replace the 'sick' man with one of their own.

He felt Wilberg's hand grip his sleeve as they both heard it at the same time: the sound of the engine.

There were no passenger trains at this time of night. They knew exactly what it must be.

Everything seemed to be coming together.

Gillier, banned from driving the trains, was nowhere now in Rameau's mind. He would never have thought for a moment that his old friend was at the head of the several hundred tons of steel and iron which was on its way down the track to meet him.

Chapter Twelve

Gillier felt the hard skin on his face crackle as he stood by Fleischer, the German-born driver, and shovelled coal into the locomotive's boiler. The old girl needed every bit of her strength as she heaved almost two dozen wagons through the countryside in the dark.

Fleischer, a thin man with a dirty cap set back on his grey face, stood on the left side of the cab, squinting in the cold wind. The German soldier with the itchy tunic was standing at the rear of the footplate, smoking a cigarette to keep awake: he had spent the night before with a girl in Neumagen who worked as a housekeeper, cooked a delicious *Kirschtorte* and entertained him with her other skills until only a few hours before he was back on duty.

Gillier had nipped through the curtains to climb onto the coal stack to relieve himself the minute they had left Trier. When he struggled down Fleischer had looked at him as if he were an old fool. It had pretty much been silence between them since, with Gillier staying close to the boiler, trying to warm himself up.

'Keep the fire in its belly,' Fleischer said over his shoulder, his eyes flashing at Gillier through the large goggles he wore. 'I don't want to be out here all night.'

The locomotive couldn't move too fast with all those wagons behind it and it laboured on the track.

But when it came into sight, Wilberg knew just when to hit the detonator and send it plunging off the track and down the embankment.

Rameau did not really know what to expect.

He glimpsed the two men in the cab as a flame flickered from the boiler but just as he did Wilberg said, 'And so it goes,' and sunk the t-bar into the detonator. The track blew immediately in front of the old engine and Rameau saw a flash of flame burst through the darkness, dancing off a thousand pieces of burning metal and flying stones.

Sparks flew at the trees, lighting up the branches and deepening the shadows. A shower of stone and earth rained on Wilberg and Rameau and shook the trees for some distance behind them. The explosion echoed up the valley and then came right back at them.

Rameau knew where the track went around in the shallow curve, but the train was not following it. The locomotive rose for a moment and then lurched to the left. It was beginning to roll, its wheels cutting a fresh track through the stone ballast and throwing up waves of dust.

Afterwards Rameau could not decide if it had all happened very quickly or painfully slowly. The engine kept moving and the wagons were following. Two, three, four, five of them careered off the track as if they were each blind men with their hands on another's shoulder as the leader marched off a cliff. The engine seemed to have turned at right angles to the next wagon and then it disappeared, firstly behind fat clouds of its own escaping steam and coal smoke and then under hundreds of tons of sharp metal.

The wagons kept going. There was a break in the chain now and with the first few losing their own shape in a single crushed pile, the next just ran straight past and into the edge of the trees. More wagons came to a rest just off the edge of the track.

And then almost silence but for the creaking of aching metal; it was as if each wagon were an injured knight in heavy chainmail, groaning and gasping his final breaths. Rameau felt almost sorry for it.

'And so it goes,' Wilberg said again, standing up in a crouch and throwing the Sten over his shoulder with the air of a man with a job well done. 'And, now, so do we.'

The way he headed off into the forest defied both his size and his collapsing lungs. Rameau stood looking at the twisted metal for a moment longer than he should and when he turned and started running he struggled to find Wilberg. Maybe all those years at the pithead gave Wilberg a sixth sense in the dark: he was away.

Rameau watched him disappearing on his bike as he turned to head cross country back into his homeland.

Chapter Thirteen

It was only a second in time on a quiet section of country railway track in the Nazi's Gau Moselland. But when Kurt Wilberg's detonator ignited the two-pound mould of plastic the consequences rippled outwards like the destructive energy of the explosion itself.

The three men in the engine died soon after the locomotive lost the left-hand rail over which it had been running as sharp as a guillotine a second earlier.

Fleischer, who was 45 and had developed an ulcer in his gut worrying about his son in the *Deutsches Afrikakorps*, was thrown clear as the rumbling metal began to plough off the track, only for his whole body to be crushed as the first wagon began to leapfrog its stricken engine.

A loud bang and the feeling that the train had dropped ten feet in an instance was all the German soldier knew about the crash. He was lifted forward towards the boiler, burning his face and hands and breaking his skull.

Bertrand Gillier saw the explosion break like a huge firework over the front of the engine and reached for the brake. He held on as the engine lurched, burning his hand and seeing the German flung past him like a rag doll. Gillier's body had already been broken in the splintering cab when it was decapitated by a piece of broken wheel which catapulted from the second wagon and struck him like a meteor burning brightly as it hit earth.

It did not end at the scene of the explosion. To Gustav Simon and his administration, Rameau's naïve - self-delusional – belief about the border did not matter. This was Simon's *gau*. The 'sick' fireman who had not turned up for work died under torture. A dozen Czechs who had been working on the track the morning of the crash were put against a wall and shot. A drunken businessman was startled by a patrol, ran and took a bullet in the spine. He lay bleeding a mile from the crash with the flames rising in the distance. A Jewish family living near the steel plant was arrested, the eldest daughter was accused of seducing two German soldiers; they were freed after two weeks but the Germans would later return and take them all away.

Wilberg escaped and never saw Rameau again.

And Claire Winter found herself sitting on the first floor of the German administrative headquarters in Luxembourg *ville*.

She was 26, wearing a black coat with turned-up collars. She had it wrapped around her as it was cold in that large, hollow, echoing corridor and the army officer at the desk was far too engrossed in his paper work: she knew he kept sneaking a look at her legs. Her black skirt reached just below her knee. Her legs were folded, her hands crossed in her lap. She had been teaching at a school in the city for four years and looked now as if she were silently adjudicating an exam. Every teenage boy in the class dreamed of Fraulein Winter, just as Hauptmann Karl-Heinz Fischer, the officer at the desk, was letting his imagination run now.

His 'office' was one large corner of the floor. He had only just arrived in the *ville* and was having difficulty prising space off some of the other departments.

He listened to the boots marching through the foyer at the foot of the curving staircase at the other end of the corridor.

This was not how he expected to fight this war, pouring over petty arguments between angry traders who claimed their shop or motor car had been damaged by a soldier of the Reich or counting the price of the small but increasing instances of enemy terrorist activity.

Hauptmann Fischer's real war ended early, during an ambitious attempt to take Willems Bridge in the heart of Rotterdam. His unit of one hundred and fifty infantry and combat engineers landed early one morning in May 1940 on the river in a dozen old Heinkel float planes.

It was a nightmare. A suicide mission. They rode ashore in inflatables and into complete carnage and confusion. When an explosion lifted the vehicle he was hiding behind and smashed it into the ground, the last thing he heard was someone screaming. It had been him.

For 24 hours he had drifted in and out of consciousness. Once he came around and saw a tramcar rattling up the road. It stopped and a dozen German paratroops spilled out, firing as they ran. He could hear a bell on the tram ringing above the machine gun fire. He had to be dreaming. It was only later when he was out of that hell, back in an army hospital in Germany, that he was told that the airborne unit had come in and saved them, dropping down at Rotterdam sports stadium, commandeering tramcars and arriving at the battle in a certain style. He had laughed then.

But the world had changed forever. His left hand and forearm had gone and his left eye socket was filled with a glass mould. *I'm 25 and half a man*. He thought of all the girls back home in Hamburg who had admired him in his uniform. All those lingering glances. Not any more, he thought. Now they turned their eyes away. Not in pity, but disgust. They adored the idea of the hero, but not like this.

This one here would do the same. Not just because of the uniform, but the half-body underneath. But, with his head turned down, he could not help sneaking a look at her. Strange, he thought, as he craned to look, even the eye he left in Holland seemed to hurt.

This was Claire's third visit to the building since the death of her uncle, Bertrand Gillier, but it was the first time she had been invited up the shining, broad staircase. She knew little about her uncle's death, even though several weeks had now past and Bertie had been buried in the same church in the small village on the German border where he had been christened forty-eight years earlier. The church had been less full than she had expected, probably because the questions over his death and Bertrand's communist past were well known; both left many people a little frightened to be associated with Bertie, even in death. Claire knew many of Bertie's firebrand friends had grown passive through their fear of the Gestapo.

There had been no information over Christmas and it had been a miserable end to 1941 for Claire. Although she had seen less of Bertie than she should, he had been her only living relative: her father, Bertie's brother, had died in a fall downstairs four years ago and she had been alone since then. She should have made more of Bertie, but he was fiercely independent and lived in his own particular way, mostly with the help of a bottle. She had visited his decaying house occasionally but he felt uncomfortable in other people's home and never once set foot in her apartment overlooking the *Vallee de la Petrusse*, one of the breathtaking gorges which break up the city. Claire turned her head to the man at the desk and sensed him duck down. His right hand gripped a pen and scribbled something; his left arm was an empty sleeve pinned to his tunic. It drew attention to the shining silver wound badge on his left pocket. The paper shifted under his pen and he seemed to instinctively try to move his left hand to steady it. He swore.

He looked up, embarrassed.

Claire broke across his blushes: 'Will I have to wait long, Herr Hauptmann?'

Fischer studied her for a moment and then gestured to a chair on the other side of his desk. Claire came forward. She could see now the captain had perfect young skin except for tiny scars under the dark eye patch. He took a file off a pile to his right - everything was concentrated on that side of his desk – and opened it. He studied the top page, reading every line rather than pretending too. He did the same with the next two pages.

'My name is Fischer,' he announced finally. 'May I begin by saying how very sorry I am for your loss. This was an appalling and unprovoked terrorist attack. A number of arrests have been made and, as I understand it, a number of people who were linked to the attack, have received justice according to the laws of the Reich.' Although Fischer's sentiments were genuine, his words sounded mechanical and he knew it.

He sat back in his chair and took a breath. Adolf Hitler looked down from a portrait hanging high on the wall behind his head; Claire got the sense that he had put it there so he did not have to look at it on a daily basis.

'Is there anything in particular you would like to ask me, *fraulein*?'

'I have nothing but questions, Herr Hauptmann,' Claire said flatly. She did not think emotion would help her here in this cold, soulless building. 'I know so little about my uncle's death. I have had no response to my questions. I have been here twice before and not been allowed to speak to anyone. I do not know why he died.'

Fischer waved a finger in the general direction of the report.

'Herr Gillier was one of three people killed in this atrocity,' he said. 'It was a cold act of sabotage. Futile. The target was...economic. As to why,' he hesitated, but had obviously never intended to finish the sentence. 'As to the terrorists involved, *Fraulein*, I am afraid these are matters of state security and, as such, as I am sure you will understand, are matters of great delicacy.'

He reached up to unbutton the pocket of his tunic. 'Do you smoke, *fraulein*?'

Claire could see her uncle's name at the foot of a list of three but she could not read much else of the tight type from this angle. She looked up at Fischer. He had a soft voice and the sympathy in his expression seemed genuine. She wondered if his kindness were down to his appalling injuries, a kind of extension to his own self-pity. He seemed resigned.

She silently took a cigarette from his silver case.

'It was a present from my father,' Fischer said, waving the case, 'when I joined the army. He was very proud.'

The captain looked at the case but it reminded him of something painful and he quickly tucked it back in his tunic. He struggled for a moment with the button.

'Fraulein Winter,' he said, closing the file, "I sincerely wish I could be of more help but there is really nothing much else I can do. However, I can repeat our pledge to track down the terrorists who killed your uncle. And I can assure you, *fraulein*, we will find them.'

As Fischer finished speaking there was a clicking on the stairs, a steady booted footstep. Whoever it was had stopped to listen while the Hauptmann spoke.

Fischer raised his head and looked over Claire's shoulder. She turned to see a man reach the bottom of the stairs from the floor above. He wore the black dress uniform of an SS officer and walked slowly with his hands behind his back. Claire felt he was difficult to age: he had a young face but light grey and thinning hair. He was tall with strong shoulders, but his waistline had obviously expanded in the last few years. He looked like he had enjoyed a little of the good life. He could have been as young as his late thirties, as old as fifty.

As he came to stand over Claire, she smelt a cologne and saw his piercing blue eyes. He did not look at the army officer but said: 'And who is this delightful young lady, Fischer?'

Fischer was on his feet now. 'This is Claire Winter, Herr Standartenführer.'

'*Fraulein*,' the colonel smiled, and nodded his head. As he moved, the glint of the Iron Cross First Class which was pinned to the left side of his tunic caught her eye.

He picked the file up off Fischer's desk and examined each page. Fischer and Claire were quiet as he read. He tutted. 'Absolutely appalling!' he said, raising his voice. 'I trust Hauptmann Fischer has assured you that we will do everything in our power to bring these criminals to justice?'

'Yes, Herr Standartenführer.' Claire felt as if she were defending the young army officer.

'Very good. Carry on, Fischer. *Fraulein.*'

He clicked his heels and nodded at Claire again and walked to the stairs. Moments later, Claire was following him down to the foyer.

Little puffs of hot breath hit the cold air as she walked quickly down the steps at the front of the building. She reached the pavement when a car door opened and she heard a voice: '*Fraulein.*'

It was the colonel. He was sitting in the back of a large black Mercedes staff car. He had swung one leg out and had a foot on the pavement in front of her. He smiled gently. 'May I offer you a lift home?'

Claire hesitated.

'Come, come,' he smiled and got out of the car to gesture to the back seat, 'I insist.'

Claire felt two passers-by look briefly at her, the Nazi and the cold leather seats and then, frightened, continue quickly on their way. It was embarrassing, dangerous, and the quicker she got out of sight the better.

She ducked into the back seat of the car and, as she shifted across, the man got in beside her. The uniformed driver shut the door after him and then got back in the front.

'Fraulein Winter," the officer said gently, turning his body to face her, 'I am Standartenführer Buchner of the *Sicherheitsdienst*. Both my car and myself are honoured to be at your service.'

Chapter Fourteen

It was Erhard Buchner's proudest boast and favourite joke with his close friends that his first act of the war had been to attack a German radio station. And though he shouldn't tell anyone, his natural overwhelming arrogance would not allow him to keep it to himself. The mission, for him, summed up the absolute commitment with which the war must be fought.

Buchner had been born in 1900 in a village near Munich and had served briefly in the Great War. He'd been injured by a British gas grenade in the last year of the war and taken months to recover. Like his Führer he was convalescing when the 'November criminals' signed the armistice and betrayed their people.

He studied at Bonn University, where he started the first in a number of obsessive and sometimes violent affairs. Walter Schellenberg – now Himmler's aide - had been a contemporary at Bonn. Schellenberg read medicine and law, and the pair had not met. Buchner now said that they had and believed it. It was all a long time ago.

He had joined the Nazi party in 1933 and the SS in the same year. He switched to its intelligence branch, the *Sicherheitsdienst* or SD, in 1935 after being recommended personally to Heydrich by a friend who talked of Buchner's hatred of the Bolshevik menace. The organisation was then enjoying huge injections of cash from the state treasury, which had been seized by Hitler when he came to power. Buchner was personally interviewed by Heydrich, as most new members of the SD then were, and was successful despite not being a natural choice for the SD: it preferred the young, intelligent brain, to the *alte Kampfer*, the old fighters, the street brawlers. But Buchner had a good education and a lightning mind.

He was also a politician, capable of tailoring his racial theories to the work in the hand: the administration, the inter-office relationships. He had animal cunning and saw the structure of the SD as one in which he could progress. It was his career.

His intelligence had lent itself best to counter-espionage. He was hugely successful at developing and nurturing informers. He became an agent overseer and contacts made through a middle-aged lover in Poland helped him establish a small operation to monitor anti-Nazis over the border. He also worked to encourage tiny alarmist factions who called for union with the Reich. He was happy spending his time making up stories of harassment and prejudice against German peoples living in Poland, and spending the evenings lying in the diamond-encrusted cleavage of his Polish mistress, a baroness eager to please the Nazis. He even travelled to Crackow twice to stoke extra fires and that took guts. The Poles were extremely alert to German spies.

Then, his first act of the war. Or rather his act that helped *start* the war. One of the reasons he loved this struggle so much was that he was right at its heart.

In the summer of 1939, a small group of SD men were brought together to carry out three 'attacks' on German targets on the Polish border. These incidents were designed to provide Hitler with an excuse for attacking his neighbour.

Buchner went to the town of Gleiwitz with a man named Alfred Naujocks. Together with the others they booked into the Oberschlesischer Hotel as mining engineers, signing false names in the register. When an inquisitive member of the hotel staff asked about the mineral survey he thought they were doing, Buchner bluffed him so well the man became bored and had to make an excuse to get himself away.

Time passed slowly as they waited for the codeword which would spring them into action. They hung around for days; *God*, he thought, *it was two weeks!* All had been threatened with death if they breathed a word of what they were doing, although they did not know what they were going to do until the code came through – 'Grandmother has died.'

The success of the invasion of Poland depended on the success of the operation. It would not begin until he, Naujocks and the others had completed their task.

The plan was to attack a small radio station at the town. Its two senior staff were in on the deception. They waited as Hitler's nerves increased, as German columns moved east ready to drive into the heart of Poland in 'retaliation', to 'protect' Germany. In London, Neville Chamberlain was guaranteeing the Poles protection.

Then a car arrived at the hotel and a body was left for the group. He was still alive. Drugged and bloody.

The unit put on Polish and civilian clothes and went to the radio station where the staff let them do as they wished. The best Polish speaker then screamed into a microphone. 'We, the Poles, want war with Germany.' Or something like that. Buchner could not remember the exact words as he was only concerned with his moment in history.

The broadcast over, the men ran outside, firing their pistols into the air. Those shots broke the peace. For ever.

The drugged man – Buchner understood it was some local man with Polish sympathies - was shot at the scene and left as a 'casualty' of the raid. Buchner had dragged him in but did not get to shoot him. He regretted that. He had wanted to be the one to pull the trigger and would have been proud to have struck the first blow for the Fatherland.

In the end he was glad to have been there and, after all, history could not be sure he wasn't the one to fire the first shots of the war.

Buchner barely knew the other men on the raid and they all disappeared back to their own units afterwards. But he himself had caught someone's eye and the following summer he found himself in Berlin as part of a special SD unit formulating plans on how to administer Britain once it had been conquered. As the *Wehrmacht* rushed across France, Buchner was with Schellenberg helping to put together Special Search List GB. It was a list of writers, journalists, politicians, thinkers, foreign leaders who had escaped the Nazis but would now be arrested when the German army crossed the Channel. They had basically just gone through Who's Who and decided who would be handed to Amt IV – the Gestapo. In particular, Buchner had looked forward to seeing degenerates like JB Priestly, Virginia Woolf and Noel Coward being led out. Buchner shared Schellenberg's enthusiasm for their rushed work although he had later heard that Heydrich may not have been so impressed. Even now that concerned him. Perhaps that was why he was stuck in this shitty Luxembourg office. The thought made him shiver, but the fear quickly rose into anger and his jaw tightened.

One of the files he had been asked to work on concerned what to do with the able-bodied males of Britain. It had eventually been decided that all men aged between 17 and 45 would be interned and transported to the continent. The final order, he knew, had come from Hitler's Army Commander-in-Chief, Field Marshall von Brauchitsch, but he hoped his work had been somewhere in there too. Unlike some of his colleagues, he had never been sentimental over, or especially admiring of, Britain.

He had returned to Poland, then part of the Greater Germany, in the spring of 1941 as plans were continuing for Operation Barbarossa, the invasion of the Soviet Union. He was making contacts with anti-Soviet Poles, trying to pick up pieces of intelligence about Soviet military and economic secrets. He'd met Heydrich there during a meeting outside Cracow.

It was after the launch of the attack on the Soviet Union that Buchner had found himself promoted and transferred to Luxembourg.

His office was on the second floor of that miserable building. He feared he had become a simple civil servant, and there were few comforts to that - Fraulein Winter was one of those little rays of sunshine.

By the time he said goodbye to her on the step to her apartment block, she had agreed to go out with him the following night. He acceded to her request that they should eat out of town and he said his driver would bring her to a favourite restaurant in Arlon. There he insisted she share a *pate de gaume* with him and when he was filled with the pork, white wine and parsley, he joked about needing a larger uniform.

Only once did he allow himself to inject a note of seriousness into the evening. He told her he was an expert in rooting out enemy of the state saboteurs and gave her his assurance that the murderer of her uncle would be caught.

Five days later he walked into the killer of Bertrand Gillier.

Chapter Fifteen

Claire Winter sat alone in her room, drinking black coffee and reading some of the schoolchildren's work. Most spoke German at home and their writing was excellent. One slid into *Letzebuergesch* and she placed that book aside. Although the language had never been officially taught in schools, she had taken it as a subject herself. Now, though, it had to be eradicated and she would have to speak to the child's father.

There was a knock at the door, two timid taps. She stubbed out a cigarette and found a tall, slim man standing in the corridor. He wore black trousers and a dark corduroy jacket buttoned across a brown sweater. There was mud on his boots and his black hair was tangled and untidy. He was obviously from the countryside.

'*Ja?*'

He responded in the mother tongue she had just stumbled upon in one of her pupils books. 'I am a friend of your uncle's,' he told her. 'I have come to offer my condolences.'

Claire saw now the man had a cap in his hands. He seemed nervous.

She stepped back, continuing in German. 'Come in.'

Marc Rameau stepped into the room and Claire closed the door behind him.

'Would you like some coffee?'

She poured him a hot black drink which he sipped without waiting for it to cool. They each lit one of her cigarettes and sat in silence for a moment.

'It has been several weeks,' she said.

'I know. I have just heard,' Rameau responded. He looked her briefly in the eye and then turned away. 'I worked with your uncle several years ago on the railway. He was very good to me.'

'He was very popular at one time,' she said.

'I had not seen him for some time.'

The oven was on and the room was hot. There was sweat on Rameau's forehead.

'Have the police made any progress on their investigation?'

'The Germans promise to catch the killer,' she stated, watching her visitor carefully. 'I am sure they will.'

Rameau stubbed out the cigarette.

'I am very sorry for what happened,' he said, standing. 'I will not keep you any longer.'

Claire did not try to stop him leave. He was more uncomfortable than her but all the same she did not want him to stay. 'What is your name?' she asked.

Rameau hesitated, and caught her studying his face. She held his gaze and he decided not to lie.

'Marc Rameau,' he said and opened the door. 'Goodbye.'

When he was gone, Claire stood staring at the door. That face had nagged her and while they were talking she remembered.

And now she was wondering why someone who had been sitting quietly at the back of her uncle's funeral a month earlier was saying he had only just heard of his death.

Rameau hesitated and took a breath on the other side of the door; but then just wanted to get out of the block as quickly as possible.

He skipped down the stairs quickly and almost bumped into the black-uniformed figure coming up. Rameau brushed his arm and the man grabbed him.

Standartenführer Erhard Buchner stared into Rameau's eyes for a moment, his fingers tight into his arm.

Then he remembered the girl he had come to see and let go. Rameau walked on, his heart beating in his mouth.

A moment later he sneaked back up a flight and saw the door to Claire Winter's apartment open and Buchner being invited inside.

Marc Rameau was well aware that the ranks of the collaborationists were growing as the rations shrunk, but to think that Bertrand Gillier's only living relative was among them had made him feel sick.

As he cycled out into the countryside he wished he had never found out about this woman. It made him weep for Gillier all over again.

It was getting dark and he had to wipe the tears from his eyes and concentrate on the road.

Meanwhile Buchner was opening a cognac and toasting the future with Fraulein Winter.

He was extremely ebullient that night. The security checks which he put out on all his women had come back satisfactory on Claire.

Her uncle had been a communist, yes, but she had no contact with him. A collaborationist neighbour had never seen him or any other male visitors. There was no hint of Jewish blood. And, very importantly, she was teaching in accordance with Nazi doctrine.

Claire cooked for the officer and let him kiss her goodnight. He pushed towards her, hoping she would invite him to stay.

She smiled but said it was too soon.

He looked at her closely and she feared he was angry. But then he put on leather gloves and said: '*Fraulein*, I feel sorry for the children in your class. I fear you rule them with an iron hand.'

He smiled and kissed her hand.

She stood in the window and watched him cross the street below to where a driver waited with his car.

As it drove off she lit a cigarette and noticed her hand was suddenly shaking.

Chapter Sixteen
Britain

He had been in danger before but this was the first time Philip Mortain knew with absolute certainty that he was going to die. And the suddenness of the shock made his blood ice cold.

He was in the twin-engine Oxford trainer banking and turning over the Midlands countryside. It was so easy. He had even started to forget the miserable moustachioed instructor who sat at his side, his hands ready to grab the duplicated flying controls.

For the last eight minutes they had been following a railway line which ran into the town a few miles from the base.

Each pilot had to learn how to manoeuvre the Oxford on one engine and Philip had already been through the procedure. When the instructor cut one engine for landing Philip could see the strip lined up perfectly ahead.

He lost his concentration for a moment and, as if waking from a dream, he suddenly realised he was far too low.

The instructor's voice cut in: 'What the fuck are you doing, Mortain?'

The trees had been pushed back a couple of hundred yards from the end of the runway but the Oxford was already easing down towards the level of the highest branches. They would be impaled on those hard spikes.

Philip tried to pull the nose up but the Oxford – so light on the controls - was responding much slower on the one engine. It took an age before the runway started to dip away from view, and the trees with it.

Philip could hear the air underneath them rush through the branches. Something hit the bottom of the aircraft and the port wing dipped. The propellers seemed to be cutting through the trees. *They're going to drag me into the ground*, he thought.

But the aircraft was still rising and then levelling out. He'd done it.

It was then Philip realised the instructor had taken over the controls.

His brush with the trees fortunately did not see him being kicked right out of RAF Flying Training Command. He had excelled at ground school, despite being largely bored by the new round of lessons and exams. He had taken the Oxford to its limits and had previously impressed his instructor. He had experienced the terror of G-force, feeling his body pressed hard into his seat and the blood draining from his brain.

The instructor did not speak to Philip on landing that day but simply followed him into his room.

Philip stood to attention as the instructor pushed powdery brown tobacco into his pipe.

'What's the difference between a fighter pilot and a bomber pilot, Mortain?' He lit a match and sucked hard on the end of the pipe. 'I'll tell you. A fighter pilot has few fucking problems. He's up there in a dinky little kite which responds to his slightest touch. He presses a button and the canon fire rips into his target. Most of all: he is a single man. And single men have nothing to worry about but themselves. Now, a bomber pilot,' he put a foot up on a chair, crumpling Philip's grey sweater which was folded neatly on top, 'he's a family man.' The instructor's pipe smoke was filling the room and turning Philip's stomach. Perhaps he was in shock. 'He has to sit freezing to death at the controls of an aircraft carrying several thousand pounds of high explosives. He is responsible for his own life and for those of his crew. He must understand their concerns, their fears, their weaknesses. He must know how to do their jobs. They will be your colleagues, your friends, your children. Do you want to be responsible for the deaths of your children, Mortain?'

'I rather think not, sir.'

The instructor lifted an eyebrow. 'Then today is the last time you ever come home with leaves sticking out of your arse.'

The training got harder, through formation, low and night flying, and Philip never made another mistake.

Shortly after Christmas 1941, the course was finished but he was thankful there was no ceremony: while friends were learning to accept anything that meant parade, or square-bashing, he hated it; he reckoned he had grown up freer than most. He was sent to the Orderly Room and picked up the small emblem which now represented his training and skill. He went back to his room and sat looking at his wings before sewing them on his uniform.

The next stage would be a posting to an operational unit and so, during the brief period of leave which followed, he and Alice went to her mother's home to tell her they were getting engaged. Alice wore her favourite pleated skirt and a brown bodice with tiny buttons down the front and a neat turned-down collar. Lillian Dearmont had made a casserole for them with a small portion of beef. She forked out the pieces to make sure they all had a share of the meat. Her heavily-lined face broke into a warm smile when she heard the news and she called in a neighbour to show Philip off.

Before returning to Howell Grove in the Welsh hills, they went to a hotel at Mumbles near Swansea and spent the afternoon walking along the front. It was freezing cold.

Alice had been the driving force that had kept the relationship moving forward. Despite Philip's deep feelings for her he was always a little uncertain.

He had never returned the admiring glances from the girls in the villages around the station, and had never gone through the kind of emotions he was feeling with Alice.

He had grown up around men now. He was a strong figure among his friends in that world where everything had changed.

But with Alice he was hesitant while she approached him with a worldliness about these relationships which he lacked.

She was the one who took his face in her hands and kissed it; she was the one who took his hand and placed it upon her.

And, if anything, he found their engagement made him more unsure. Not because he doubted his feelings for her, but because he was aware they were so strong. After all, soon he would be flying ops, and thinking and worrying about Alice.

When he whispered his fears to Alice she assured him they had to grab happiness while they could.

She was sitting now on the edge of the bed facing away from him and smoking a cigarette. She was wearing a smooth white slip and knickers made from parachute silk. Each had a pink frill at the bottom and was so thin he could see right through. One of the thin shoulder straps had slipped from her shoulder. Her skin was so different from his. It was white as marble with only her hands revealing the hard physicality of some of her work. His skin was tough and darkened by all those years on the farm. Those parts of her which were naked were still new to him. Even the arm and hand which she leant back on held a fascination. He studied her splayed fingers, wishing to reach out and touch them but not wanting to disturb her. She seemed unaware he was looking at her.

Both were suddenly quite uninhibited in each other's company as they let their warm skin cool in the grey hotel room. Philip looked at the window and realised it had suddenly gone dark.

His watch on the bedside table said it was only 4.30. Alice turned to look at him. They had the whole evening ahead of them.

Bachelor had returned to Howell Grove and insisted on taking a walk before dinner with Philip.

Despite his round body and short legs, Bachelor moved quickly up the slope behind the house and was out of breath by the time they reached the spot where the path flattened out. He loosened his heavy black jacket and the thick woollen scarf around his neck.

They were in amongst the trees and brush now where two men were cutting back nettles. They wore brown caps and tightly buttoned jackets, and muttered a greeting as the walkers past. Bachelor stopped talking until they were out of earshot. He stopped at the other side of the trees, seemingly to study a group of a dozen brown cattle and their dirty white feet and bellies.

'There are many jobs to be done in wartime, you know, Mortain,' he said at last, pushing a leaf with his walking stick. 'And it is not always a clean business. It is not all MMC rules, do you follow my drift? And you know skills that might mean little to you in days of peace become priceless, do you know?'

Philip stood silently. No, he did not know. He looked ahead to the dark slope of a mountain and to the evening mist which was dropping into the valley ahead.

'We must begin a war inside France,' Bachelor went on. 'Who knows, maybe inside Jersey. Do you think the islands will fight?'

Philip thought of James. 'Many of us came here for that reason,' he said. 'But there will be a lot of anger at home.'

'Resistance needs organisation,' Bachelor said. 'Without it chaos and anarchy. With it, you have an army inside the belly of the beast.'

When he returned to his station in the Midlands he waited for his posting. Scottish Harry went off to fly Wellingtons in Cambridgeshire, but weeks past and nothing came for Philip.

Then he received two letters.

The first was a Red Cross message posted more than 15 months earlier from Jersey. Philip cried as he read James' message. He could hear his voice describing the large swastika that now flew "right across the front" of the town hall. His mother, Grace, had written at the bottom. 'We are both fine. The farm is fine. We pray you are safe. Your loving mother.'

It seemed like he was there with them for a brief moment, but they were not only in a very different place, they were in a different time. Were they still "fine"?

He wept so long and steadily that it took him some time to turn to the second letter.

It was from a Mr Bachelor at the Ministry for Economic Warfare.

Chapter Seventeen
Jersey, July 1942

This was not how a soldier was supposed to look. He was a stocky man with a belly that made his tunic bulge over his shiny black belt. His knee-length boots looked heavy and uncomfortable and every few moments he shifted his feet. He had a thin smile which never seemed to reach the eyes half-hidden in the shade of his dark steel helmet. The sun was shining directly on him and there was sweat on his top lip and on the heavily pitted skin of his cheek and jaw. He looked easily old enough to be James' father.

The soldier's teeth glinted as he grinned at a woman passing on the street.

This was the man whom James Mortain hated the most. This clerk in uniform with a rifle sloped over his left shoulder. A soldier who seemed irritated by his own gun.

It wasn't that James had ever taken any interest in the building at which the man stood guard. The stone-walled town hall meant nothing to the teenager. But the way he looked down the street and held James' stare made him a figure of hate.

Him and that large swastika flag which flickered and snapped in the brisk breeze high above his head.

It flew from a pole which reached out into the street from the building's roof. As James looked the other signs remained, from the days before the invasion of the "greenfly", the signs for Lyon's Cakes and Craven A, for Oxo and Smith's Jersey-made ice cream and for Randalls beers – the island's best – but it was the red, black and white of the swirling flag which dominated the scene. They were conquered.

James had managed to hang on to his bike, despite seeing a number of soldiers eyeing it jealously and being aware they could simply take it if they wanted it.

He pushed the pedal now and turned away from the town hall. It had become a ritual to cycle past and check his enemy was still there.

But now he had to get home. He had Grace's shopping in the basket, although not as much as she had hoped. Sugar had risen in price again and he had only been able to find a couple of ounces of a dreary, dirty-looking salt which would need immersing in hot water (so the dirt would drop to the bottom and the salty water could be boiled to collect the salt). He also had two small loaves of bread, which were rather heavy as they were largely made from mashed potato. But there had been no meat at all in the shops today.

At home he found Grace in the kitchen. There was sweat on her face and she kept wiping her hands on her green apron. She had her hair held up in a clip.

When she checked inside the oven a waft of hot air blew out into a room already warmed by the summer sun. James could see she had the oven full with a few of the new recipes forced on the islanders by the shortages.

On the top shelf was a potato tart. Jersey was not yet short of that particular vegetable. She had tucked slices of raw potato the size of five shilling pieces into two rounds of potato pastry, then sprinkled on a little sugar. It was now beginning to brown. After an hour or so she would take off the top and add a little cream. It would make a couple of meals for the two of them with some vegetables from the patch they had expanded behind the house. James was doing his best with the soil, even cultivating a growth of stinging nettles to boil up like spinach. Grace had used two of James' carrots to make a pudding and had just placed it into the heat. She had grated them and mixed them with breadcrumbs, a little butter and sugar and egg yolk, before adding the beaten egg whites. Eggs were one of the most precious of food stuffs, never seen in the shops. These were from the Mortains hens. Sometimes the Germans came for them but when they could Grace shared them with neighbours.

Finally, she was making a Yorkshire pudding for them to eat now. It was James' favourite, although Grace thought it dry and felt it only reminded her of how little meat they had to enjoy. James could see the thick batter was just starting to darken and his mother would soon be making the gravy.

The farm was running okay. The Germans had visited, seen there were only two bedrooms in the house and decided, to both their relief, not to billet any soldiers there.

James had taken on part of a neighbour's dairy herd and was up every morning at dawn to tend them. His friend, John, a Guernsey-born minister's son, helped him virtually full-time now.

A couple of days earlier they had been walking near Trudi's farm, now the home of a German officer, when they had been struck by a heavy, rancid smell. It seemed to drift on the breeze between the tall summer hedgerows and they both sensed it at the same time. It was like a stale and musty old pantry, thick with mice or rat droppings.

The two teenagers stopped and heard a dragging sound, as if someone were pulling a huge body along the narrow country lane.

They stood aside and saw two German soldiers come into view and stand on the verge, their rifles held across their chests.

Slowly a grey mass of ripped and ragged clothes, rough, bearded faces and matted, dirty hair shuffled into view. It was a group of around twenty people who moved as one, leaning on each other, stumbling, holding each other up. Their feet and boots were shredded, dragging on the hot tarmac. Their eyes were sunken but fixed. Only one looked at James and John as they passed, herded by a handful of bored-looking soldiers. The stench was overpowering as they drew level with the teenagers and a Nazi soldier came to stand between them.

There was a commotion and the rhythm of the shuffling was broken. One of the group right at the front had stopped, dropped to one knee and then fallen to one side. His skull made a dreadful noise as it cracked the pavement. Another had tripped and fallen over him. James could see that the others had halted for a moment with half of the narrow lane closed to them and one soldier had come around to the front, shouting some of the basic words the boys had been forced to learn.

The soldiers who walked around St Helier smiled and rang their bicycle bells but these were different. The one in front turned and gestured angrily to the boys with his rifle. 'Move away,' he said in English. 'Go!'

John stepped back and stumbled, twisting his ankle in the rough grass. James took his arm and they started walking. James risked one look back. The soldier was still watching them but the group seemed to have started moving again.

The smell had been in his nostrils when he got back to the farm.

The picture was still in his mind now. His mother had found out they were all young men from a village in Russia which had been over-run by the Germans. They had been shipped all the way to France in the back of freezing, covered trucks. Many had died on the way, according to gossip which had apparently started at the hospital.

It was gossip which anybody who saw the state of the new forced labour force arriving on Jersey could well believe.

There were no other ways of getting news now. Not long after the invasion, the Germans had ordered the confiscation of wireless receiving sets – but then changed their minds. So the BBC had remained a connection to the outside world for the people of the island – something other than the German-controlled local press and the cinema films describing the *Wehrmacht's* continued successes.

This summer a new order had been announced again making the possession of a radio punishable by a massive fine and a six-month jail term. They all had to be given up.

James told his mum he reckoned it must mean the war was going badly for Hitler. Therefore, he had persuaded her to let him keep their small set. He planned to have it wrapped and hidden in the vegetable patch, but Grace said she would only let him keep it if she were in charge of it. He was her 16-year-old son and, although he had grown up quickly, she was afraid of his over-enthusiasm for the war. And she thought if the radio was discovered, his ignorance of where it was might spare him punishment.

So the radio came out when Grace said it could and they sometimes listened to a tea-time request show on the BBC but mainly tuned in for the news. James was told not to discuss it with anyone but he did and she often heard him telling everything to John.

But the young pair had ideas of their own about the war. They had already begun their own minor campaign to chalk V for victory in as many places as they could, taking turns to keep watch. It was hugely exciting at first, as well as frightening as it was likely to land them a stiff jail sentence. But soon James grew tired of it.

In the winter and spring they had found a new game, defying Nazi orders which kept people off the beaches around the new coastal defences and going looking for cockles, mussels and ormers. It was a dangerous business. Guards could shoot you and much of the sand was mined. The ormers were their particular favourite, a small shellfish which could be collected from beneath rocks at low tide. They could sell a catch of a dozen for around four shillings or give them to Grace Mortain to cook them something. But the season ended with the first flush of summer and the boys were now eagerly waiting for October to begin their little trade again.

Reverend Morris, John's father, had not married until he was into his early fifties when he met and fell in love with one of his parishioners. She suffered a heart attack soon after John's birth and left his father alone to bring up the child. He had retired to Jersey in 1938 and was one of those who seemed to have aged most quickly during the occupation. The woollen blue jumper that he had taken to wearing on even the warmest day seemed to be getting looser on him and he had now almost completely lost the thin crown of white hair which had been all that was keeping him from complete baldness. He was about five feet eight, shorter than James had now become, and the teenager always found himself looking down at the liver spots sprinkled across his pate.

James had believed him to be slightly ponderous and timid, always sitting in a red leather chair in his study reading a book and drinking port or whisky from a heavy glass as the teenagers wandered around the house. But as time went on he began to discover little pieces of information about John's father that interested him. Firstly, whenever James would get carried away and blurt out something about the war he could only have gleaned from the BBC, the reverend would discuss its implications or even match it with some fresh fact or discovery of his own. He must have a radio too, James thought.

Secondly, and this amused rather than just impressed the teenager, the former man of the cloth had a thick clump of tobacco plants growing like a rampant weed right across the length of the foot of his garden. It was something the States had been trying to control through a licence but they were generally failing. The reverend always had his pipe in his mouth or peeking out of a pocket so the way the plants grew rapidly without any attention – and the simple ways he had found of drying and curing them - pleased him greatly. It pleased James and John too because one of the habits they had picked over the last eight months had been smoking. They felt saboteurs and people who flaunted the jackbooted adults' rules deserved a man's habit. "Soldiers smoke," James had said once to his friend.

Thirdly, there were the foreign workers. Hitler believed that with Britain beaten out of all of Europe – apart from Malta and Gibraltar – it would want to regain footholds at North Africa and in the Channel. And that if the islands were retaken the British would cause severe disruption to German convoys in the area. The Germans had therefore started a massive fortification programme, turning each Channel Island into an apparently impregnable fortress. The Organisation Todt, led by Dr Fritz Todt, the engineer who had built the autobahns, was charged with creating the islands' defences. Military zones were declared, often on the most beautiful coastal areas of Jersey, with gun emplacements, concrete bunkers and minefields created to deny raiders a place to land.

Todt's architects and builders were the foremen in charge, but the hard work was being done by slave labourers from Russia, France and other corners of the Reich. The first to arrive in the middle of 1941 had been 'Red Spaniards', ex-socialists and communists, who had fought General Franco during the Civil War. They and the workers from the other conquered nations found themselves living in terrible conditions, and could regularly be seen wandering the countryside, scrabbling in the dirt for potatoes or begging for bread. The island had become as much a prison as a fortress and so the Germans seemed to let them move about if they slipped out of their camps – knowing they would have to return. However, islanders risked being sent to a concentration camp if they were to help escapees.

Reverend Morris had met a forced labourer when visiting a friend in the St Ouen area. The man, a Russian, had escaped from a camp near St Peter and was in a terrible state. His face was scarred and bruised and his eyes bloodshot, and his clothes were ground through with dirt. He had already been beaten following an earlier escape attempt and was then living in the backroom of someone's house. He survived there for two weeks until, cleaned and shaved, he had decided to go for a walk and had been recaptured.

But the clergyman's interest had been sparked and, once he was aware of an injustice, he could not ignore it. He travelled around in an Austin Seven using a doctor friend's petrol allowance and looking for groups of desperate workers to feed. And he was only too happy when a Spaniard named Joseba arrived at his home, asking for help.

Joseba had escaped from a camp at the racecourse at Le Quennevais, where he had been kept while working at the harbour in St Helier unloading boats bringing cement for the fortifications. He had easily escaped, slipping under barbed wire and past the bored guards. He had wandered across the island and been discovered by a woman in Grouville. She had directed Joseba to Reverend Morris.

Morris moved him into the attic of his rambling old house and he had been there a couple of weeks when James saw him sat in the study, sipping a large glass of dry Jersey cider and holding a stilted conversation in English. James was following John up to his room and took his arm. 'Who is that with your father?'

'Joseba. He's Spanish.'

James was angry with John for not telling him about his father's guest. It was the biggest bit of news they'd had for ages and John had been working at his side for a fortnight without breathing a word. There was an awkward silence until John promised to ask his father if James could come to dinner the following evening and meet the mysterious visitor.

'He fought in the war in Spain,' John said excitedly, 'against German divebombers. And he doesn't mind talking about it.'

Close up, Joseba was even more interesting. He had a thin face, split by a long narrow nose. His cheeks were pitted and sunken, hanging slackly off his high, prominent cheek bones. A greyness was pushing through the natural tan of his skin and his lips were the colour of ash. He had thick scars around his mouth and one in the shape of a half moon over the top of his right eye. The skin and hair of the eyebrow were burned away. His eyes, though, flashed a rich green when he talked, struggling to describe the journey he and his comrades had made from Spain. They had been defeated by Franco and had fled over the border into France. There, they were held in internment camps until the war started and many of them were handed over to the Germans. They had been forced to work on coastal defences on the French coast before being moved to Jersey.

The Spaniard talked as he tucked into a rabbit which Morris had bought on the black market. The stew was hot and surprisingly tasty considering there was little with which to season it. He was washing it down with more of the vicar's cider and was still chewing when he lit a rolled-up cigarette.

There was a quick discussion about the reverend's tobacco plants.

'Thank God for the father,' Joseba laughed loudly to the boys. 'And for his tobacco. See!' He pushed out his tongue and went "Aaah!" as if he were at the dentist. It was as black as coal. 'What I have been smoking did this,' he said, poking his tongue out again.

The four of them laughed and Morris poured himself a glass of vinegary wine from a half bottle bought for him many years ago by a parishioner.

At 8pm Reverend Morris said it was time for James to leave. Grace Mortain insisted her son was home well before the hour of curfew, which the Germans kept changing. Joseba stood and shook James' hand. His bony fingers were long and closed tight on James' so that he could still feel their grip as John walked with him to the front door.

'See you tomorrow at the farm,' James said as his friend clicked the door shut. James took his bike from where it was resting against the creeper at the side of the Morris' house and wheeled it out onto the road. It was a restful summer's evening, calm and gentle, part of a different world to the patches of burnt and sallow skin which pieced together Joseba's face.

James climbed into the saddle and freewheeled away from the house; the soft clicking of his wheels seeming to break through the evening silence. But something made him pull up a short distance away and drag his bike up onto the pavement. He stood against a tree and turned. A German NCO and three soldiers were striding towards the Morris' house, the metal studs in their jackboots striking on the roadway, then stopping as they moved through the gate and onto the short gravel path.

James felt his stomach tighten and his heart miss a beat as one of the soldiers lifted his rifle to bang on the door with its butt.

There had been nothing James could do. He would never have got around to the back of the house in time to warn them. He found his hands shaking. Everything inside him told him to ride off but he could not turn his back on his friends – even though he knew it was useless. He got on his bike, pushed forward and let his momentum take him back past the house. He could hear the NCO's voice, barking out in English as loud as the rifle butt.

James turned his head. Reverend Morris was just inside his door, the palm of his hands turned up in front of his body. The NCO had stepped into the house and looked like a giant beside the clergyman. He was saying something about "consorting with and assisting prisoners of war". One of the soldiers turned, his rifle held across his chest. He tipped his helmet back off his eyes and stared at James, who wobbled before pedalling away. He expected a shout or even a gun-shot to follow him, but none came.

James found himself in a state of panic. He hit the curb twice on the way home, his pedals spinning out of control. He cut his hand on the gate and could not talk to his mother when she asked him what was wrong. He lay awake, listening for the field police to come. Every time he heard an engine in the darkness, he waited for it to stop at the gate, waited for the doors to swing open, the shouts, those awful boots on the ground.

What could have gone wrong? No-one could have seen Joseba. He imagined the Morris' house in his head: no, there were no windows in the Morris' attic. He had prided himself in staying out of sight, he said so as he ate down the rabbit. *Would that be his last meal?* James had heard such things about what the Germans were doing to people. He saw Joseba's black tongue. *Didn't they cut them out of some prisoner's heads?* He thought of John and his poor father. What would happen to them? Prison, for sure. But on the island or France or Germany? Some had come back from those places but for lesser crimes. Then he thought of himself. Both could say he was there, knew about Joseba, although he trusted them not to, unless they were tortured. But the Germans wouldn't need torture: they could easily link John to James – and to his mother – through the farm. And a soldier could identify him from outside the house.

He thought of the way they had strode to the door. Tomorrow they would do the same at the farm. There was no rush. They knew he could not go anywhere. Besides they probably had plenty of evidence: of the V signs, of the 'trespassing' on the beaches which the Germans had made out of bounds to them, of the meeting with Joseba. James had heard people talking to Grace about Morris as one of those who was rocking the boat. Rocking the boat! Because he dared do something. *How dare they!* James gritted his teeth: *Lousy collaborators and conchies, the lot of them!*

He got out of bed and looked out over the countryside. Total peace, but the thin clouds around the moon looked like thin slivers of ice. It was a cold sky which looked down on him and it made him shiver.

Chapter Eighteen

It was Grace Mortain's guilty pleasure. She chastised herself for it as if she were just taking an extra slice of cake, but she was risking her life.

She looked at the clock and re-tuned the small radio set in time for the first request. She heard the opening bars to A Foggy Day (In London Town). *What was that from? Astaire, of course, in A Damsel In Distress.* It made her smile as she leaned and pulled off her muddy boots to place them at the door.

The weather had changed. A bright morning had given way to a fine rain which covered the countryside and was bringing evening on early. James had disappeared a few hours ago when the weather was fine. He was wearing shorts and a light blue shirt, and would be soaked through. John had not turned up for work that morning and James said he was going to find him. Grace had spent the whole day sorting through a crop of potatoes only to discover that about six out of ten were rotten and totally unfit to be eaten.

She needed cheering up and the sinkful of dirty pots, pans and plates would never do that. They were to be ignored for the next half an hour while she listened to London.

She had heard it before but the music had deceived her. But now she heard it again.

James' dog Annie was barking away from her shelter in the shed. That meant only one thing.

Grace pushed her hair back from her face and leaned to look out of the kitchen window.

A dark grey German *Kubelwagen* had pulled up outside the gate, its canvas hood pulled up against the rain.

Two soldiers, one with a peaked cap, the other wearing a helmet, were already on their way to the house. The officer had his hands behind his back as the other swung open the gate.

Grace turned, fumbling with the switch on the radio, cutting the music off so that the march of the boots on the yard became loud in her ear. There was a banging at the door and a shadow fell across the window. Grace stood between it and the table and calmly took her mother's knitted burgundy tea cosy and fitted it over the small brown set.

She opened the door and was immediately forced back by the peaked-capped officer who stepped inside the house.

'Good afternoon, madam,' he said, rain dripping from his cap onto his tunic. He wore an Iron Cross on his pocket and, unlike many of the soldiers on the island, must have seen action early in the war. The other soldier come over the step behind him and rushed into the living room, pushing back chairs.

'What is it? What's going on?' asked Grace, pulling her thick grey cardigan around her.

The officer was in his early-20s with bright white skin and a perfect set of teeth. He took off his cap and ran a hand through his short blond hair. He gestured and Grace moved back into the kitchen.

'Please sit down, Mrs Mortain.' He was smiling but it was an instruction rather than a request.

For a moment Grace was shocked that he knew her name but every home and its residents had been noted, of course.

'We called for you earlier but you were not in,' said the officer, sitting opposite Grace at the kitchen table and placing his cap next to the tea cosy.

They had to have heard the radio, hadn't they? He's playing with me.

Grace took a breath, trying to keep the terror from her voice. The soldier had ran upstairs now and was going through the bedrooms. She could hear him slamming cupboard doors and turning over the beds. The kitchen ceiling shook. Two or three other figures were in the yard. The hens had been forced out of their little shelter and were calling out. Annie was barking. She prayed they wouldn't shoot her.

'I was probably in the fields,' Grace said, remembering the officer's words. 'I don't understand what's going on.'

A soldier appeared in the door. He was wearing a waterproof cape over his uniform and the water was running off it. It was raining harder now.

'Nothing, Herr Leutnant,' he said, looking up to see the soldier return from upstairs. He shook his head too.

The lieutenant turned to face Grace.

'Mrs Mortain,' he said, 'where is your son?'

The look of surprise on Grace's face was genuine.

'James? What's James got to do with this?'

The officer showed no signs of having heard her. 'Where is he, Mrs Mortain?'

Grace looked at the two soldiers in the doorway. A puddle of water was running from them into the centre of the kitchen.

'He's running errands. Working. This is a farm,' she replied. The lieutenant's eyes were like two clear blue rock pools.

He reached into his pocket and took out a notebook.

'What time did he go out?'

Grace felt composed now, because inside she was not frightened for herself but for James.

'Before the rain started,' she said. 'Around midday.'

'What time are you expecting his return?'

'I don't know. He's 16. My husband is dead. James runs this place as much as me. There are many things for him to do.'

'John Morris works for you, does he not?'

What was going on? 'Yes, yes, he does.' It was no secret.

'Do you know his father,' the officer looked at another page of his notebook, 'Charles Morris?'

'Not very well,' Grace replied; her first lie. 'I know what he looks like.'

'He has been aiding prisoners of war. We fear your son may have been helping him. I am afraid that is an offence triable before the court of the *Feldkommandantur 515* and is punishable by a prison sentence.' Grace knew about the court of the German civil affairs unit which was running Jersey; she also knew the officer did not have to tell her why he was here.

He stood and as he reached down to pick up his cap, his hand grazed the tea cosy: Grace noticed it; he seemed not too.

'You have a very pretty home,' the officer said. 'I am not a farmer but I like the cottage.'

The other soldiers had moved off the step and were standing in the yard. Grace could hear the drumming of the rain on their helmets.

The officer had stopped in the door and cocked his head to one side: he was listening to something. 'Ah-ha,' he said and turned into the other room.

Grace strained to listen to his boots on the stone floor of the living room, and stood up quickly. Alone in the room, her mind was racing with a thousand things. Her palms were sweating as she placed her hand on the woollen cosy.

The officer was talking to himself in the other room.

'What a beautiful clock,' he said. 'A wonderful movement.' It was the noise which filled the house; that Grace no longer even noticed.

The German returned to the doorway.

'Remarkable. Such a wonderful German timepiece. Here, in Jersey. Where did you get it, madam?' Another question. Still frightening. *It's just about the clock.* There were soap suds on her hand as she wiped her fingers in the back of her dress.

'It was my husband's,' she said. 'He bought it about 20 years ago in France.'

'Really,' said the officer. 'It was second hand then. Maybe already 40 years old. But it is still as beautiful.' He answered her next question before she asked it. 'My father worked all his life for one of the finest clockmakers in the *Schwarzwald*. He is still there. He is an artist. As was the gentleman who made that clock.'

The officer was smiling, but just with that perfect set of teeth. His eyes, at least to Grace, still looked cold, clear, emotionless.

They had settled on the open flap which was standing out from the kitchen cupboard. Grace's mixed pieces of crockery filled the shelves. On the flap itself, dead centre, was the tea pot from which about two hours ago she had been drinking foul sugar-beet tea – one of the substitutes to the real thing everyone was now forced to consume.

The lieutenant's smile was fixed.

'You are aware, Mrs Mortain, of the order of June 6 regarding the use of wireless sets?' he said.

She was looking at the tea pot as well now. It was round, brown, so utterly normal.

'Yes, of course, lieutenant,' she said.

He stepped across and touched the pot with the back of his hand. The other casually lifted the tea cosy.

Grace's breath was tight in her throat as the officer's blue eyes locked on hers.

He put the cosy to one side and moved towards the door.

'My apologies for the distress we have caused you, Mrs Mortain,' he said. 'Would you please ensure that on your son's return he reports to the *Feldgendarmerie* headquarters at Tudor House. It is in his interests. If he does not, we will be back.'

He raised his arm in a Party salute. 'Heil Hitler.'

There were puddles forming in the yard and the *leutnant* had to skip across them quickly to where one of the private soldiers was holding open the gate.

The soldier diligently locked the gate and got in the *Kubelwagen*. It was gunned into life and made a three-point turn. Another identical vehicle which had been parked behind it did the same and the noise of the engines slowly disappeared into the drumming of the rain on the window.

Grace turned and pushed both her hands into the sink. The wooden radio, encased in soap suds, clunked against the china plates and iron pots. She placed it to one side and felt her eyes sting.

She wondered suddenly if she would ever see either of her sons again. She suddenly felt light-headed and found herself slumped on the floor, her eyes streaming with tears.

The house was so empty, apart from her short, breathless sobs and the relentless ticking of her husband's favourite clock.

Chapter Nineteen

The Morris' house looked so different to the way it had 24 hours earlier.

The small wooden gate was the same and was even pulled on the catch as the reverend insisted. The post box was still labelled with the family name. The heavy green curtains of the front room were drawn half across as they generally were and the curtains of the upstairs bedrooms were open. It was John's house alright, but whereas last night it had been the place James loved to visit, to talk and to smoke in the overgrown corners of the large garden, today it seemed more like a grave.

It looked empty and unattended, as if it had been deserted for years. The rain and growing wind lashed it. The summer and its surroundings had turned on it. And the people who lived there.

Or so it seemed to James.

He was standing under the same tree at which he turned the night before to see the soldiers arriving.

He was shivering and wet, with the rain having caused his shirt to stick to his skin. He pulled it free but it just came back to wrap around him, suffocate him.

He had been stood there for half an hour, maybe more, but virtually nothing had come past him. Perhaps, people sensed the house was now cursed and no-one dare go near it for fear of arrest.

Maybe they were right. It did not matter. James had to go near it. He had to walk to it, open the gate and knock at the door.

He had to know if John and his father were alright and he knew no other way. He could not go to the police or the Germans, or inquire next door. He feared he might simply be arrested or turned in.

He had to know about his friends, and know now.

He wheeled his bike closer to the house, lay it against the privet and put his hand on the gate.

It opened and, as the rain lashed against his face, he thought he heard a car. He turned, but the road was empty. He breathed a sigh of relief as any vehicle was almost bound to be a German.

He stood at the door, breathed in once and then knocked. It was a timid knock, one which did not really ask to be answered. Silence. He half-turned and then hesitated. *I'm not coming back*, he thought.

He knocked again, this time almost bringing the brass knocker off its hinges.

But the result was just the same. The house never blinked.

James got back on his bike and was heading home when he remembered overhearing Reverend Morris discussing a hut on the edge of the beach near Gorey. It was attached to a fisherman's cottage but the man was elderly and let the clergyman store his rod and tackle there. James and John had vowed to make use of it, but had never liked the look of the old man and had stayed away.

Morris, though, was always thinking ahead. James wondered if he might have told Joseba about it. Maybe he even gave him a key to the heavy rusted padlock. Could Joseba have escaped the house? If he did, James was suddenly sure that that was where he was.

He could be there and back to the house within a couple of hours or so.

He headed off quickly, the rain blowing into his face, his shirt hanging heavily around him. The faster he cycled, the more the rain stung his bare legs.

The war had made him feel so grown up. Now, suddenly, with John arrested, and alone on the country road in his short trousers, he felt like a little child.

How he wished Philip were here!

The sea was spreading out in front of him and he could almost see the fisherman's cottage when he saw two Germans step out of a roadside hut. One had his rifle held at his side; the other was holding his as if about to raise it.

'Hey!'

James' tyres skidded in the road as he slammed on his brakes. The soldiers were less than 30 yards away.

'Hey, there, lad.' The first soldier was coming up the hill to meet him, both hands on the rifle, its muzzle pointed down at the road.

His colleague at his shoulder lifted his helmet off his face and wiped his face. He was a heavy man with a large belly. He was puffing in the sea-spray which was coming in off Grouville Bay.

James could see the pitted skin of his cheeks and around his chin. The slow walk. It was the man from the town hall.

Just to his right there was a small ridge off the road with a path running down towards the sea. With a quick push and by standing on the pedals, James was off the road and on the short spiky grass of the pathway.

He heard more shouts behind him and the clatter of boots running on the roadway.

He ducked down over his handlebars, the wind filling his shirt like a balloon. The tyres hit ridges and stones in the path but he kept up the pace, expecting a shot to ring out. The Germans were still shouting, still following, but he dare not look around.

His eyes were virtually shut now, the wind and rain causing them to stream with tears. But he could see dunes, the line of the coast, in front of him.

Then he couldn't. His front wheel suddenly found a thick patch of wet sand in the pathway and almost completely stopped. He was thrown forward over the handlebars, spinning in the air to land on the compact ground at the side of the path. He heard the air squeezed instantly out of his lungs and felt his head crack against something in the grass.

The first time he tried to lift himself, he failed. But he heard a German shout again and forced himself on to his side, then his knees and then he was running.

He felt a stabbing in his neck with each step and the grass was just a blur beneath his feet. He couldn't hold his head up anymore and was limping along the battered-down line of the path.

This time though when he fell he had his hands in front of his face and he did not go completely to ground.

Like a runner on the blocks, he was ready to go again, but something was dragging on to his left leg. Wire. It had bitten through his trousers and was clinging to his skin. The tiny cold metal spikes seemed to rip right against his shin bone as he pulled his leg free. There was a thud as something fell to his right but he raced on into the sand.

James could make out the sea now, an expanse of bluish-grey with white surf turning and foaming in the downpour.

One of the soldiers had stopped to pick up James' bicycle, making sure his friend did not claim it. There were not many left unclaimed now. He was not letting this one get away.

The heavier one had passed his comrade on the path and had slowly gone on after the bike's owner. They would have to find out why this youngster had wanted to run.

His boots crunched on the sign that James had pulled down as he ran into the wire stopping locals from going on the beach and warning they were now entering a minefield.

The soldier's grip tightened on his rifle as he took another short step forward. He took a breath and shouted 'You must stop.'

As the last word carried in the sea breeze, an explosion echoed back towards him, and a family of gulls, squawking in distress, rose into the wind, and flew out to sea.

Chapter Twenty

It was six o'clock in the morning when they came, but Grace was already up.

Even on a normal day there were always plenty of things to do at that time, but this night she had not slept at all. She was worried sick about James.

So when they came she watched them, pulling the two *Kubelwagen* into the space outside the gate and rushing out.

What astonished her was that they were shouting. Why? She was just a middle-aged woman, feeling older by the hour.

The blue-eyed officer was back, his hands crossed behind him. She could see him clearly. It was quite light and the previous evening's rain had left a cloudless sky. It looked like it was going to be a lovely summer's day.

An NCO was doing all the shouting as two grey figures went around either side of the house. Two others stood at the front door and banged it with their fists. Annie was already barking in the shed but they all ignored her.

Even though Grace was expecting the soldier's knock, it made her jump. She watched the wooden door shudder and the metal latch rattle.

She pulled her gown around her and lifted the latch.

'Frau Mortain,' said the officer, and then continued in German: 'You must come with us.'

Grace stood stock still. The three brutal faces made her shiver.

'Get dressed, Mrs Mortain,' he said now in English.

A soldier ran up, his boots heavy on the stones of the yard. He held an object out in front of himself for the *leutnant* to see: it was the radio. Grace had buried it in James' vegetable patch thinking she might get it repaired. They had gone straight to it, although she did not think of that now.

She turned, leaving the door open, and slowly climbed the stairs. They seemed steeper than before and strange, like this was not her house at all.

One soldier stood in the doorway as she changed and put together a small bag containing toiletries and a change of clothes. She slipped three small photographs into her purse and put it into the pocket of her grey cardigan.

As she stepped onto the landing she saw that the boys' bedroom was still in the same mess it had been the night before, after the Germans' first visit. She had straightened the furniture everywhere else but had not gone in there. She regretted that now: it should be left tidy.

Two soldiers walked each side of her to the rear *Kubelwagen* and helped her inside. They waited then for the officer to appear, stepping carefully out of the house and through the gate. He had a sack in his hands and it might have contained two dozen eggs for the care he took with it. It was bigger than that though. And, as she watched him take a seat with the bag on his lap, Grace realised it was just about the size of her husband's clock.

The Germans had taken over two blocks of Jersey's Gloucester Street prison. The larger building was reserved for German servicemen and the smaller for civilians who had fallen foul of the occupying authority.

It was here that Grace Mortain found herself sitting inside a square, granite-walled cell. She sat on a hard bed and looked around at the small stool and table-top attached to the opposite wall. She put out a hand to touch the raised wooden head piece that served as a pillow and cried. But she did not cry for herself. She thought of Philip and James, fearing now that they must be lost from her for ever. Others had disappeared and not returned: friends who had inquired about them had hit walls of silence from the Germans.

Time stood still for Grace that first day. No-one came to her cell and it stayed light for hours. She found herself sat on the stool, her stomach empty, her bladder full. She went to the bed, lay on her side and pulled her knees up. The wood was hard under her head and she ached.

She tried to think about James. She imagined him returning to the house and finding it empty. She heard Annie barking over and over. James would wonder why she had abandoned the dog. He would hate her. She realised her mind was running away with her. James had disappeared first, remember. He was looking for John Morris. So was the German lieutenant. And Charles Morris, he had said, the reverend. Aiding prisoners of war, that's what he had said. But that's not why they had wanted her: it was that stupid radio. *A foggy day in London town, had me low, had me down.* Oh, you stupid woman!

She could hear a door slamming, someone shouting, laughing, but she could not work out if it were real or imagined.

When she awoke it was light again and she could barely move her shoulder.

Two *Feldgendarms* with shining brass breast plates came to take her out of the prison some time that morning. She stepped into the street, feeling an intense sense of shame. Her hair felt tangled and lank, and her clothes were crumpled. She could smell sweat and, as she was driven through the streets, she suddenly felt embarrassed that the two Germans might smell it too.

They brought her to Victoria College House, which had been taken over by the administrators of the *Feldkommandantur 515*. One of the *Feldgendarms* took her arm and gently guided her upstairs to an office occupied by two men in plain, dark suits. She was made to sit on a hard wooden chair opposite them and the *Feldgendarms* left, closing the door behind them.

The room smelt heavily of cigars and there were several stubs in an ashtray on the table. The man sitting directly opposite Grace was sitting bolt upright with both hands on the table, palms faced down. He had short, cropped blond hair and almost unnatural square face. His ears looked like two handles on a box.

The second man looked so relaxed that he barely seemed interested in Grace, although his cruel eyes never left her. He gave her the impression that she were nothing to him and that, although his hands were folded in his lap, he could reach out and strike her at any time. His skin was rough and he had the thick, wracking cough of a heavy smoker.

The first man had a beige folder in front of him. He opened it and Grace noticed his smooth hands and long fingers. He might have been a concert pianist preparing to perform his favourite symphony.

'It is very wise that you have chosen to co-operate with us,' he said at last.

She did not know what that meant. Did they mean that she had not tried to fight the people sent to make the arrest or the prison guards? What did they expect her to do? She was not a fighter. She was 45 and feeling very, very tired. She wanted to ask about James. Maybe she could now. She was co-operating, they could tell her about her son in return. But what if he were on the run? Would she make things worse for him? *Best just shut up.*

'But,' the square-faced man continued turning a page in the folder, 'how lamentable that you should choose to ignore the simple laws of the administration in the first place.'

He closed the file. It was a thin file, maybe three or four pages.

'Now perhaps you would tell us about the resistance ring of which you were a part,' he folded his hands and sat back, as if preparing to listen to a long speech.

Grace felt a strand of hair in her mouth and reached to remove it.

'We already have your co-conspirators in detention,' the man said. 'You and they have nothing to lose by your co-operation.'

When he did not speak, the silence in the room was painful. Grace could feel her body shaking and clasped both hands tightly together.

'I'm afraid I don't understand.'

'Come, come,' said the man, his tone was still gentle rather than mocking or threatening. 'We know all about it. Save us from putting you through all of this.' He gestured with his hand at *all of this* and to Grace it seemed to refer to his silent colleague with the cruel eyes. 'We know how you were helping to interfere with our construction of defences on the island – we know all about that. All about Reverend Morris. We just want you to talk about it."

The man leaned forward: 'Tell us, Mrs Mortain, how did you make contact with the British officers and how many were involved?'

Grace thought about Charles Morris and John and wondered if they were already dead.

'I don't know anything about the defences or the British officers,' Grace said, trying to keep her voice calm. 'I don't know what you mean at all.'

The other man stood and took a thin cigar out of his pocket. He lit it with a silver lighter and stood at the window. He seemed suddenly interested in something way off in the distance.

'Your eldest son is a British officer, is he not?'

It seemed so long since anyone had talked about Philip. Little Jimmy and her just communicated about him through a fond smile over some shared memory at the farm.

'Philip? I don't know. He is in England, yes.'

'Perhaps he was involved?'

'I don't know what you mean,' Grace said.

'I mean it is only natural that you would wish to make contact with him, or that he would want to contact you. We all miss our homes – we, Germans, understand that, I assure you.'

The man at the window seemed to be blocking out the light. His broad back was more frightening than anything.

'The resistance group, Mrs Mortain: who was involved?" The man at the desk had opened the file again and had a pen in his hand.

'I don't know anything about a resistance group. You must see that. As for Philip,' she looked at her hands, 'I really don't know how he is. I wish I did.'

'John Morris worked for you,' it was a statement not a question but she found herself saying 'yes' very quietly. 'And you knew his father, Charles.'

She hesitated. 'Not very well.'

'You were once his whist partner.' It seemed the most innocuous statement but it was presented like an accusation of murder on his lips. Grace did not know what to say: the card evenings were part of another world, before the Germans. For one moment she imagined German spies living among them all these years but then realised it was just information given to them now by informants. Perhaps there was someone out there who really hated her, had told them she was a saboteur, dealing with the British. Perhaps Philip really was here, leading a resistance group, and he had got James involved.

'Please,' the man was saying again, sounding almost hurt, 'do not insult my intelligence, Mrs Mortain. You know Charles Morris?'

She looked at the man at the window. His cigar smoke was drifting up the side of the window and then dancing in a draft.

'Yes, yes, I do,' she said.

'How well? Perhaps you were lovers?'

'No, no, how could you say…?'

The German interrupted her, holding up his hand: 'Thank you, Mrs Mortain. Thank you.'

A cloud of blue cigar smoke broke across her face. The other man had turned and stepped towards her. She instinctively flinched but his cold eyes fixed on hers and his monotone voice came whispered from between thin, bloodless lips.

'Now, Mrs Mortain,' he said, 'would you please tell us about the radio?'

Grace did not know the game they were playing. She had no idea where the questions were going or why over the three days the second man said so little. She only knew that she knew nothing.

She denied knowledge of the radio, saying it was old and had just been dumped in the soil years ago. They asked why it was wrapped up; she said she did not know and 'Did it matter?' They asked again and broke for lunch. She was allowed a sandwich and then the questions started again. Who listened to the radio with her? Had strangers been staying at her house? How many British officers had she met? Had she heard from Philip?

And then: 'Which broadcasts did you listen to? Where would you sit? Where would the others sit?'

And all the time all she knew was that she really knew nothing.

On the afternoon of the third day, the cruel-eyed man sat on the edge of the desk and watched her eat her sandwich.

As she chewed self-consciously on the thin slice of pork and white bread, the man said flatly: 'Failing to surrender a wireless receiving apparatus is an offence. The reception of wireless transmissions is prohibited – it is an offence. Aiding and abetting prisoners of war is an offence.'

He reached behind him and fumbled in her file and pulled out a blue sheet of paper.

'This is a *Nacht und Nebel* order,' he said, waving it so that she could see there was a copy underneath. 'Once I sign this you go to Germany and,' he clicked his fingers, 'we no longer care what happens to you. You are an enemy of state, Mrs Mortain, in a time of war, being a woman or a mother does not protect you.'

Grace was no longer eating, despite her hunger. The man took the half-eaten sandwich from her hand and threw it into a wire wastepaper-basket under the desk.

'The minister led the resistance group,' the man was counting people off on his fingers, 'and you worked with him. His son and your son couriered prisoners of war from one safe house to another. Whose houses, Mrs Mortain?'

There was a long silence. Grace could see that the skin of her calf and ankle between that awful brown dress and her shoes was white and bloodless. She could no longer sleep in that cell and all day she found it so impossible to concentrate on their questions. Yesterday, she had asked about James and received no reply.

The square-faced interrogator – whom she had learned was called Kerrl - said: 'You are going to prison, Mrs Mortain. A name will guarantee a shorter sentence.'

Grace wanted to say something but she found herself just shaking her head.

The next day only Kerrl was in the room. She sat down and he immediately pushed a clump of paper across the desk.

'Read this and sign it,' he said, barely looking up from more paper work.

Grace looked at it. Each page was typed. Her name was on the last page with the day's date.

Kerrl looked up.

'It is your statement,' he said impatiently.

He was different today. As he spoke he barely opened his mouth as if he could not spare the energy on her. His jaw was tight, holding back anger. Grace had allowed herself a secret joke about his square face and prominent ears, but it did not amuse today.

'It's in German,' she told him nervously and then flinched as he reached out quickly and took the statement. He read through, translating it for her quickly. It seemed to accurately reflect what they had been talking about and, apart from the fact that her lies about the radio sounded ridiculous even to her, she could not hear much in it to frighten her. She could not even force herself to listen to it all.

'Sign here,' he said, jabbing a finger at the last page, before reaching for the black telephone on the corner of the desk. He spoke briefly and then carefully hung up the receiver, using his other hand to coax the cord to lie exactly as is had before.

Grace signed, wondering if he had translated the document accurately for her. She found it hard to care as all this seemed to be happening to someone else anyway.

Kerll took the statement and checked the signature.

'Good,' he said and placed it inside the folder.

The two *Feldgendarms* charged with taking her back and forth from the prison were at the door. One stood just inside the room as Grace stood and felt his hand at her arm.

She knew she was leaving that room for the last time and disappearing into the silence of her cell.

She turned and said: 'Herr Kerrl, could you please tell me what has happened to my son, James?'

It was then she knew what he was. The administrator who had ticked all the boxes on her file. The calm, flat voice which disguised a cruelty defined not by violence but by being unable to recognise another's suffering.

'Your son was a terrorist,' he said, glancing up not to look at Grace but to indicate to the soldier to take her out. 'He was killed trespassing in a prohibited military area.'

The door clicked shut and the *Feldgendarm*'s arm appeared to be holding her up as much as guiding her down the corridor.

Everything changed then although Grace found it hard to understand what was happening to her. She felt the pinch of the handcuffs but the pain did not seem to register in her brain. She felt her body buffeted at the dockside as she was loaded onboard a busy ship but her feet seemed to be moving of their own accord. The soldiers on the quayside, the crates being unloaded from the troopship, they did not belong to her world. *Why was she walking through all of this? Surely they could not see her?* The noise of the ship's engine only drove her further into her other world. It was like she was asleep but could see everything going on around her. Perhaps she never got any real sleep at all. The engine rumbled and vibrated through the ship's hold. Someone pulled at her clothes and another forced a piece of bread into her mouth. And then she was climbing back up the iron ladder of the hold to be out in the open air again.

People were mumbling around her as they shuffled through the town. Gulls were swooping low over their heads. They were in France. She hadn't been in France since before the boys were born.

It was only the train which brought her around. It had been so long. Gaston and her. He loved to travel through his country by train, even taking her all the way to Biarritz one summer. He had made her feel like royalty in the old resort.

This time she was in a carriage with three other women and two *Feldgendarms*. She looked at the Normand countryside as it passed her window. The cattle turned to watch them pass, then ate on. How she envied them.

She found the *Feldgendarm* looking at her. He was a young man with a kindly face. He was good looking enough to have his photograph in a film magazine. He even tipped his helmet back off his face like she had seen Gary Cooper lift his cowboy hat.

He leaned forward towards her.

'You are very lucky,' he said in English. His accent was thick and he shouted so that everyone could hear. His hand reached out and she felt his fingers squeeze her knee through the dress. 'You are off to Paris, old woman, and then you go all the way to Germany.'

He was mocking, his face lied: he was not kind at all.

He laughed, held his hand on her knee a moment longer and then turned at the others to see that they were enjoying the joke.

In the distance Grace could see the spire of a small white church and a small red tractor turning into a field. Was everything on the train now part of the other world, while outside people sang hymns and worked their farms?

Chapter Twenty-One
Germany, Luxembourg, Summer 1942

People were scurrying back and forth on the Simeonstrasse in the pale morning sunshine.

While the last winter had kept up its tight grip into spring, the days were now long and a thin cloud moved slowly across a blue sky. In the winter the people moved quickly to keep warm, now they hurried to catch what was available first thing in the shops. *It was not meant to be like this*, some of the shoppers were thinking. *The war was meant to make us richer. We accepted rationing. But did not think it would last this long.* Those that grumbled to themselves as they wandered along with their groceries at their sides did not complain out loud - especially not to the officer standing proudly in the centre of the street, his gloved hands forced deep into his dark SS greatcoat.

His cap was low over his eyes, his body still, the tails of the coat billowing gently in the breeze. He was studying the discoloured sandstone of the *Porta Nigra*, the Black Gate, Trier's most famous landmark. It was eighteen centuries old. The northern gate of the city walls. A massive structure, whose light-coloured stone had turned black with age hundreds of years ago. The Rhinelanders here boasted their town was the oldest in the Fatherland; that it was "old when Rome was young".

We have been here for too many generations to count. The French occupation of the city after the first war, he thought, was simply a criminal act. *And that was just our foundation. It is all still to come.*

'Erhard.'

He hadn't heard her approach, although when he turned he had the impression from her face that she had called his name more than once. He could see as she came closer that she was breathing excitedly. She wore a brown coat buttoned tight up to a thin red scarf at her neck. Her lips were coated with a glossy lipstick to match the scarf and her thick blonde hair was held back at the sides with two clips. She had a long straight nose, bright blue eyes and a wide mouth, which Buchner kissed eagerly. She was big-boned, matronly but attractive. As they embraced Buchner felt her heavy breasts through her clothing.

'*Meine leibe* Anna-Louisa,' he said as she faced him, her hands on his arms. She loved his uniform, the feel and look of it. She flexed her fingers in the thick material.

Buchner could smell that sweet perfume he had bought for her a year earlier in Paris. *She must only be wearing it for me.* He stroked his hand down her back.

'You're a naughty devil,' she said and took his hand, leading him away from the *Porta Nigra*.

Buchner had met Anna-Louisa long before his posting to Luxembourg, at a celebration of the Führer's birthday thrown by the Nazi party magazine, *Der Adler*. Her brother, Josef, was a *Staffelkapitan* with a fighter squadron which in 1936 had been one of the units to start righting the wrongs of Versailles: occupying the demilitarised Rhineland. She was very proud of him. He was now somewhere in Italy.

She was 33 and had never married, although Buchner knew she saw him in the role of husband. That would never be.

When they got to the apartment, he led her straight into that familiar bedroom. The big brass bed creaked loudly as she kneeled on it and watched him undress, hanging his clothes neatly in her old oak wardrobe.

She giggled and pulled the clips from her hair, and only half stripped before climbing on top of him.

She still pleased him, only now she was beginning to bore him in equal measure.

Afterwards, he lay naked in her bed, his hands behind his head, and looked around the room. There was a narrow table along one wall with a bust of Beethoven in the centre and a photograph to the side. It was a portrait of a *Luftwaffe* officer – Josef. He wore his cap at a jaunty angle and there was a smirk on that wide family mouth. He had the same nose as his sister too. It seemed as prominent as the peak on his cap.

Buchner crossed his legs under the yellow silk eiderdown as the door clicked open.

It was Anna-Louisa. She was naked too, a thick flicker of hair falling over her right eye. She was carrying a tray with two mugs of coffee and a plate with two slices of *Apfelstrudel*.

Yes, she would make the perfect *Hausfrau* and her devotion meant she argued less than some of his other conquests.

So why did he keep thinking of the other girl? It usually came so easy to him to put each section of his life into different compartments. One group of thoughts rarely contaminated another. But Fraulein Winter had not yet yielded to his power and he wanted her all the more for it. When he returned he would hold a birthday dinner, invite his closest friends and show the schoolteacher off.

And Anna-Louisa? She was sitting on the bed, holding out a coffee cup. He smiled. He would not return here again until he had conquered Claire Winter. Anna-Louisa would wait.

He put his hand to the back of her head and gripped her hair tightly in his fist, pulling her face towards his.

Each time he felt cruel and ruthless, it reminded him he was also inventive and creative, and the same wolfish smile broke across his lips.

As he felt the woman's mouth upon his a wave of excitement rushed through him like a surge of electricity.

Whenever Erhard Buchner thought about his birthday, memories came back of the rolling fields around his childhood home in Bavaria. In his mind's eye he was playing tennis in the shadow of the *schloss.* He was like a leaping white tiger in his flannels playing his good friend Otto off the court. His sister Maria and a childhood sweetheart Mitzi were watching and the churchbells were ringing down the valley, as if honouring him. Now, if he were honest, he could not even remember if you could see the tree-encircled *schloss* from the courts. But that is where his mind wandered to. *Strange*, he thought. Before uniforms. Before the first march to war. Before the *Weimar* disasters. Before, even, the Führer. Maybe it was just because his family was gone - even Maria, dying so young from cancer - and so was the slim, tiger-like Erhard of the powerful serve and deft backhand.

His waistline had grown again tonight with the thick cuts of veal that Richter had produced for the Standartenführer's birthday celebrations. Where Richter or his chef got the fine meat from was anyone's guess. None of those at the table was going to ask if it was the black market. *He must get it the same place he gets the good wine and old brandy*, thought Buchner. *The brandy which is making this 42-year-old sentimental and maudlin.*

He looked to his left and smiled to himself. Claire Winter was wearing the white blouse with the stand-up collar he had bought her especially for the occasion. Where it swelled over her chest it was open slightly at the buttons and he enjoyed a glimpse of flesh. She looked beautiful, a young rose among this bunch of jaded old thorns.

The schoolteacher was talking animatedly with Frau Falkenberg, a large red-faced woman whose tennis player days had disappeared even further into the distance than Buchner's. She had a strong Saxon accent which rose above the throng of voices, each talking over the other.

They were sitting upstairs in Richter's bustling little inn. Richter had made sure they had the room to themselves but it still seemed cramped around them. There was a dark beamed ceiling and the roof sloped at each side towards the white stone walls. The more Buchner drank, the smaller the room seemed to become. It was certainly thick with smoke. He did not smoke but had let the others, as a gesture of goodwill for joining him.

Claire and Frau Falkenberg were talking over Buchner's aide, Wiedler, who was sitting quietly between them. Weidler was a tall thin man with thick glasses and a clerk's attention to detail.

The Falkenberg's daughter, Liesl, sat at the farthest end of the table from Buchner. Her father, Max, was opposite her.

Somehow Richter had got the table plan mixed up so that the other side of the table was the wrong way around. Buchner had wanted Max Falkenberg, one his oldest friends opposite him. Falkenberg was 20 years older than the colonel but represented something Buchner admired: power. He had built up his own chemical firm during the 1920s when times were near impossible for the businessman with the Versailles reparations to be paid to the French and inflation rocketing. Falkenberg's fertiliser firm flourished largely due to its owner's canniness and ability to deal with anyone, even the French. By the time the Nazis came to power he had some of Germany's greatest chemists in his laboratories and he was to gain financially and socially from the Party's interest in what his research and development people were up to. When his business was taken over by the industrial giant *IG Farben*, German's largest company, he not only made a not-so-small fortune but maintained a place on its board. He was grey now with rheumy eyes, but his mind was still as sharp as a tack. He was watching his wife talking to the teacher, and absent-mindedly fingering the Party badge on his black jacket.

Buchner looked through the smoke to Ritter, a business partner of Falkenberg, and his wife, who had a hooked nose and a snorting laugh. Both were talking to the handsome *Luftwaffe* captain to their left, Hauptmann Joachim Voss, the room's hero with a Knight's Cross at his neck and, despite the smell of good food and cigars, and the crisp, freshly-ironed white tunic, an air of aviation fuel and cannon fire around him. Buchner did not like the airforce too much and would have encouraged Voss, his sister's son, to follow him into the SS if he had had the influence over him. But Voss had not taken Buchner on as a surrogate father when his mother died and his father's boat went down in the Mediterranean. They were comrades in the war, and Buchner tried to disguise his intense pride in his nephew. Voss for his part showed little warmth for the older man, preferring to ignore the look of his mother's eyes he saw in Buchner's. Voss was a fighting man, a straight-thinking Nazi hero, with no time for sentiment about some peaceful life. The only peace he had seen had been shattered by his mother screaming her lungs out in agony. He believed in the Party but more than that he believed in the war. It was the fighting which interested him most, not the reasons behind it. He was committed to his unit and to his country, and determined that neither would lose. Voss was on leave from the Eastern Front, although the discussion with the Ritters appeared to be about Malta and the continuing siege.

'Such a small island,' Frau Ritter kept saying, for apparently little reason.

Having the Ritters boring both Falkenberg and Voss was a disaster, thought Buchner, turning to his final guest and feeling even worse.

Buchner emptied his brandy glass and looked at Hauptmann Karl-Heinz Fischer. He was chain smoking and largely quiet. Buchner was not unsympathetic to his mutilated body but he seemed so utterly defeated.

Not for the first time that night Buchner wondered why he had invited the *Wehrmacht* officer. He poured more brandy into his glass and heard Claire's soft laugh to his right. *But, of course, she had suggested it! She'd said he had been very kind during the search for her uncle's murderers.* And then Buchner realised why Fischer was so quiet: he was studying Claire. Looking at her hand on her glass, the way she smiled at Frau Falkenberg and laughed at the way Voss would close sections of conversation with a curt aside, sometimes comical, sometimes menacing, but always sharp like a bullet.

Was Claire looking at Fischer too? Did she return his affection? Buchner turned to Claire and found her so close he had to refocus to make her out. She was still in deep discussion with Frau Falkenberg.

There was a bang behind them and everyone jumped. It was Richter opening another bottle of champagne. They all laughed and Buchner reached over to put his arm around Claire Winter.

It was obvious to Claire Winter why Liesl Falkenberg, who acted like a teenager but had to be well into her twenties, barely said a word during the meal.

To her parents Liesl was a loyal wife – her husband was serving in France - and mother to two young children. While such a role was a supremely honourable one, it was still their son they wanted to talk about. Wilhelm was an officer of the *Adjutantur der Wehrmacht beim Führer und Reichskanzler*, working with Hitler's chief *aide-de-camp*. 'He is with our Führer every day,' Frau Falkenberg stated. 'He travels everywhere with him.'

That, according to the proud mother, meant the Old and the New Reich Chancellory, the *Berghof* on the Obersalzberg mountain in Bavaria, a new headquarters in the woods of East Prussia and, it was stressed, the Führer's special train with its eight coaches. 'All of the Führer's personal retinue went everywhere with him,' was Herr Falkenberg's only contribution to the discussion. 'But my son is of course proud to be among them,' he added. 'And we are honoured also.'

Frau Falkenberg was not concerned about telling all this to Fraulein Winter, who was a non-German and whose use of the language, though extremely competent, seemed incongruous in the present group: she was a guest of Erhard Buchner and that was certainly good enough for her, and besides *you don't miss an opportunity like this to talk about Wilhelm!*

Claire thanked God for her. She was great company while they sat through the endless dishes and refills – Claire thought about friends of hers who were close to starving. Wiedler and Liesl were virtually silent; Herr Falkenberg was aloof; the Ritters were mesmerised by the medal at Voss' neck while he kept glancing at her chest and nodding his head each time he caught her eye. Fischer, who she had wanted at the party, shifted uncomfortably and kept looking to her for help. But it was impossible to bring him into much of the conversation.

Erhard, of course, was drunk, so much so that when his driver stopped outside her flat, he had to discreetly help the Standartenführer out of the Mercedes. In the cold air she realised she was drunk too and neither noticed the twitch of curtains as they laughed and talked their way across the street.

Inside her apartment Buchner took off his cap and threw it across the room.

'Take off my tunic,' he told her, his breath hot with brandy.

Claire put the cigarette in her mouth and moved towards him, watching his eyes twitch with the smoke.

She pushed the sides of his tunic back and he let it drop to the floor.

'Today," he said, ' it is my birthday.' He reached out to take both her arms in his hands. His grip was tight; she staggered slightly with the drink as he forced his face into her neck, kissing her noisily, moving his hungry mouth up towards her lips. His cheek burned against her skin.

Chapter Twenty-Two

On August 20, 1942, a message was received in Moscow containing thirty five-figure cipher groups. It was sent by an agent working in Belgium, named Eva Heigl, who used the three-letter Soviet call-sign TCV. She had been a courier there for the Soviet Comintern since the mid-1920s and since the start of the war she had worked for a growing Soviet spy ring.

Her message not only reached its intended target, *Glavno Razvedyvatelno Upravlenie*, the GRU, Soviet Military Intelligence, it was also intercepted by a German *Funkabwehr* unit monitoring the airwaves.

The Germans were increasingly interested in the long wave Morse code messages being tapped out to Moscow. They called the operators pianists and the spy ring *Die Rote Kapelle*, or Red Orchestra, and had been trying to smash it since its discovery shortly after the invasion of the Soviet Union in the summer of 1941.

They could not decode this message but filed it in case the cipher could be broken.

To Moscow there was nothing of outstanding interest in the transmission either: Heigl had sent more than 500 since the war began.

But Heigl had finally restored contact with an old GRU agent who was looking at a fresh system of getting messages to Moscow Centre.

The agent, the source of the information in the message, was known to Heigl by the German codename *Steinbock* or Capricorn.

When the message was deciphered at the GRU headquarters in Kropotkin Square in Moscow, they found it contained Capricorn's first reference to an industrialist named Falkenberg.

Chapter Twenty-Three

There were two narrow old woodcutter's paths marking the entrances to Marc Rameau's new home. They were each on a steep incline and surrounded by a seemingly impenetrable tangle of trees and thicket. Apart from the reddening of the leaves of the bushes at ground level, the autumn made no impact on this area of the forest: a thick pine ceiling virtually blotted out the sky.

He had positioned himself on a blanket underneath a single shaft of hot, watery sunshine. He had one leg across the other and his eyes shut. He was wearing a crumpled black waistcoat over a brown shirt. A captured Mauser 98K rifle was propped against a tree stump at his side.

Behind him, fitted tightly among the trees, was the place where he, Jean and Maurice lay their heads and cooked their meals.

They had made a large bed, which they shared, from a frame of rods and stakes, together with straw, twigs, branches and some stolen material. So far the weather had been kind and the big black railway tarpaulin had not sprung a leak.

They cooked on a fire covered with corrugated iron and kept their weapons at their sides.

They had separate caches of guns, grenades and explosives buried at two spots in the wood and at a safe house in a nearby town.

But getting about was no longer so easy. Luxembourg was part of the Reich and young men could be called up to fight for Germany at any time. If you avoided wearing a *Wehrmacht* uniform then you could find yourself working as a forced labourer. Rameau had been expecting them to come for him anyway, waiting for his past to catch up. And then, when he saw the Nazi calling at the home of Gillier's niece, he knew it was time to go into hiding.

He joined up with old friends in the dense forest of south eastern Belgium and aimed to continue his own private war.

He had taken provisions and money from some of his old comrades who had joined the large underground movement, the *Front de l'Independance et Liberation* (FIL). But he had generally tried to remain independent, with Jean and Maurice happy to accept him without question as their leader. Through an extended network of farms and peasants they would attempt to get their own weapons' supply by attending downed American bombers, seeing what could be salvaged. Everything would then be passed down a line for Rameau's inspection. Unwilling to invite any other volunteers to their little base, Rameau hoped in time to be able to set up a series of satellite groups around the area.

The last ray of the sun dropped into the trees and Rameau pushed himself to his feet, the carpet of pine crinkling as he walked in the canvas *espadrilles* he wore around the camp.

He stretched and suddenly felt a thirst. He reached into a dark corner of the hut and found a half-empty bottle of red wine. He blew into a dirty glass, poured the wine to the brim and drank. It was sharp but they had no water or milk at the moment.

Soon after there was a rustling in the trail that led the quickest way to the nearest village.

A gangly figure wearing black trousers and boots and a heavy brown shirt came into view. He was over six feet but with the round face and puffy cheeks of a much fatter man. He wore his dark hair, like Rameau's, brilliantined back. This was Maurice, a 19-year-old Belgian who was fiercely proud to be with the underground. He kept his guns the cleanest of the three. Rameau had shown him how to strip them down and every evening since Maurice would take apart his .38, small in the palm of his large hand, and his Schmeisser. As he stepped into the small clearing, he lifted two sacks off his tall shoulders and stooped revealing Jean.

Jean barely reached Maurice's shoulders, although he was five years older. He had the build of a boxer and a narrow face which scowled permanently underneath a shock of auburn hair. He had been a soldier in the *Corps France* when the war started. After the Armistice he went back to his home village near Lille and found the Germans had been through his house and taken what they wanted. Most of his belongings were on trains back to Berlin and Hamburg, and so he decided not to stop fighting. He had killed four Germans but had only just started. Before the war, it was said he had been a misfit. Now he had a reason for being.

A heavy satchel on the end of a long shoulder strap was slapping against his thigh and a dead chicken hung down from his right hand. Its wings were spread in a lifeless fan. Jean walked to the bed, sat down and began to roll a cigarette.

Maurice was kneeling in front of Rameau, unfastening the tie on one of the sacks.

139

'How did it go?'

Maurice looked up and smiled. He pulled open the sack and Rameau could see a dozen or more packets of cigarettes.

'And we have wine and sugar and tinned peaches, salt ham and bread,' Jean stated without a note of celebration in his voice. Rameau noticed his cigarette was already stuck to his bottom lip.

Maurice held up a brown paper bag. 'Boiled sweets,' he stated. 'And,' he rummaged in the other sack, 'a dozen pairs of socks.'

'Good,' Rameau said. It had only been a small raid on a small store owned by a known collaborator a few villages away but it was a decent enough haul. Rameau reached out for a pair of socks and held them to his face. They were of a rough wool but they smelt clean.

He handed what was left of his bottle of red wine to Maurice and said: 'Break open a packet of those cigarettes.'

The men sat quietly in silence for some time. It was cold in their little glade now. Although the sun had been shining all day, the ground was too well shaded to warm through. Maurice and Jean had been panting with the exertions of their day when they arrived but now the sweat was turning cold on their skin.

Maurice sneezed and then wiped his nose on the back of his hand. Rameau could tell there was something they were both waiting to say.

He lit another cigarette and watched Maurice coax to life a low fire with a flame just large enough to warm his hands. Maybe it was because it was a Sunday and Maurice had missed Mass. He always held it against Rameau that he could no longer go, but it was too dangerous: it was the place a stranger was bound to stand out.

'Any news from the valley?' Rameau said. Maurice did not look up so he turned to Jean, who was sat on the bed, slicing butter off a slab with his knife and placing lumps on coarse bread. He had a British Sten gun across his knee. He called the gun his *clarinette*.

'There is bad news from Luxembourg,' he said, still eating so that Rameau could see the bread being crushed between his discoloured teeth. 'Simon is beating and killing. Workers are being sent to a camp in Germany. He has started on the Jews. Families are being rounded up and taken God knows where. All of Germany's laws now they say are Luxembourg's laws.' He looked at Rameau. 'You have no more country, my friend.'

'It is not that which matters,' Rameau said, without elaborating. Maurice and Jean exchanged glances: they just wanted to fight Germans; they knew no more politics than that and often did not understand Rameau.

'None of us have anything until every Nazi is dead,' Jean said, shrugging his shoulders and tipping wine into his mouth. Some spilled down his front.

'We saw that rogue, Gerard,' said Maurice, looking up at Rameau.

'And?'

'He wants our help with some of the forced labourers working the valley.' Maurice made it sound like it was the kind of work he did not join the underground to do.

'To do what?'

'Some are Belgians, some French, some Dutch. Most are trade unionists or socialists. They deal with German workers too, some of whom want to know about their politics.' Maurice stood facing Rameau, reaching into his pocket and pulling out a crumpled up page of a newspaper. 'Gerard says it's a case of passing information to them, literature, encouraging them to work slower, cause trouble, sabotage.'

Rameau opened out the paper and found it was a page from *Freiheit*, an illegal German-language Communist newspaper. He read: *'Happily, the German people's solidarity with the foreign workers and civilian prisoners is generally continuing to grow and is driving the Brownshirt criminals into a desperate state of fear and panic.'*

Rameau nodded his head, a gentle agreement that they would help Gerard.

'I don't like him, Marc,' added Maurice. 'I don't trust him.'

Rameau had reservations about Alain Gerard too but he had known him long enough to trust him. He was flash and a loud mouth, yes, but not a traitor. He frightened Rameau because he was dangerous to know, driving around the countryside in a small gas-powered car with a commercial traveller's pass. Rameau had heard he had even been giving out stolen *Wehrmacht* boots to some villagers and that really frightened him. Gerard was careless and appeared to have nine lives – the fact that led some, like Maurice, to mistrust him – and he could certainly get them all killed.

At the same time, though, they had to keep working and Rameau was becoming afraid he was getting too comfortable hiding out in the forest, eating butter and drinking wine.

'It's our duty to help our comrades,' he said. 'Let's remind them they are not alone. Whatever help Gerard needs we are there to help.'

Chapter Twenty-Four

The cobble-stoned central square in Grunburg always proved a good measure as to how the economy of the town was performing. And at that moment it was thriving.

The soldiers loved it, especially those enjoying a short leave from France, Belgium and the Netherlands and wanting a brief taste of the Fatherland. They stood around the fountain, laughing and joking with local girls, listening to the clip-clopping of the horses on the drayman's cart as he bought more beer for them to enjoy. They stayed in the town's finest hotels, which stood either side of the *Rathaus* on either side of the square. They each flew large red swastika flags that had turned slightly pink in the sunshine and faced each other down like gunfighters in the Wild West. But there was no need for competition when things were this good: there was enough for everybody. The Baron's family had even cleaned up the castle after which the town took its name. It was looking as fine now as the original building must have looked when the soldiers of Charlemagne, the Holy Roman Emperor, built it well over a millennium earlier. Some locals even joked that this was the first rebirth of the town since those days. In the Eighth Century it had benefited from the Emperor's arrival in Aachen, 30 miles or so to the north-west. Now it was industry.

On the other side of the hill the grey and dusty criminals worked the quarry. The townsfolk knew they were thieves, idlers and foreign workers or *Gastarbeiter* from Belgium, Luxembourg and Russia living in a camp in a large clearing cut from the forest. They were carving a road into the hill and could often be seen in small groups cutting pine trees from the forest. On this side of the hill was a similar, smaller camp for women. Locals could see some of the women working in Grunburg's factories making gas masks and life jackets or watch them through the fence if they simply walked past the camp. Both work camps held around 300 people and were simply satellites of a concentration camp called *Natzweiler*, the only concentration camp on French soil. They were there to provide labour for the quarry and the factories.

Everyone had work and they were even bringing in the workers from as far away as Saxony now. They talked funny and seemed as alien as the foreigners but they paid their bills and were stuck in the middle between the *Gastarbeiter* and the locals, forbidden from talking to the former and largely ignored by the latter.

Back in Luxembourg *ville*, Giles Wallis was providing papers for a widening group of Soviet agents throughout the Low Countries. His paperwork now came from the Comintern's forgery branch, which provided its outstations with papers as good as the original. By now, many in the field knew they were so much better than those coming over with agents from London. The passes that took Rameau and his two comrades to Grunburg were from Moscow. Jean's cover as the owner of a company making window shutters – a business which actually existed – allowed him to travel over a wide area without arousing suspicion. According to their papers, Rameau and Maurice worked for Jean and the van they travelled in contained a variety of instruments and tools and had the company name, *ATF*, painted on the doors of the cab.

They arrived in Grunburg from the south-west with Jean driving and Maurice sitting between him and Rameau. It had begun to rain so heavily that the single wiper on Jean's van was struggling to keep the windscreen clear.

At the narrow bend which leads into the square, Jean slowed for a German army motorcycle combination and lorry. He then crunched into gear and carried on through town.

Rameau again felt Maurice shift uncomfortably in his seat. He could see that the youngster's palms were sweating and again he regretted bringing him on this journey. Jean and he could have handled this. He should have gone with his instinct. Again he heard Maurice's words when Gerard described what he needed them to do. Jean, he had said, had the right papers, he could easily slip into Grunburg and then it was just a matter of slitting a man's throat.

At the north end of the town they saw a dark stone cross in the growing gloom and passed a large church. Its grey stone had turned black in the rain. Beyond it lay a narrow graveyard and then a single, redbrick house behind a neat wall and hedge. It was here Rameau made contact with a man named Dieter, who wore a constant frown and spent most days tidying and cleaning the church of St Michaelis. Dieter was broad-shouldered and strong and a veteran of the first war. But he had worked for Moscow for 20 years, spying on his fellow worshippers and townsfolk, and detailing factories and industrial sites throughout this part of Germany. He disguised much of his activities through his love – which appeared genuine – of birdwatching. There were sketches, photographs and oil paintings of birds throughout the downstairs of his house. Nothing was out of place in Dieter's home and his floorboards shone.

The three men sat in a large room watched by the dark eyes of an eagle which swooped out of a huge painting above the fireplace and listened to Dieter describe the man they were to kill. He was a *kapo* at the female labour camp, a supervisor of the working groups known as the *kommandos*.

'A Lorrainer and a criminal named Carnand.' For a big man Dieter had the softest voice, almost a croak. Rameau had seen a photograph of him in uniform in the hall and wondered if he had been wounded in the war. Maybe he was ill. 'He was one of the cruellest men in the work camp. Most cruel to his own.' Dieter knew from Maurice's accent that he was not French. Jean had not spoken until now.

'A traitor,' he said. He knew of others. *Killing this bastard would be a pleasure.*

Dieter sensed that in the little man's face and played on it.

'The German's use him for their dirtiest work. Carnand's work as head *kapo* is essential to their levels of production. He will humiliate, beat and kill for them.'

Rameau said: 'How do we get to him?'

'As a reward for his exceptional work, the Germans allow him off the camp to organise deliveries for the SS guards. He comes here to Grunburg and when he does he visits a house near the square.' Dieter hesitated, the others' eyes upon him. 'There is a girl.'

Dieter went to the window and faced the town. He was talking now as if he could see the girl's house from here, although he could not. He was looking out on the graves and then a stone wall which was close to giving in to the ivy which was slowly strangling it. There were houses on the other side of the street and back towards the town, but the centre of the town was obscured by the church. The street outside was empty.

'He goes to her house and stays for an hour or so. The SS know about her but she's Dutch and they do not care – as long as she doesn't go near their own.'

Dieter turned back towards them. 'He comes to her house early in the morning, around 7am, after he has led roll call and got the poor souls to work. He stays with her and then goes about his SS business. You could be waiting for him when he arrives.'

Maurice said: 'What about the girl?'

Dieter looked at him but then addressed his response to Rameau. 'Her name is Pelser,' he said. 'It might be best not to leave her alive.'

Rameau said: 'It might be best to be in her room waiting. Would that be possible?'

'You could go there at night, see to the girl and wait.'

'What if he does not arrive alone?'

'Usually he is brought in with the SS,' Dieter stated. 'They then have their own work to do. They meet again in the square before nine.'

'And so the sooner he is dead, the further away we can be by then,' Rameau said.

Dieter gave the slightest nod but the room as silent.

'He will be there tomorrow,' the German said at last.

'Good,' Rameau said firmly and smiled reassuringly at Maurice, 'because I have a plan.'

The *ATF* van would have been seen going through town, despite the weather and so Jean and Maurice drove back into town and found a room for the night. Then they sat at separate tables to Rameau in a busy café across the street from the girl's. She lived on the third floor of a tall narrow building with tiny window boxes and heavy pinned back shutters.

Rameau picked out which room was Fraulein Pelser's and watched the rain battering on the glass. From his seat he could see both sides of the street as they waited for her return. According to Dieter she finished work in one of Grunburg's war factories – making gearboxes for tanks - at 6.30pm. Fifteen minutes later Rameau saw her. She was as Dieter described. Short, a little over five feet, with a slightly hunched walk. Her hair was held in a head scarf against the rain. As soon as Rameau picked her out, he picked up his newspaper and turned it over. On the signal Jean got up and stepped out into the rain. The street was busy; she was not the only person returning from work. Fraulein Pelser skipped up the three steps to the front door of the building and Jean calmly turned up his collar and walked across the road. She was shutting the door when he reached it. Rameau watched them barely exchange a word, but she let Jean in. Dieter said there were up to 20 people in the building and, although Jean's German was not good, he had said he would easily mutter a few words to explain why he was coming in. Besides in those kinds of buildings, all Fraulein Pelser would consider her own were her small, front-facing rooms.

The café was closing. Rameau rummaged in his pocket for change. Then he saw the curtains of Fraulein Pelser's room close. It was done already.

Maurice left next, returning to the room he had booked with Jean. They would see him next in the morning with the van.

Then Rameau picked up his small workmen's bag and put it over his shoulder. He walked across the road, waited a moment and then heard the door click. He stepped inside and followed Jean upstairs.

The Frenchman took the stairs two at a time, in spite of his height. Rameau tried to move quickly but quietly; the last thing they needed now was for someone to step out of any of the dark-doored rooms off the staircase. There was no carpet on the stairs and both men's boots sounded far too loud for Rameau.

Jean had Pelser's key in his hand and quickly opened her door.

It was a single L-shaped room with a bed under the window and a sink at its side. Because of the shape Rameau did not see the woman until he had taken four or five steps inside. She was lying face down between the bed and the wall. Her head was under the sink and Rameau could see there was a large bloody gash behind her right ear. The hair was matted in a thick clump. It was almost the same shade of auburn as her killer's.

'Is she dead?' Rameau regretted his words as they left his lips.

Jean did not look at him. He had taken Rameau's bag and was sorting through its contents.

'This is the top floor. There is no-one above us. There are three rooms on this floor, plus a toilet. If we need to piss in the night, we will use the sink. You might want to move her.'

Jean seldom spoke so much, but Rameau found himself listening in something of a trance.

'What is it, Marc?'

Rameau was looking at the woman's stockings. One had ripped open like a wound at the back of her calf. Her skin was very white underneath. He had seen something like it before, a dead woman during an air-raid in Barcelona.

Jean began to strip the dead woman's body.

Rameau could hear the wind at this height. It joined forces with the heavy rain drops to make the window creak and shake. Sometimes it seemed hard enough to break through.

They heard Carnand long before his key slipped into the lock. They heard his boots on the stairs and the jolly tune he was whistling. He had heard some birds singing in the drive over from the camp and they had put him in a good mood. They had been celebrating the end of the rain and the appearance of the worms from the damp forest floor. He was looking forward to a quick hour of excitement. The squalor of the camp and the constant need to cajole the members of the work *kommando* got him down but here in the house he could get rid of his frustrations without those damned workers or the SS.

'*Cherie?*' She loved it when he spoke French. The curtains were drawn as usual. She slept until he arrived, waiting for him to slip in bed beside her. When he left, she went to work.

He took off his dusty black cap and shut the door. There was enough light coming through the gap at the top of the curtains to allow him to see the mop of red hair on the pillow. His knee touched the end of the bed as he began to unbutton his heavy jacket.

Jean stepped out of the bathroom and right up behind Carnand, his nostrils filling with the *kapo's* odour, something of the filth in which he worked. He reached around Carnand's face and covered his mouth with his hand, his fingers pinching his nose, feeling the hardness of his teeth.

The *kapo* struggled but he had been in the process of slipping the jacket off his shoulders when he was struck and the sleeves now trapped his arms.

But he was a strong and desperate, and quickly recovered from the shock to begin forcing Jean back towards the door.

His leg kicked a stool over as he fought. He was getting the better of his attacker, kicking off balance, and he began to laugh madly as he twisted the fingers off his face.

Then he saw a figure move across the window.

Rameau had stood up from the other side of the bed, his knife glinting in the dark as his body brushed the curtains allowing Carnand to see a last chink of dawn. Rameau came forward and without hesitation stabbed Carnand twice.

Jean felt the man choking between his fingers before he sunk to his knees and fell forward so that his head and shoulders were on the bed.

Jean leaned down and quickly began undressing the *kapo* before pulling back the bed clothes to reveal Fraulein Pelser's white naked body. Her skin looked like marble. He put the two in bed together and then pulled over the bed clothes.

Rameau watched him and then heard Jean laugh. He took one of Carnand's hands from under the blanket and put it on the woman's face.

'Farewell, *cherie*,' he said.

Rameau silently went to the bathroom to wash his hands and the blade.

When he returned Jean had taken a small container of petrol from Rameau's bag and poured it over the bodies. He now had the cigar shaped time bomb that Gerard had provided in his hands. It was a lead tube, divided into two halves by a thin copper disc. Each half contained an acid which ate away the disc. When activated the acids would combine and form an intensely hot flame.

The building was slowly emptying. Rameau hoped the destruction would be confined to the room.

He opened one of the valves on the small fire on the wall opposite the bed. It began to hiss gently. The bomb was set to go off in ten minutes by which time the room would be full of gas. The bomb would create just a small flame but it would be enough to obliterate the room and hopefully enough to persuade the Germans that Carnand's death was an accident and not sabotage. He doubted they would spend too much time investigating the deaths.

The pair slipped out of the room and went downstairs. The street was already busy again with everyone seeming to move one way, towards the factories. Rameau and Jean joined them and saw Maurice in the van near the main square.

All Rameau wanted to do was run and get out of the town but he forced himself to walk to the van. As he approached he could see a strange look on Maurice's face. He was staring and at first Rameau thought Maurice must have spotted someone following them. He resisted the temptation to turn and then realised Maurice was staring at him. He looked at himself, holding his hands out quickly. They were clean. Then he noticed the sticky mess on the front of his brown shirt. Carnand's blood. Neither he nor Jean had noticed it in the darkened room and in their hurry to get out. But Maurice could see if from there. He suddenly became aware of just how many people were around him. One bumped his shoulder. *Jesus!* Then he was at the van.

'You!' It was the voice of an officer of the *Ordnungspolizei*, who was striding across the square in a striking green uniform and shining black knee-length boots. Beneath his helmet was stern face which was well used to dealing with nuisance law breakers. His army-style shoulder straps indicated he was a *leutnant* but his manner indicated that he was the person that made Grunburg run smoothly.

Rameau was at the passenger door, across the stumpy bonnet of the van from the German.

'You, I am talking to you,' the German said almost at the van. 'Is this yours?' he struck the van with a gloved hand and looked Rameau in the eye. Then he noticed Maurice. 'Or yours?' In the cab Maurice's fingers tightened on his Smith & Wesson .38 and he brought it up to rest on his knee. A row of German army vehicles moved across the other side of the square and moved slowly towards the narrow bend that marked one way out of town.

'It's mine,' Jean said firmly, stepping between the German and the van and pulling the door handle. 'What of it?'

Rameau let out a tiny breath and quietly opened his door. He slowly fastened the two buttons of his waistcoat.

The officer looked at Jean and put his hands on his hips.

'You cannot park it here," he said, putting his hands on his hips. 'What are you, a Frenchman?'

'Oui, m'sieur.' Jean turned to face the officer.

'What are you doing here?' The German held out his hand, 'Where are your papers?'

Jean reached into his pocket and handed the documents to the German. He looked through them, disappointed to find them in order.

There was a beeping of a car horn along the street and someone shouting in German. Another man began to shout back.

The army policeman looked down the road, letting the hand holding Jean's papers drop to his side. He was wondering what the hell was happening in his town this morning. He could see an army truck and another vehicle facing each other at the bend. Two soldiers were on the pavement arguing with an old man.

Rameau stepped up into the cab of Jean's truck as the German began to walk off.

'Herr Leutnant?' Jean called, and the German stopped and turned. Jean pointed to his papers.

The policeman looked at them as if suddenly wondering how they had got into his hand. He stepped back and virtually threw then to Jean. 'Get that van out of here,' he said, and walked off to sort out the next mess.

The three men sat in the cab. 'There are clothes in the back,' Jean said. 'You can change.'

Rameau nodded.

'Turn this thing around first,' Maurice said, 'and let's get out of here.'

As Jean pulled out of the square the acid flame ignited the gas in Fraulein Pelser's room. The explosion blew the door off its hinges and clean through the balustrade to land on the stairs of the next floor. It blew out the thin interior wall behind the fire and destroyed the next room. The man who lived there had left just after Rameau and Jean. The window and a large section of the wall around it crashed out into the street, showering dozens of people with glass and splintered wood. Two people leaving the café across the street after breakfast were caught by the fall-out of the blast as if they were right on the exact range of the arrows from a hundred archers.

The bodies of Carnand and Fraulein Pelser were still burning as the truck wound its way into the countryside outside Grunburg.

Chapter Twenty-Five

It took a few days for the people of the labour camp to find out what had happened to Carnand. The first rumours said he had been executed by the SS for being a black marketeer. Then they heard he had been killed by a woman. That changed slightly to say he had been executed for catching a sexually transmitted disease. That was the tale many of them preferred and, even when it was settled that he had died in a gas explosion, many still talked crudely of his sexual organs having "fallen off".

In moments when her terrible hunger subsided and she could think straight, Grace tried to consider her reaction to Carnand's death. She felt pure joy that he was gone and absolute horror that this was what she had come to. His death made her smile and she thought of Kerrl, her interrogator in Jersey, and wished the same on him. A few months ago she had met no-one so cruel as Kerrl and even in Paris, where they held her in a cell for weeks, she was not treated with brutality. But that was before her arrival here, after the bone-shaking truck journey through the forest which was then slowly being stripped by the cold autumn. The trees were thin and stark and so were the figures which ran by her that first day in the camp, the *kapos* sticks cracking on the camp inmates' skinny arms and legs.

This *sonderlager*, special camp, was square, about 200 yards across. It was surrounded by a two-metre high wire fence which was topped with a thick curl of barbed wire. The wire looked unsurmountable to Grace, to them all. There were four watch towers, one at each corner, with machine guns trained on the camp and an SS soldier smoking or staring at the women. Dogs patrolled the perimeter. The huts and fence posts were cut from the pine which formed this part of the forest. Strips of wood had been laid across the camp as duckboards connecting the huts and tracing the edge of the central exercise and *appell* square. With the onset of winter these became slippery but the only way to get around without losing your shoe in the thick mud.

The soldiers were camped in a group of barracks outside the main gate. The kommandant had a hut of his own, from which he appeared for some of the camp's daily roll calls, the *appell*, at 5.30am. He normally looked uninterested in what was presented before him: lines of around 350 women, mainly from France,

Luxembourg and Belgium, who had been involved in or suspected of some sort of anti-German activity and so had been disappeared into the Night and Fog.

They knew early on they were in Germany - they had travelled through a frontier post on the train – and there was talk about a men's camp nearby. But they could see nothing from their dark corner of the forest, which turned bitterly cold in the weeks after Grace's arrival, the damp and chill leaking through every corner of the hut.

On arrival they were stripped and forced to remove their wedding rings. Grace had already lost weight and the ring came off quite easily and for the first time in years. It was the first act that was not only humiliation but theft. Then they were made to run to a hut where one man cut at their hair with a pair of heavy shears and another shaved the hair down to the bone. As the clumps of hair fell to her shoulders, thighs and to the floor, Grace watched without interest. She wondered why it was not breaking her heart but then she remembered James and realised her heart was already broken.

Outside again they were each made to take a razor to the rest of the hair on their bodies and then they dabbed themselves down with rough cloth that had been dipped in a barrel of disinfectant. All the while the *schupos* ran back and for, the tails of their green overcoats flapping. Most of the shouting came from the *kapo* called Carnand, who screamed in French and German and lashed out at some prisoners with his fist. Every time he directed his attention to a prisoner, a *schupo* would arrive before her and shout or push or beat her with a short club. '*Eine Laus, der Tod*!' Carnand screamed as they winced to the touch of the stinging disinfectant. The smell and pain made the young woman at Grace's side wretch but there was nothing in her stomach. She doubled over and Grace turned to help her. As she did she saw the flash of the *kapos* bright armband as he punched the woman full on the side of the face. 'Dirty bitch,' he said in French. Grace struggled to pick the woman up, noticing the scars and cuts across the top of her skull. Carnand had a gloved hand on both women pushing them towards the rising steam if the shower block.

This woman was Louisa. She was a 19-year-old machinist from Liege and was the main reason Grace become so overjoyed by Carnand's death. Carnand never forgot the moment he first saw

Louisa at the lice table and every time she had to give him the four-digit figure which identified all the prisoners instead of their names, he said, 'No, you are dirty bitch,' and struck her.

The prison uniform was a grey-blue shirt, jacket and trousers, awkward wooden clogs and a scruffy cap which had to be taken off for every *kapo* and soldier.

Grace and Louisa were put in a quarantine hut for a week, watching fellow prisoners being made to exercise on the yard before being taken to one of the large huts to work. It seemed these were involved in sewing, making and repairing uniforms for the front. The news heartened Louisa who thought she might escape the worst of the treatment when the guards realised how good she was with the machines or the needle and thread. She took to massaging her hands and fingers, a gesture which in time became like a nervous tick and would later irritate some of her fellow prisoners. Not Grace. To Grace, Louisa became a surrogate daughter, a reason to live on and to put up with the harsh cruelty of the camp. She coped with what they did to her by concentrating her efforts on keeping Louisa safe.

Each night when Carnand arrived at the hut and made them stand to attention, Grace urged Louisa to be strong. He made them take their caps off quickly, and then put them back on. It was a hideous game and anyone who was not quite quick enough took a snap from the *kapos* stick. Once one had been struck, one risked further blows by falling to the floor. Collapsing to the ground in the camp did not make one safe from further punishment; just the opposite.

Soon the women were put to work and even the horrors of the camp became structured in a routine set to the sounds of shouting, the crack of stick on bone and the piercing screech of whistles which echoed through the trees, and punctuated by stubby cuts of bread and bowls of thin, colourless soup. The camp was startled into life at 4.30am with each prisoner being ladled a cup of weak, watery coffee. There was a roll-call and then the run around the exercise yard, cold toes curling into the front of the clog to try to stop it from coming off and getting the wearer a stick across the shoulder blades. Work began at six with the women sitting in rows down six long tables which stretched the length of one of two long huts in the compound. Some prisoners were taken outside of the camp to factories in a nearby town, which Grace learned was called Grunburg and was only just inside Germany.

After a break at noon for soup the women returned to work until around seven in the evening. They were then given a bowl of stringy turnip soup, which was sometimes hot but was normally cold, and only occasionally contained tiny strips of meat.

They were then returned to their hut but could not go to bed until between nine and ten when Carnand and one of two drunken SS NCOs would turn up for the bunk inspection and to hear the prisoner's shout their number in German. Sometimes this was when people took a final beating of the day. If Louisa was standing at the front Carnand always kept a punch for her. Only days before he was killed he caught her a blow on the knuckles with his club. Her hand began to swell up and she became afraid she would not be able to work. The two women sat next to each other the next day stitching pockets to a tunic. Grace could smell her own clothes and carefully kept her eyes on the dirt ingrained deep under fingernails so that it looked like she were concentrating only on her work. But she could feel Louisa wince with every movement and knew that any time soon one of the *schupos* would become aware of the problem. She willed Louisa not to stop, not to cry out. Somehow the young Belgian managed to work on.

Christmas had passed with just a whisper in the morning from one of the prisoners in the hut and then brief hugs from one to another. When Grace held Louisa that morning, she felt her ribs tight against her own. She looked into Louisa's eyes. They had been a striking blue that morning a few months ago when they ran to the shower room together; now some of that colour appeared to have drained out of them. Her skin too was grey, her cheekbones pushing through. Grace smiled the warmest smile she could find in her own despair and said: 'Merry Christmas, Louisa.' Louisa laughed back, although there were tears in her eyes by the time the whistles began ringing and the soldiers' feet began drumming on the duckboards outside.

The ground was still hard that late January morning when Grace, Louisa and around 50 others were kept back after the *appell* by the *rapportführer* who had taken roll call. He told them they would be leaving the next day but did not say anymore. As they dispersed quickly, they caught each other's eyes suspiciously.

The following morning they were awoken by the usual sound of whistling and shouting echoing through the still air and into the stripped trees of the forest. They were hustled to the showers and then made to stand in front of the clothing store. The *kapos* brought them their clothes and made them dress.

Grace felt the thin bones of her legs as she bent down to step into her dress and pull it up. She was used to being naked now in front of so many strangers. This did not beat her down. She was used to shivering too. She just pulled on her clothes and felt the comfort of them. She did not know where they were going but they were leaving. There had to be hope.

As she pulled her cardigan sleeves tidy over the sagging skin of her upper arms she watched two large green trucks enter the wooden gate of the compound. Their wheels crashed through the thick puddles, emptying the pot holes and letting the water find new channels in the frosty ground.

The two vehicles pulled up with their closed tailgates facing the women. Their brakes squealed as they stopped and the engines belched out dirty grey smoke. The smell of burning fuel cut through the usual smells of cut wood, damp clothes and human odour.

Grace turned her head back to face the *kommandant*, who had started a speech about their continued 're-education'. His breath broke in friendly puffs in the cold air as he spoke. It reminded Grace of the soft clouds she often watched drifting over the coast at home. Grace watched them closely and for a brief moment felt the touch of a warm sky. Not for the first time she felt as if her mind were split in two: one half trying to trick her; the other acutely aware of the deception.

When he finished speaking he turned and walked briskly along the duckboards, keeping the dirty ground from his shiny boots.

The women were split into two groups and pushed towards the trucks. Somehow Louisa, who had been so close at her side as they dressed that their elbows had touched, was heading for the other truck. *How had they let themselves get separated! Never mind*, Grace thought, *they would be with each other at the other end, wherever that might be.* The canvas flaps of the trucks were pulled back and the tailgates dropped. Grace found herself seated next to one of the *schupos* sat at the tailgate at the rear of the second truck to leave the compound. One of the flaps had been left pinned back so that the prisoners could watch the camp gate close behind them as they left.

The trucks swayed and bucked on the country road. The women too weak to hold themselves steady. They pushed and buffeted each other. The ones sat on the floor were perhaps most comfortable, although they were kicked and kneed by the ones on the benches at the sides.

The truck moved around one hundred yards along the road, changed down a gear with a lurch and then turned a corner to follow the route through the forest and the camp was gone.

The crews of 2 Group, the light bomber component of the RAF's Bomber Command, were not unhappy when they were shifted from the direct air attacks on German shipping. The Bristol Blenheim crews, in particular, were suffering appalling casualties from flak despite the bravery of the crews and the high levels of tonnage of German ships sank. So the switch to *Ramrod* operations, for many, was something of a blessing. These were daytime flights involving the new Lockheed Venturas, Douglas Bostons and Blenheims. The bombers flew with a fighter escort over France and the Low Countries to strike at airfields, factories, power supplies and communication centres.

It was a shock to many in the border areas of the *Greater German Reich* that British bombers would strike them. They were too close to the towns and workers of the British Allies in France, Luxembourg, Belgium and France. The *Tommies* would not want to turn their friends against them.

That is how it was in Grunburg that Sunday morning in January 1943. Cologne and Mainz were alerted for possible attack within thirty minutes. Alarms surrounded in towns between Koblenz and Trier and policeman ushered people off the streets.

But in Grunburg they were sure the target would be further south in the Ruhr. The people grabbed their ten Reichsmarks gas masks and headed for the shelter but did not know that the small cluster of factories on the edge of their town had been chosen for attack.

So when the first marker flares for the bombers dropped near the town the two-lorry convoy kept going until the drivers could see over Grunburg, from the smoke of the factories two miles to their east to the meadows and vineyards stretching out towards the short border with Belgium. The driver of the first truck noted that some of the flares were burning in bright red fires in the meadows to the west of the town.

The flares could be seen too by the pilots thousands of feet above them that clear frosty morning. One crew coming in from the west felt the shockwaves of flak bursting ahead of them. The guns were concentrated on the far side of the town as they flew in from the west. They were there to protect the factories. So when the crew saw the first flares to the east no-one could blame them for releasing their load and banking away before hitting the heaviest flak.

A line of five 250lb high explosive general purpose bombs – each about the size of a man – streaked into the countryside outside Grunburg. The first landed near a bright flare throwing up a huge crater of ground, disturbing earth and clay which was probably centuries old. The others followed in a line, about the length of a football field apart.

The sixth bomb landed directly on the first truck turning the skin and bone of the four *schupos* and 25 forced labour workers, and the metal, wood, rubber and canvas of the vehicle, into a million pieces and scattering them over the roadway and hard green grass around it.

The second truck had dropped behind the first but its cab was still struck by lethal sections of roadway and deadly shards of material from the heart of the fireball. One of the *schupos* in the second cab died instantly, the driver was mortally wounded turning his slowly lumbering vehicle off the road. The ground had shook with the explosion sending shock waves through the passengers in the back. The canvas ripped and Grace saw rose red holes explode on the women around her. A front wheel struck one of the stumps of the trees laid flat by a forest *kommando* of workers from the men's camp. Heads and arms clashed together and Grace glimpsed streaks of cold blue sky as the roof of the truck collapsed and began to twist itself around her.

A whole new series of explosions seemed to be echoing through Grace's head as she was pushed towards the tailgate of the truck. The *schupo* at her side was forced over the metal frame and out. The truck was going over and she was falling backwards, slowly. Then her bones were crushed again and the tailgate gave way and she felt her teeth smash and her mouth was filled with grit and dirt. She lay with her cheek on the cold ground, feeling her head bounce as the earth rippled with explosions from ten feet or ten miles away. She felt a shocking pain in her ear-drums as pockets of displaced air burst around her head. Then the rain streaked on her face and lay in a puddle before her eyes and she put out her hand to wipe her face with the water, but it was thick and heavy and red.

Sometime later she was walking through a countryside smelling of smoke and fire, and over a roadway made of huge chunks of earth, broken metal and clothes. She stood on a glove but it was full and dripping with blood.

Then she saw a black cross rising out of the ground ahead of her. It got very close until it seemed to be falling down on her. She heard a man's voice but it was a croak, a whisper. She felt his breath in her ear and then she was lifted up and carried towards the cross. Her eyes were too heavy to remain open but even as they clamped tightly shut she could see the dancing lights of a hundred fires on the inside of her eyelids.

Grunburg had taken a terrible battering. A town which had stood virtually unchanged for 500 years was transformed, with half its homes left uninhabitable.

The flames leapt across each narrow street, from block to block like a dragon's tongue. Broken gas pipes sparked like blow torches. Some buildings, being just piles of masonry and broken bricks like giant dusty molehills, acted as fire breaks.

But there was little luck on the side of the firefighters tackling the blaze. The once-colourful timber framed buildings around the square collapsed and crackled like matchsticks and burned for hours as the crews struggled against red, orange and white walls of flame and a shortage of water. One firefighter suffered such terrible burns from the heat of his own clothes that he died three days later.

Three of his comrades died trying to rescue people from a public shelter which had been filled with the terrifyingly hot breath of an explosion. They were killed by a gas explosion when only yards from breaking through into the shelter. They had not known that all 40 people inside had already been dead.

The bodies of some townsfolk had been melted to the cobbles by the heat. The whole town was caught in a thick black blizzard as paper and ash, the homes and belongings of the residents swirled into the air hundreds of feet above their heads. Survivors wondered around in a daze, asking after people they already knew they would never see again. Some walked in the fields as if they had escaped from a lunatic asylum.

The street where Carnand's woman had lived had been completely destroyed by a single 500lb bomb.

Many of the factories were destroyed too. No more rubber parts would leave Grunburg for the torpedoes of the Admiral Doenitz's U-Boats or for the cockpits of the Heinkels. The huge black complex at the head of Adolf Hitler Strasse was least damaged with three out of four of its factory blocks unaffected by the bombing. Its supply of fuses and ignition sets for tanks on the Eastern Front continued uninterrupted.

Several women in Grace's truck had stumbled from the van after the crash. Many walked back towards the camp. Two were shot dead in the woods. An SS *Stabsscharführer diensttuer*, or acting sergeant major, took three privates armed with sub-machine guns to find the women. Ignoring the chaos around them they discovered by mid-afternoon that one of them was missing. They began a door-to-door search on the outskirts of town but called it off after being told a woman with bleeding hands and face had been seen walking towards a burning wing of the town's municipal *Krankenhaus* shortly before the hospital collapsed. It was good information. From a Nazi Party member, a Great War veteran who had run a Hitler Youth camp that the NCO had attended when he was 18 in 1937. The *Stabsscharführer diensttuer* gave a party salute and returned to the camp to report.

Dieter Moller returned the salute, looked up at the church again. He could believe it had survived without a scratch. It remained unaffected by the war: apart from the fact that only one bell remained; the other having been stripped the year before because the metal had been needed to produce army equipment. He hurried back into his house.

To the townsfolk, Moller had been a good Catholic – like most of them – who had joined the Nazi Party to work hard with a generation of the town's youth. The party may not agree with his religion but it had never interfered with his politics. Besides he rarely attended services these days and was linked to the church because he lived next door and was good friends with the sickly old priest. He kept a key and made sure the church was tidy.

However, in his head he had no time for religion at all and cared only for politics, although not that spouted by the Führer.

He had taken Grace into the church during the SS search. Now that it was over and the evening was drawing in, it was safe to bring her into his house. He had been nursed for four months in hospital after shell fragments ripped through his chest and neck in 1917 and it all came back to him as he looked after the thin woman with the shredded clothes and shorn off hair. Her physical injuries appeared limited but she was suffering from heavy concussion and she had lost several teeth. When she was well he had to decide quickly what to do with her. He would send a message to Alain Gerard and seek out the men who had dealt with Carnand.

Chapter Twenty-Six

Alain Gerard's men were living in a farmhouse which to Marc Rameau summed up the small underground group: it was more about comfort than security.

It was luxury compared to the recent lifestyle of his group but it was only one hundred yards from the main road. It would only take one German vehicle to break down and the *boche* could stumble across a pretty stack of machine guns, pistols, explosives and radio parts.

Gerard was sat in the kitchen pulling at a round loaf of bread with an omelette *fines herbes* stuck in the middle. He was a dapper man of about 40 with a neatly trimmed moustache. His hair was cut in the short style now being favoured by the *Wehrmacht*. He wore a black suit which was only a little threadbare at the elbow and knee, and from which he carefully brushed away crumbs of bread with every mouthful.

Two members of his group were outside washing at the pump before heading into the village. At least he was getting that right now: there was nothing more dangerous than walking around looking like you were living rough; it was a give-away.

Rameau guessed the improvement was down to the Englishman who arrived to organise drops of ammunition and to help build alliances between the resistance groups in this area of south east Belgium.

'Does your Englishman have politics?' Rameau asked. He was standing, looking out the window. Being here made him feel nervous. He could see Jean, standing at his van. He had pulled back the bonnet and his arm was moving with the turning of a screwdriver.

'He is like the rest of them, he has no politics,' Gerard said, taking a sip of red wine. He stopped chewing to study Rameau. When he spoke he sounded like a father addressing a wayward son. 'Sit down, Marc. Have something to eat.' He kicked a chair out with his foot. It scraped noisily against the stone floor. 'There is something I need to speak to you about.'

Rameau perched awkwardly on the end of the chair.

'Forget the Englishman,' Gerard said, waving a piece of bread in his fingers. 'The British are alright. But in small doses.' He laughed.

'And especially when they can arrange aircraft to drop guns and grenades.'

As he popped another piece of bread into his mouth, a car turned off the road and headed towards the house. Rameau stood again to see a grey Ford V8 pull up near the pump. Three men got out. Two stopped to talk to the others who were now standing around smoking while the third headed for the house.

'That's him now,' said Gerard without turning to the window.

A door slammed. Rameau listened to the footsteps approach the door. There was a knock.

Gerard winked. 'The Englishman,' he said.

The man who stepped into the room was around six feet tall, about the same height as Rameau but he was much broader than the slim Luxembourger. His hair was dark and wiry, and he had heavy brown eyes which settled quickly on Rameau. He looked like he had lived an outdoor life and Rameau was surprised to see a redness in the man's cheeks: he had thought all Englishmen were bank clerks and shopkeepers.

'Marc Rameau,' said Gerard, 'This is Henri, our Englishman.' The newcomer flashed a look at Gerard as if it were not the way he would choose to be introduced. Perhaps he hoped always to pass as a Frenchman, even among the underground.

He reached out and shook Rameau's hand firmly.

'Would you help yourself to coffee or wine, Henri? I have to brief Rameau about a little job I have for him.' He turned back to Rameau. 'Our friend in Grunburg has an escaped prisoner who he needs to move from his home as quickly as possible. It's an interesting one. A woman.'

Gerard explained the situation to Rameau, describing how the woman needed to be moved over the border into Belgium and to a safe house in Liège. There, she could wait until they could move her through France and over the Pyrenees to Spain. It had worked before with two British air crew.

'It's risky,' Rameau said.

'I know, I know,' replied Gerard. 'And the rewards are not the same as moving air-crew: at least they go back to England and bomb the *boche*.'

'So why are we doing it?'

'Dieter simply cannot keep her, you understand that? And he is a fine contact to have that side of the border.'

Henri was sipping a glass of wine and looking absent-mindedly out of the window: he was thinking about how he was going to persuade Gerard to move from the farmhouse. He did not like the set up here. If this group were broken, the trouble would spread like ripples on a pond: it had been involved in just about every sabotage and resistance activity in the area. And Gerard himself was too valuable to lose: his knowledge of safe houses and couriers would put dozens, maybe hundreds, in danger if he were captured.

So Henri was barely listening to what the two men said and they made no effort to gain his attention, after all why should they? They had no idea that the woman they were planning to rescue was called Grace Mortain, a 45-year-old woman from Jersey who now felt alone in the world.

Henri was known to them only by that field name. Neither Rameau nor Gerard, who had slept at his side these last three weeks, could have any idea that his real name was Philip Mortain and that he was the loving son Grace had not seen for almost three years.

At that moment Grace and Philip were as close as they had been since the war came to them in the summer of 1940. And the two strangers at the table eating bread under Philip's nose were blissfully unaware that they plotting to reunite them.

Philip watched Gerard's men outside, wishing they didn't look so sleepy, so much like people who had had one too many glasses of wine with their lunch. Here he was, living among the very occupying Germans he had left his family and home to escape. He thought about the road which had brought him here: and concluded he must have been mad.

Chapter Twenty-Seven

The man who had greeted Philip Mortain in that bare wooden room in the War Office in London had spent a lifetime perfecting the expressionless look.

His face was an empty mask, painted on to portray the complete absence of emotion. His eyes were dark round pools framed by thick black glasses.

The man studied the file in front of him. He was already familiar with its contents – a personal history, RAF record and a letter and notes from Mr Bachelor himself – but he liked to leaf through the documents and make the interviewee wait. *Where does Bachelor keep bringing them in from?*

'So now all of a sudden,' the man – who had been introduced as a major but was not in uniform - sneered at last in fluent French, 'after learning to fly aircraft you want to start jumping out of them?' He raised an eyebrow at the end of the sentence and kept it raised. Philip could see two strands of hair dangling down from each nostril.

'I was told you needed French speaking people to parachute into France, sir,' Philip said. He was unsure at what point he should mention the approach from Mr Bachelor of the Ministry for Economic Warfare and their recent awkward lunch at Simpsons in the Strand, or even if he should mention any of it at all.

'You have an accent there,' the major snapped and sat back slightly, his belly squeezing against the buttons on his black waistcoat. Philip saw a silver pocket watch glint beneath his jacket.

Philip held his stare. He certainly had no more of an accent to his French than this idiot. He supposed the major was more used to the sounds of Paris than of Normandy.

'Still,' the major added, perhaps sensing Philip's coldness, 'it is passable. Tell me about your father.'

Philip guessed most of it would be in the file, but he played along: 'He was from an old proud Norman family, sir. When he was 18 he left the family farm and went to work in a bank. Through hard work he found himself working for one of the largest banks in France. He travelled around the country and beyond. I think he made a great deal of money.' The major frowned at the vulgarity of the statement but Philip chose to ignore his censure. 'He made enough to retire young and buy a small farm on Jersey. Going back to his roots, I suppose you might call it, sir.'

'But your mother was English?'

'She is a Channel Islander,' Philip stated. 'We spoke English with her but French with my father. Always.'

'But you never travelled with him to France. Why not?'

'My parents seldom went after I was born,' replied Philip. 'My father was an only son. His father died young. The farm went with him. I suppose that's why he tried to start up a farm of his own. To replace something which was lost.'

This time it was the major who remained silent to hold Philip's gaze.

'But my father had many French friends on the island. We spoke with them. I know slang well, both Jim and I were keen to learn that.'

The major took off his glasses, catching one of his large red ears as he did so.

'Tell me about your personal obligations.'

Philip hesitated. He loved Alice but it was strange how little he considered her when he was in uniform. It was like he could only safely let himself really love her when they were away from all this. Then, she was all that mattered. But now here in London with these dusty old officers fussing over him this was it, this was his life.

'I am engaged to be married, sir.'

'Yes. Alice is the lady's name I understand.'

'Yes, sir.'

'What does she do?'

'She works in a house in Wales.'

'How does she feel about your being in uniform?'

'She is very proud, sir. She knew I was joining up when we met.'

'If you worked for us you might not be able to tell her what you were doing. She would not know where you are. Would that be a problem?'

'No, sir.'

The major paused.

'We need good pilots,' he said at last. 'You achieved excellent marks in training. If we send you to France, we lose a good pilot.'

'I hope that any work I can do in France will be of considerable importance to the country of my mother and the homeland of my father. I would prefer that Hitler were not able to stand beneath the Eiffel Tower. I also hope to be able to say that one day I struck at the Germans and helped release their grip on my homeland.'

Mr Bachelor, Philip thought, would be proud of that burst of patriotism. In truth, Philip reflected, he was motivated more by impatience than patriotism –an impatience to fight the enemy face to face as, he imagined, his mother, little Jim and his friends were being forced to do.

The major sat up straight. His chair creaked.

'We only take volunteers,' he said, replacing his glasses and opening a drawer of his desk. 'Do you need time to think this over?'

'Absolutely not, sir,' Philip responded.

'Good,' the major lifted a sheet of paper out of the drawer, 'then please sign this.'

Philip did so and as he slid it back the man said, 'This is not final. If we are not happy with how you are performing we will find something else for you to do. Likewise if you are not happy you can withdraw.' The major put the sheet of paper in a drawer to the other side of him. 'You are very young. You will now embark on a new period of training. It will not be easy but the rewards for you and your country may be immense. Thank you, Mortain.'

Philip stood and saluted. He left, his signature on a piece of paper shut away in a drawer, signing himself up to something he knew virtually nothing about.

Philip's tour of Britain continued. He spent a fortnight in a requisitioned country house in Hertfordshire and, passing the short preliminary stage, was sent to the western highlands of Scotland. He arrived via Glasgow and was made to walk eight miles to Arisaig, where agents of SOE would be 'toughened up'. Some of the instructors were sneering at Philip because although he was physically now well-built his features still gave away his young age. But he had come of age in RAF uniform and had never had any problem learning what he was told. He was determined that there would be nothing at which he would fail.

At Arisaig they were taught the various arts of silent killing and living off the country. Philip learned that in a fight he should put a finger in his opponent's mouth and rip as the "mouth tears easily" and he found a local crofter who was happy to share a plate of eggs and bacon with him.

There were no parades, only lectures, and instruction in how to clean, dismantle and use British, German, Dutch and Belgian small arms. Philip managed to avoid getting lost during nights outdoors without provisions and to avoid blowing himself up while laying charges. Next he went to Manchester and made his first parachute jump.

It was only then, when he had made it to the SOE finishing school, Beaulieu Manor on the edge of the New Forest, that he began to really find out what it was all about. The trade he was in, he was told, was subversion. How to damage the enemy's property, means of communication and production. How to put a strain on his manpower resources. How to undermine the enemy's morale. How to raise the morale of the occupied populations. Learn what you are told, instructors at Beaulieu said, and your chances of being picked up are small. Do not put your learning into practice and you are putting your life in extreme danger.

Philip learned the basics, from identifying Nazi insignia to meeting a contact. He had to learn to live illegally.

But instructors found the most important aspect to teach him was aggression. They picked up on notes from Arisaig during unarmed combat and tried to focus the hatred he must have felt after being driven from his homeland. They dragged him from his bed at three in the morning and shone a light and threw questions into his face.

Philip only realised he had passed all these test when things began to accelerate. A French dentist was brought in to check for any non-French dental work; he had to write a will (he realised he had nothing but had to face the fact his mother and James could be dead and therefore the farm would be left to Alice); he received French clothing and razor blades. Then he received his cover story with the name which would be on his identification documents. *Henri Mortagne*. Date of birth the same, but born in a village in Normandy which was actually near the town of Mortain. His parents would be Gaston and Greta. He had spent ten years living in Jersey between the ages of four and fourteen and this accounted for his accent. The man who gave the cover story told Philip that most Germans and few French would know where Jersey was. Philip, according to the story, now worked as an agent for a Belgian insurance company; work which involved travelling.

It was then he was told about Gerard and about the area along the river of Ourthe where he would be expected to work.

He would be leaving in three days.

Philip was studying a map of Liège when he heard a polite cough and looked up to see Bachelor.

'Mr Bachelor,' he said, beginning to stand.

'Don't get up, old boy." Bachelor pushed his head further around the door. 'Everything alright?'

'Yes, sir.'

'All set?'

Philip did not know what he knew or what he was really asking.

'Yes, sir.'

'Jolly good.' He seemed a lot less up-tight than normal. He made to disappear and then popped his head back again. 'What about the girl?'

Philip hesitated. 'I am seeing her tomorrow. Mrs Pembridge has been very kind.'

Philip forgot to book them a table and they walked around half a dozen restaurants before finding one where they could eat. Alice had been surprised to see him still in his RAF uniform. The Official Secrets Act may stop him telling her what was going on but she was not stupid: other girls were going out with aircrew and, while some had gone to Canada to train, their instruction had not seemed as drawn out as Philip's.

Alice fingered the narrow silver engagement ring and talked cheerfully about her work. She wasn't going to let this get her down. Philip looked at her and realised he loved her but could only think about the aircraft which was about to take up over France and drop him into the darkness. He wanted Alice but was not free to have her until all this was over. He reached across the table and held her hand but she was afraid his touch would make her cry, and she would not break down in public. She moved her hand away and bit her lip.

The food and the emotion made him feel sick and when they booked into a shabby hotel that afternoon he wished he had not drawn out this goodbye. *I should have written*, he thought and immediately rebuked himself for his selfishness.

They made love but both felt like a stranger to the other. Afterwards, Alice sat in the dark in silence as the room filled with her cigarette smoke. Philip had his cover story running endlessly through his head and that only served to widen the gulf between them.

They lay side by side on the bed. They did not look at each other but their hands were touching.

It was in the street next morning that they truly felt the strength of each other's love. They stood on the pavement waiting a taxi to take Alice away. Philip was selfishly glad now that she was leaving, not him. He did not know how he could turn his back on her. When they hugged and their faces were hidden they both felt the full emotion: it was in the strength of the arms that gripped them and the way they pushed their heads into each other's shoulders.

They gripped each other so tightly it was as though they were leaving a gentle impression on the other's soul.

And when Alice's cab turned the corner, Philip lifted his hand and waved to an empty street. He turned and, as his eyes swelled for a moment with tears, he tried to express his grief in his head for her in French.

By the time Philip reached the bleak surrounds of Tempsford airfield 50 miles north of London he was wearing a pair of dark blue tweed workmen's trousers, a thick and rather itchy jumper and a black leather coat which reached just below his waist. He was given a knife and a .38 and three sets of pills: knock-out drops to put in some villain's drink, as in the movies; benzedrine to help him stay awake; and a single cyanide capsule, which would take him on a five-second slide into oblivion.

Overalls and a parachute harness were then put over his clothes and he was introduced to the aircrew.

The pilot, an Australian with teeth that glinted in the dark, told Philip they would cross the French coast at a gap in the German's anti-aircraft defences near the mouth of the Somme and then turn westwards towards Belgium.

'You frighten'd, mate?' he said suddenly.

Philip shook his head. 'No.' But his mouth was dry.

'Don't worry, mate, we'll have you dangling under the moonlight in no time at all. As long as the flak and night fighters don't knock us out of the sky.'

Then the Whitley's engines opened up and Philip could see the tarmac running past. The ground was shining in the moonlight as he left it behind.

Chapter Twenty-Eight
February 1943

Erhard Buchner's gleaming black Mercedes cruised through the Rhineland countryside towards the curve in the river between Mainz and Koblenz. It was a journey he normally enjoyed: the sight of the hilltop castles which stand guard along *Vater Rhein* as he swept north in the darkness between steep and thickly wooded hills towards Cologne.

But tonight he very much wanted to get to his destination and had urged his driver to keep the accelerator to the floor.

Buchner's body lurched forward as the car braked heavily for an oncoming horse and cart.

The obstacle negotiated, the driver squeezed the accelerator once again and they were back up to near full speed.

'Don't worry, Erhard,' Claire Winter said from the backseat beside him, 'we've plenty of time.'

'I'm not worried, Claire,' he said, shifting in his seat and adjusting the charcoal jacket of his woollen suit. 'I just do not wish to be late.'

Claire picked a piece of fluff off her black skirt and thought about the weekend ahead. She had been nervous when they had first made this journey to the Falkenbergs' country home, but now they seemed to be heading there once or sometimes twice a fortnight. She looked out and knew that soon they would be crossing the river and heading into the countryside east of Wiesbaden, the ancient city almost directly across the river from Mainz. Falkenberg, Claire had guessed, liked Wiesbaden's associations with the wealthy leisure classes of the nineteenth century who had made the city so rich in the years up to the Great War.

It was not the most entertaining place to stay as Frau Falkenberg could be a terrible bore and Buchner spent most of his time walking and talking with Max Falkenberg, but their daughter Liesl, obviously tired of her parents' company and missing her husband awfully, had adopted Claire as a kind of surrogate sister.

This weekend, Erhard seemed especially agitated. The Falkenberg's son, Wilhelm, who worked in Hitler's inner circle, would be there. 'It's only boring business,' Buchner had told her, but the calming smile that went with those words was forced.

It was a cold February evening and it was black dark when the Mercedes swung off the main road and its tyres splashed through a series of puddles on the narrow country road which led to the house.

Then the headlights caught the twin stone pillars of the house and the wheels crunched on a gravel drive.

Claire could not see much in the darkness but sensed when the car passed over the small bridge which crossed a shallow dry moat. Out to the right a wall stretched to a small copse of trees which led back to the roadway. To the left the dry stone ran unimpeded for two miles. Ahead was the Falkenberg home. Three storeys of white stone caressed by a thick green ivy. To the rear, two short wings reached backwards a short distance creating a U shape with two minor upstrokes. In between the three sides was a broad patio and the head of a well-tended garden. Beyond that was the open fields, rich with deer and boar.

The butler opened the door to Buchner and Claire, but the host himself was just behind. He was wearing a black suit and silver spectacles with thin frames.

'Erhard,' Falkenberg said. 'Heil Hitler.' He saluted. Buchner responded and then the two shook hands warmly. Claire noticed Falkenberg always took Buchner's hand between both of his; he always wanted to be in control.

'My dear Max,' Buchner said.

'Fraulein Winter,' Falkenberg stated, taking her hand. 'How are you?'

'I'm very well, Herr Falkenberg,' she replied, 'if just a little cold.'

'You're right. Come through.'

Falkenberg led the pair through to his private sitting room, a large space with oak-panelled walls and a green and red carpet which reached just short of the walls. A tapestry hung along the length of one wall and a pair of black and silver duelling pistols on another. A log fire burned in a stone hearth.

'A warm drink for a night like this, I think,' he said, directing them to the red leather couch and taking a seat himself.

They waited while the butler brought them brandies.

'May I apologise for Frau Falkenberg,' their host said. 'She has a terrible chill and has spent the day in bed. Liesl has been looking after her. I am sure she will come down soon.'

'And Wilhelm?'

Falkenberg shot Buchner an almost reproachful look and Claire sensed the name should not have been mentioned in front of her.

'He is delayed, Erhard,' Falkenberg said flatly. 'But he will be here tonight.'

There was a short silence, until Claire said: 'Perhaps I could be of some help to Liesl?'

Falkenberg studied her for a moment and then gave a cold smile.

'I suspect she must have gone to bed, my dear,' he said. 'You will see her tomorrow.'

'Then, if you do not mind, perhaps I could have an early night as well,' Claire said, putting down her brandy glass. She had barely touched a drop.

'Of course,' Falkenberg said, a little too eagerly. 'I will get Otto to show you to your room.'

Both men stood with Claire as Otto appeared at her shoulder.

Buchner gave Claire's arm a squeeze. 'I will be along later,' he stated.

As she pulled the door, she heard Falkenberg say, 'Come through to the hall with me, Erhard.'

Claire and Buchner's room was dominated by a four-poster bed and a large window which drowned it with moonlight. It looked out over the front of the house and she had only been in bed an hour when she heard a car pull up and a door slam shut. By the time she had got to the window the driver was at the front of the house. She saw a shaft of light hit the gravel as Otto let the visitor in and then silence returned.

She knew the room where Falkenberg had taken Erhard. It was at the centre of the house, a cavernous space built in the style of a great hall of a *schloss*. It was where Falkenberg went to show off. He held board meetings there or talked to people like Buchner about his businesses and how well they were doing. It had stone floors and a large oak table with high-backed chairs. One wall was lined with thick red curtains which covered a large window overlooking the patio. Falkenberg had installed torches on the walls. They burned continuously.

Leaving her room Claire could move down the first floor corridor to a small archway. Behind a heavy curtain were three angular and uncomfortable wooden chairs where Claire could sit in the darkness and listen to what was happening in the hall below.

Falkenberg was sitting at the head of the table. Buchner was to his right. He was being introduced to Wilhelm Falkenberg. Claire could only see the top of his head.

'Wilhelm has arrived from the *Wolfsschanze*,' Falkenberg said, referring to the Wolf's Lair, the Führer headquarters in woods near Rastenburg in east Prussia. 'How has it been, Willi?'

'There has been much to discuss,' the young man said. He was hesitant, seeming almost frightened to hear his words as they returned on the room's echo.

'Wilhelm, as I have told you, Standartenführer Buchner is of one mind with us. He is committed to this war. He honoured himself in Gleiwitz in '39. I have told you that, haven't I? I have brought you here this weekend so you can meet the Standartenführer. Together, there is much we can do. But, as I suspect your news will confirm, there is no time for hesitancy. From any of us. We must be frank as well as decisive and courageous.'

Wilhelm Falkenberg cleared his throat. 'Father,' he said, 'in the last few weeks our armies have capitulated to the Bolsheviks at Stalingrad and we face humiliation in North Africa. Tripoli has fallen. Almost all of Libya is in British hands. The Americans are in Tunisia, at our soldiers' rear. The Italians have gone to...' Claire heard him click his fingers and sit back noisily in his chair. The other two men were waiting for him to continue. 'Two weeks ago, the Führer summoned all the *Gau-* and *Reichsleiters* to him and described the events of the winter. He talked about the Russian successes but gave no hint of the catastrophes we face. They left convinced, filled with enthusiasm that all was well.'

Herr Falkenberg cut in now, teaming up with his son and warming to the theme.

'You know what the Americans and the British did last month, Erhard?' he said, his voice rising. 'They told us there was no going back. It is to be unconditional surrender or nothing.' Buchner stayed silent, well aware the businessman was talking about the Allies' conference in Casablanca. 'That means those among us who think we can sue for peace are deeply misguided, one might say, tilting at windmills. Weakness should never have been considered; now it is no longer an option.'

Claire leaned forward carefully to sneak another look at the three. Herr Falkenberg was leaning forward now, physically pressing his point on Buchner who appeared calm and still.

'Two days ago,' Falkenberg continued, 'I was in Berlin to see Goebbels speak at the *Sportpalast*. Did you hear what he said, Erhard?' The businessman clenched a fist dramatically. 'He said: "Do you want total war? Do-you-want-total-war?" And then, and I repeat his words faithfully, "Do you want it, if necessary, to be even more total and radical than can ever be imagined today?"'

Somewhere in the corridor behind Claire heard the click of a door and a soft footstep.

Down below, Falkenberg continued: '*More total and more radical than can ever be imagined.* Do you know what that means, Erhard? The only way. Total and complete annihilation of the enemy.'

He stressed the last words and they hung over the room, reaching every hard stone corner.

'And do you know what I thought when I heard those words, Erhard? No, you cannot know. They took me back to a small room at the rear of my father's house. It was a dark room or so it always seemed to me. The forests came right up to the back of our house, the trees almost touching the window. It seemed the only light in the room fell on the photographs on the wall. German heroes. Frederick the Great, Goethe. The only non-German was one of the fathers of the golden age of Greece. Do you know who that was, Erhard? Pericles.

'This was my father's study. Ah, you had no idea that I came from academic stock? You are surprised, eh? My father was a professor of Ancient Greek history. Pericles was one of the men he most admired.

'Like Herr Goebbels, Pericles was a great orator. He addressed Athens during the Persian and Peloponnesian wars. He ensured that the people did what *had* to be done. Like us, he understood that war is not a fight you undertake with a hand behind your back. "If we go to war, be determined that we are not going to climb down," he said. "For it is from the greatest dangers that the greatest glories are to be won." His wisdom is cited by our own Führer in *Mein Kampf*. It is all or nothing, Erhard. There is no other way to fight a war.'

The three men fell so silent Claire was afraid they might hear her breathing.

'Claire!' it was the sound of someone shouting a whisper. '*Claire!*'

It was Liesl's voice somewhere behind her and for one terrible heart-stopping moment she thought Liesl Falkenberg had caught her eavesdropping on her father.

Claire shuffled backwards and realised Liesl was standing down the hall outside her room. She was standing in a blue night-dress and tapping gently on Claire's door. She had pushed her blonde hair back off one ear and was listening for movement in the room.

After a moment she gave up and turned away.

Someone was on their feet in the hall and two voices were talking over each other. Claire could feel her heart racing in her chest as she turned into the corridor and tip-toed to her room.

When she awoke Buchner was already out of bed and watching the maid place a jug of hot water on the wash-stand. She looked over the sheet to see him start to shave as the maid coaxed the stove into life.

'Good morning, my darling,' she said lazily.

Buchner turned. He had soap on his face. He studied the sleepy face and the long mop of blonde hair, and gave a wolfish grin.

'My darling,' he said, coming over to give her a kiss. He playfully put a little shaving soap on her nose and they both laughed.

'What time is it?'

The maid left the room although neither of them seemed to notice.

'It is seven-thirty,' he replied, continuing to shave.

'I didn't even hear you come to bed,' she said, sitting up and stretching her arms. He eyed her breasts in the mirror as they pushed against the white night shirt. 'It must have been very late.'

'It was,' he said, 'and I am afraid I will be away from you today.'

He patted his face with a towel.

'I have to visit one of Herr Falkenberg's factories.' He moved to the wardrobe and chose a plain black suit. Claire wondered why he seemed to stay out of uniform when visiting Falkenberg now.

'Will you be long?'

'Most of the day, I'm afraid.'

Claire reached across for her cigarettes and lit one, knowing that it would irritate him.

He glanced at her reproachfully.

'I have to do something,' she pouted.

'I am sorry, my darling,' he said. 'Perhaps I should not have brought you along.'

As he came to sit on the bed she leaned forward and put her arms around him.

She put her mouth close to his ear.

'Don't be silly,' she said. 'Don't worry about me. You have your boring old factories. I can help Liesl. She always needs the company.'

Buchner knew it pleased Falkenberg to have someone be with Liesl, even if the businessman seemed always cold towards Claire.

'Excellent.' Buchner kissed her, rose and knotted his tie. 'Then I shall see you this evening.'

He put on his jacket and shoes and studied himself in a full-length mirror. He took his party badge from his grey suit and placed it carefully on his lapel.

After she stubbed out her cigarette and watched him and Falkenberg drive over the little bridge, she realised the room still smelled sweet from his cologne.

When she went down for breakfast Claire found Wilhelm Falkenberg deep in conversation with his sister.

He was wearing brown trousers and a knitted roll-neck sweater with the sleeves pushed halfway up his muscled forearms. He was handsome in an arrogant way, with very fine blond hair. Claire noticed his eyebrows were so light they were almost invisible.

He stopped eating and stood as she came to sit at the table next to Liesl. She felt his eyes on him and fumbled with the spoon.

'Delightful to meet you, *Fraulein*,' he said in a confident or maybe mocking tone. Claire suddenly began to see him as a bully, strong now in what he felt was weaker company. 'I understand you are from Luxembourg?'

'Yes.'

Liesl said needlessly: 'Claire is with Herr Buchner.'

Claire smiled. She appreciated her friend's effort to help, but Wilhelm now had stopped eating and was studying her. He had leaned back with one hand on the table.

'The birthplace of the emperor, Henry VII,' he announced. 'Luxembourg.'

'I had a letter from Kurt,' Liesl said, aware that Wilhelm could not ignore news of her husband.

He turned to her. 'And how is he?'

'He says he is still bored but I'm worried,' she said. 'The British have started bombing the U-boat base at Lorient. I'm afraid for him.'

'Our wolf packs are sinking their ships as if they were ducks at a fun fair,' Wilhelm smiled. 'The bombing will not last. They can not reach the U-boats because they are hidden under tons of protective concrete. Kurt is not even at the base itself. Do not worry, sister, he will be safe.'

'I can not help worrying,' Liesl sniffed. She had tears in her eyes. Wilhelm gave Claire a look and Claire moved towards her to put an arm around her shoulders. Liesl began to cry. Wilhelm stood, nodded in their direction and left the room.

Liesl had one of the largest rooms in the house, complete with a new white suite of drawers and two huge wardrobes. A large mirror dominated one wall with stacks of soaps, perfumes and *Schwarzkopf* shampoos laid out in front of it. Most of her friends, and the ordinary people of Germany, Claire knew, stank for the lack of soap. Liesl's wardrobe was lined with hangers filled with dresses and jackets created by German designers copying their pre-war French counterparts. One shelf was lined with felt hats, each in different colours and styles.

Liesl brightened up when she was back in her room, suddenly flinging open the doors of both wardrobes in search for something which she was promising to Claire.

'Ah, here!' she said, dragging out a thick fur coat and pushing it towards Claire. 'This is what I am looking forward. It would look wonderful on you.'

She was holding it up in front of Claire, imaging what she would look like. Claire reached out and touched it. It was so smooth, a soft sandy-coloured yellow and brown.

'It's beautiful,' Claire said, 'but it looks new.'

'It is,' replied Liesl proudly, pulling it off the hangar. 'Daddy got it for me.'

She was starting to throw it around Claire's shoulders and as she did Claire noticed the label inside showed signs of wear. She wondered if the coat were not new at all but was from one of the clearances of goods from Jewish homes that were affecting Luxembourg and, she was sure, Germany too.

Liesl was chattering into her ear. 'It will look wonderful on you,' she was saying again. 'Oh, yes. Very pretty for Herr Buchner.' Liesl laughed. 'Or Herr Voss.'

Claire stopped and looked at Liesl. Her eyes were still slightly damp from the tears and they sparkled as she began to smile.

'What do you mean?' said Claire, the coat now wrapped fully around her.

'Oh, come now, Claire, you saw him,' Liesl stood back and turned quickly, her shirts swinging. 'At Herr Buchner's party. The flier. Hauptmann Voss.' She caught Claire's eye, her face tilted. 'Some might say he was very handsome.'

Claire hesitated, then laughed. 'Who would? You or I?'

'I'm married,' said Liesl indignantly, but smiling as Claire admired her new coat in the mirror.

'And I'm very happy with Erhard,' said Claire, who without turning to face Liesl added: 'Is there something you want to tell me?'

'No, nothing,' Liesl said, but she was acting like a child, her hands clasped in front of her. "It's just that I heard Daddy talking about Herr Voss, saying that he wants Herr Buchner to bring him here and I thought it would be lovely to see him.'

'I didn't know your father knew Herr Voss very well,' said Claire.

'He doesn't. But I know he wants Herr Buchner to introduce him more properly. Herr Voss rushed off the night of Herr Buchner's party – not that *you'd* remember - and I think father was...angry with Herr Buchner.'

Claire looked at her reflection and smoothed her hands down the thick fur at her sides.

Her interest now was apparently in the coat. 'That is between them,' she said.

Max Falkenberg and Buchner stood on the east bank of the Rhine, north of Koblenz. The river was wide and straight here, with a cold breeze seeming to blow right off it. Across the water was Max's factory, a complex of buildings behind a tall wire fence standing guard along the top of the steep riverbank. Buchner could see three main buildings, each with a grey chimney stack reaching about 80 feet into the air, but there were several other buildings besides.

Alongside one, Buchner's eyes followed a twisted maze of pipes and shafts, heading horizontally along the side of the concrete wall and vertically upwards to the roof. Each found its way back inside the building.

'Where were you in May 1919, Erhard?'

Buchner looked thoughtful but he knew what was coming and did not think an answer was required.

'Shall I tell you where I was?' Falkenberg said. 'At Versailles. In protective custody. A businessman pleading for his livelihood. I was pleading to save all this.' He nodded at the plant and watched smoke curl from one of the stacks. 'They almost stopped me. Had they annexed that,' he spread his palm in front of his face and moved it from right to left indicating the whole sweep of the west bank of the Rhine in their view, 'they would have set me back. Instead, as you know, demilitarisation. *Huh!* They tried to smash us, Erhard, they tried to smash us so hard that, even with the stench of the battlefields still heavy, we considered resuming the war.'

Buchner remembered the sickness he felt on the day of the surrender. He was lying in a hospital bed and heard the nasal accent of a Saxon soldier in the next bed mutter, 'Thank God!' He still felt the hatred rise in him when he thought of that man and of the way he had welcomed defeat.

Falkenberg went on: 'And so the peace was signed. *Their* peace.'

He began to walk the bank and Buchner followed. The ground was damp and they had to pick their steps. Buchner felt like he was walking with his father. Falkenberg was talking about a time Buchner himself had lived through. He realised how much he had pushed those years into the back of his memory, denied them. Falkenberg at the time had been making money, working on the mustard gas that went to the front to hang over the Tommies, to pull at their skin and hair. Buchner had been there.

'But I fought on,' Falkenberg said proudly. 'I made deals with the French so that my companies could get around their attempts to destroy our chemical industry. I gave their industry something and had their military loosen the reigns in return. I might have looked like I was pleading, but I was negotiating a business deal. "The people are starving," I said, "I produce fertiliser. The farmers of Germany need me," I said.' Falkenberg stopped and touched

Buchner with a pointed finger. '"The farmers of France need *us*," I said.' He winked, gave a self-satisfied smile and carried on walking.

Buchner did not. He was looking across the fast running river to the coiled mass of pipes with which they had drawn level.

'And now, Max? Tell me all about what you are producing there now?"

Chapter Twenty-Nine

The train moved interminably towards Berlin. It had a slow, disjointed journey but now finally they were criss-crossing a maze of lines at the north-western edge of the city. As the lumbering engine groaned, Hauptmann Joachim Voss dozed in the carriage, his face turned to the window; he was oblivious to the others in the same compartment. He hated returning to Berlin, in fact, he no longer felt comfortable among the civilian population. He hated the long faces, the *greyness*. He had no interest in their problems, their petty complaints. Even their suffering did not touch him. There was only one place he wanted to be: among the men of his unit. And the more viciousness, horror and violence he witnessed, the more the bread queues, shopper-filled trams, the children in the street, the aimlessness of ordinary life, repulsed him.

He took a long slow drag on his Russian cigarette filling the compartment with black smoke. They no longer made his throat rasp. *How strange that you can get the taste for anything.*

It was a year now since he had stepped forward on the ice-packed ground of the airfield at Dno to receive the Knight's Cross which now hung at his neck; it seemed so much longer. The award provided a much needed boost for the unit. They had only recently taken possession of new aircraft: Stukas again, updated now, but still Stuka, just as he and others had flown over France, Norway and Malta. Most in the *staffel* had groaned. They knew the Junkers Ju 87, the screaming *Sturzkampfflugzeug*, dive-bomber, the symbol of the *Blitzkrieg*, was obsolete, no matter what high command said.

But Voss greeted the arrival of the new Ju 87D with grim determination. It was still slow, yes, doing only a little over 200mph, but it was easy to handle and packed a 1,800kg bomb, two fixed 7.92mm machine guns and a fixed twin 7.92mm machine gun. It was all he needed until something better came along. It was for someone else to create the weaponry. He would use whatever was to hand.

Soon after he was out on his 300th combat sortie. It was minus 30 degrees Celsius in that area of Demyansk where 100,000 troops were encircled by four Russian armies. Some were taking a pounding from an armoured train when Voss and his squadron came screaming out of the ice blue sky at 9,000 feet. Voss dove against the wind until the white-painted wagons of the train filled the front screen of his cockpit canopy. He released the bomb-load and felt the aircraft lurch as he pulled out of the 70-degree dive and turned away from the target. Three Gs of pressure took hold of his body as he pulled out of the dive and he tensed his muscles and cold bones. He caught sight of three wagons of the train twisting and turning over in flames but craned his neck to look above and around him. Stuka pilots knew they were most vulnerable to enemy fighters as they pulled out of the dive. He heard waves of explosions from the train behind him and felt the battering of the anti-aircraft shells subsiding as he hugged the wide open expanse of white land and flew for home. Later that day he flew again, against what remained of the train and when one of his *staffel* was forced down by Russian guns he landed and rescued the surviving crew member: the pilot; the radio operator had bled to death. Soon after the Knight's Cross was his.

The ceremony provided only brief respite from bombing runs on airfields, tank columns and the railroads east of the Volkhov river.

In April the emphasis shifted to the Soviet warships which were picking off German vessels in the Gulf of Finland. The anti-aircraft fire around Leningrad would light up the sky and Voss was one of the few pilots with the nerve to hold steady through a complete dive as loud explosions punched the air all around him. But he was losing good pilots and good friends, in the air over Leningrad, and back at their airbase well to the south of the city. Squadrons of the stubby fighter bomber biplanes, the Polikarpov I-153s, would flash over the base, their red stars glinting in the early morning watery sunshine, their 7.62mm machine guns and bomb loads picking off Stukas and Ju 88s, and standing crews scuttling for cover.

Later they would see occasional raids by the U-2 biplanes, which slowly approached their targets and dropped bombs from racks. They were nearly all ineffectual and the Germans soon stopped bothering getting out of bed.

Voss' radio operator Blum did not get up. He was shattered after a long day of missions, which had started at about 7am. He had gone to bed at 10pm, barely able to walk with tiredness. He would have been fast asleep, Voss guessed, when the lone U-2 came in at barely 600 feet, its engine stuttering like the 'sewing machine' the Germans nicknamed it after, and the pilot dropped a single 440lb bomb.

Blum was not long dead when Voss got recalled to Germany and was able to travel by train to attend his uncle's birthday meal.

Much had changed since then. Within a short time he found himself being transferred onto the staff of the office of the director of technical intelligence at Rechlin, northwest of Berlin. He did not know what to expect and found his new life a world away from the Russian Front. So far his role had been something of an administrator, helping to organise *Erprobungsstelle 2*, a booty – *Beute* - testing station, but the site's new role intrigued him. He had already been ordered to spend a great deal of time studying British and American heavy bombers.

The Eastern Front was still very much on his mind though. Germany had had three days of national mourning for the defeat at Stalingrad and he could still see the effects of that blow in the faces around him now. He had not mourned but burned with anger as he listened to the communiqués from Russia. *Damyansk now evacuated.*

So he met few gazes as he moved through Berlin that day and followed directions to a building in a street close to the Tiergarten.

Inside he rang the bell at a large apartment and was answered by a maid who disappeared as soon as Erhard Buchner appeared from a room beyond the hall with a cheery, 'Joachim!'

Buchner led Voss through to the main room and shut the door. The apartment was one of high ceilings and tall, slim doors. The windows were hung with heavy green curtains and despite the space the room was cramped with mahogany furniture. The place was storage for someone's wealth.

'How are you, Joachim?'

'I am well, uncle.' Voss had a cold voice. When he addressed Buchner as "uncle" he suffused the word with no more emotion than if he was addressing a wine waiter.

Buchner poured two glasses of schnapps and handed one to his nephew.

'I had no idea you had such a place,' Voss stated, taking out his cigarettes and placing them on the table next to his chair.

'It is very handsome, isn't it? But,' Buchner laughed, 'I am afraid it is not mine.' He nodded towards the marble mantelpiece.

Voss stood and walked across, conscious of but not caring about his boots on the expensive carpet. He picked up a studio portrait of Herr and Frau Falkenberg. She was seated, her husband was standing at her side. Another photograph showed Liesl and another man in uniform.

'They have a son?' Voss said without appearing to show any real interest.

'On the Führer's staff.'

Voss returned to his chair.

'You seem agitated, nephew,' Buchner said. 'Please smoke if it makes you more comfortable.'

Voss took out his lighter. The smoke slowly twisted towards the high ceiling above him.

'It was very good to hear from you, uncle.'

'I expect you were surprised I found you. Congratulations, by the way, on your posting.'

'I am sorry I could not tell you. It was highly confidential. Even my own unit has no idea where I was transferred. They probably think I am in some sort of disgrace.' Voss picked a piece of tobacco off his lip. 'How did you know?'

'There should be no secrets from Standartenführer's in the SS. Or from uncles. In all honesty, it was not easy. But I have many friends.'

Buchner smiled thinly and nodded his head slowly as if agreeing with himself on something most secret.

'Anyway, it is very good to see you. What is it six, seven months? Too long anyway.'

Voss crossed his legs and as he did so the Knight's Cross moved and glinted in the afternoon light from the window.

Voss could see his uncle staring at it.

'A different life, here, eh? Don't worry. Our resistance in the east is growing. We have practically encircled Kharkov. We will push the Ivans back.'

Voss nodded.

'I would like you to come and see us again soon, Joachim. Claire and I. You realise we spend a lot of time with Herr Falkenberg. He has a fantastic home near Wiesbaden. An ideal place to spend your next leave.'

Voss did not respond.

Buchner leaned forward. 'But, first, nephew, I'd like you to tell me a little about Rechlin.'

Chapter Thirty

Maurice was barely grown-up himself. His face was still pale and the hair on his chin soft and fair. But he watched the children playing in the street near the railway station at Liège with a feeling of great superiority: the games he played were for adults. He had been 16 or so when the war started. He often wondered what age he would be when the Germans finally left. *Thirty?* Not if he could help it.

He tried not to show any reaction as the people at last started to filter from the platform. A group of workmen in dirty denims came through the checkpoint first, shuffling and pushing the policemen checking the travellers. Then came the other passengers. Maurice saw Rameau but not a flicker of recognition crossed either's face.

There was a woman, Maurice saw her now. She was behind Rameau and followed him up the street. Wallis had produced papers for both Rameau and the woman, and they came through easily enough.

Grace had shut herself off from fear as Dieter had delivered her to Rameau. She had felt strangely disengaged and indestructible since the camp and the raid. Perhaps she could no longer care what happened to her. She did not feel reckless or brave, just that everything was happening to someone else.

She walked up the street, her head straight and not looking round. If she had, she would have seen the gangly youth wandering along behind on the opposite side of the road, making sure he was the only one following them.

She had got a great deal of her strength back thanks to Dieter's kindness. He had shared his food with her and she had gained a few pounds. He had found her new clothes and she was in a brown skirt, jumper, black coat and hat. The small handbag over her shoulder was virtually empty.

She was still tired and aching though, and she struggled to keep up with the tall man at her side – she did not know his name – and he appeared not to notice that she was struggling.

At last, as the street they were on entered a large square, he stopped. He gave her a quick questioning glance and she nodded to indicate she was okay.

The man's stride had been confident, purposeful, but now she sensed a hesitation in him.

He was looking into the square ahead. It was a fairly nondescript place with a café, which seemed to be empty on one side and three-storey buildings all around.

'We are going to the house on the end, the red one,' the man told her in French.

She looked directly across the square, past the small fountain. There was a street similar to the one they had just walked along. At the corner, the red house, three storeys and windows indicating rooms in the steep roof.

Grace nodded again.

'Come.'

Grace wondered if he is going to lead her around the edge of the square but he began to walk straight across, slower now so that she could more easily keep up.

In the corner of her eye she saw two green uniforms. An engine revved.

She felt the man's hand on her arm and his pace quickened.

She allowed herself a tiny glance, not being able to resist a look, and saw two German soldiers, helmets on, at a motorcycle. One was standing on the pavement, a rifle dropped low at his side; the other was sitting on the bike. Both were talking to two young women.

Rameau and Grace walked past the fountain on the blind side of the soldiers. The house still seemed a long way, although she could now see its tiniest details quite clearly. *Four front steps. A black door.*

She wished the wooden soles of her shoes were not so loud on the cobbles.

One of the soldiers shouted and Grace caught her breath. But then she heard the two women laugh.

She could see the triangular design at the top of the door, a carving of two horses raising their hooves at each other.

They stepped onto the pavement. They were now five paces from the door, coming close to the bottom step.

The door swung open and a figure stepped out of the darkness.

Rameau hesitated but then recognised Henri, Gerard's Englishman. The safe rooms in the house belonged to Gerard's group; Henri would have been checking the building's security. Breathing quickly again, he moved on but realised Grace had stopped.

She watched Philip skip down the steps, seeing his glance at Rameau.

Grace mouthed his name and Philip saw her. *I must look so different.* She touched her forehead, her hand shaking, and moved the hat off her eyes.

Philip had one foot on the bottom step, the other on the pavement, and was in the act of turning down the street which ran down the side of the safe-house.

But now he had stopped in mid-stride.

He stared at the woman, his mouth slightly open, now not seeing the baggy clothes, which seem to envelope her, and which had been all he had taken in from the first glanced. Now he saw only her eyes, watering, pleading, calling out.

All his thoughts came in English. He started to speak but then sensed movement behind him.

He saw Rameau's eyes flash and then felt his hand on his elbow, pushing him aside.

Rameau grasped Grace's hand in his and led her up the stairs past the German officer who had appeared in the doorway.

The door was big enough for two people to pass so the German seemed to pay little attention, his boots clipping on the stone steps.

Grace looked over her shoulder but Philip had gone.

Rameau reached across her and shut the door. He and Grace looked at each other. 'It was my son,' she said.

In the street, the German officer took about ten paces along the pavement. But then he turned and studied the closed door.

He thought about the way the couple who went into the house were holding hands. They did not look right together. She may have been making money anyway she could, he realised, *but what was that look on her face?*

He glanced across at the two soldiers. They were still laughing and talking to the two women. He should call them.

But then he thought of his girl. He did not want to make trouble for her in her neighbourhood. She would still be lying warm in her bed on the second floor.

Besides it may be nothing.

He walked back to the steps of the house and took out his key.

It clicked in the lock. He looked again at the two soldiers. They had not even noticed him. He would go and give them hell afterwards.

He unhooked the button on his holster and stepped inside. He left the door ajar but still hesitated to let his eyes become accustomed to the darkness of the grim downstairs hallway.

There were private rooms on each of the four floors. He saw people occasionally on his visits although never the strange woman and the hard-faced Belgian.

On one side of the hallway was a door, on the other the side wall of the house in which there was no window.

He reached up with his black-gloved hand and flicked on the light.

He glanced down the hallway ahead. There was one room at the back of the house in which an old woman lived. She stank out the house with her soup. He had passed her many times. She was half-blind and never even looked at him.

He took the first step of the stairs carefully and began to rise to the first landing. There was not a sound. *I am almost certainly being foolish.*

He shifted his body to turn and heard a creak in the flooring of the stairs above his head.

He stopped and, reaching for his holstered pistol, stepped forward. His eyes narrowed.

Rameau stood at the top of the second flight of stairs, half inside a doorway directly opposite the officer's girlfriend's room.

Rameau was staring back at the officer. It appeared to be a blank look but then the office saw the mouth. It was slightly twisted in a cruel smirk.

The man began to lift his pistol, his eyes on Rameau.

Silently, Jean slipped out of the first floor doorway behind him, knife flashing under the naked light bulb.

One hand went around the German's face and over his mouth, the other slid the blade ruthlessly into the side of his neck, forcing a fountain of blood over Jean's fist and across the flaked paint on the wall.

The officer's right leg kicked out as if in spasm and he tottered onto the top step, bringing the little Frenchman with him.

The German's cap fell off and bounced down the stairs.

Jean held onto his face as the body began to slide then, feeling the man's final kick and unable to hold him any longer, Jean was forced to let go. The body crumpled down the stairs and came to rest in the hallway in front of the open door.

Rameau vaulted Jean and skipped down the steps. As he started to shut the door, a shadow fell over him. He looked up and saw Maurice. Rameau took him by the shirt front and pulled him inside.

Maurice leaned heavily against the wall, his eyes running up from the twisted body of the German to Jean who was already rubbing at the blood-spattered wall with a rag.

'Maurice!' Rameau hissed, pushing the dazed young man on the arm. 'Let's get him in Gerard's room and then get hold of Alain. We have to dump the body.'

Grace stepped from the first floor door. She looked at the dark red stain and the bloody tunic of the soldier but she did not say anything.

Rameau waved her back in the room.

Maurice took the officer's shoulders and backed his way up the stairs, with Rameau at the man's shiny boots. They put the body inside the dark room.

Rameau wandered through the room quickly, found some rags and threw them under the tap.

'Jean, you go to get a message to Gerard,' he said. He threw a rag to Grace and said in English: 'Help me, please, clean the blood.'

Philip was still striding hurriedly through the streets. He had got as far as he could almost on a single breath before stopping in a doorway and slumping against a shop window.

His mind was whirling. For a minute he was walking in front of the Southampton Hotel, his hand tucked in his mother's hand. Every time he passed that hotel he would crane his neck, look right up to the very top and see the large figures: 1899. *'When was that, mother?'* Such a high building and such a long time ago for a seven-year-old. He would squeeze her hand and get talking to a shopper coming the other way. He looked around him to be sure he was not there or at the farm.

He saw his mother's eyes. She looked so haunted. What did it mean? He tried to remember what Gerard had been telling Rameau that day. Had his mother been in some awful camp? Oh God. And the way she looked at him: as if she was so shocked to see him, not just here, but *alive*.

What about little Jimmy? Where was he? Was he safe?

Grace looked broken, a different person; her eyes were almost dead but there was something trying to come through, to reach out, to tell him…

It was late afternoon when Alain Gerard and two of his men arrived and darkness was already falling in the street.

Rameau told Gerard they had to move Grace before trying to get the body out of the house.

'Of course,' Gerard said, running his fingers off his blond moustache. 'And we must make this place safe.'

'Make it safe, then ditch it,' Rameau told him.

'Places like this are hard to come by, comrade,' Gerard replied, grinning. 'Everything is money and hard work.'

'Maybe so, but you have to treat it as blown,' Rameau said forcefully. 'That German was seeing a girl here. We saw her leaving earlier. Now, it may have been just something on the side, but soldiers talk. They will come here looking, they will arrest her and everyone else in this house.'

'It will cost me,' Gerard said.

Rameau said no more.

'You are right,' Gerard said at last. 'I have someone on a barge who will take the lady,' he gestured to Grace, 'to Namur. She will be safe there until we can pass her onwards.' He looked at the bundle on the floor where the dead soldier had been wrapped in a rough, dark blanket. 'But I look forward to the time they come for the girl. Filthy whore.'

He stepped forward, pulled at the blanket and studied the dead man's face.

'Good work, Rameau,' he said.

Rameau nodded at Jean.

'You, Jean?' Gerard said, clapping him on the shoulder. 'Speaking of filthy whores - ' he offered Jean and Rameau a cigarette and there was a long silence as two lit off the same match and Rameau waved them away to light his own. 'Speaking of filthy whores, I would like to ask you something. You know Bertrand Gillier's niece, Rameau?'

'A little.'

'Then you will know that every time she goes with that SS scum she sullies Bertrand's memory?' Gerard gestured with the cigarette. 'It cannot go on. She must pay.'

Gerard pointed at Rameau as he spoke. When he finished, there was silence. Rameau looked away but he saw Jean nod in solemn agreement.

Chapter Thirty-One

The rain lashed against the high windows and shook the thick bushes along the sides of the garden. The lawn was lush and wet and green, the trees trimmed and smart. Erhard Buchner had got himself one of the best gardeners in the city to go with the fine chef he had borrowed from a local hotel.

Claire Winter enjoyed the use of both, although she tried to play mistress of the house as much as Buchner would let her. If he had his way completely she would do nothing outside of accompany him to parties and political evenings and be his companion in bed.

Her life had been transformed since meeting the Standartenführer. At first, she had been promoted at work over the heads of more senior staff. No-one had said a word but she knew how her former friends felt. Buchner promised to have anyone making her life difficult arrested but she had said all was fine. Then he had said she really should not be working at all.

And when he had asked her to move in to his large detached house on the outskirts of Luxembourg city, she had finally agreed to leave her teaching job.

The house had belonged to a Jewish banker and it was one of the finest in a wide street of late nineteenth century homes. It was surrounded by high trees and a large iron gate. She had moved in away from whispering neighbours and colleagues, and had at first felt very safe.

But Buchner did not like her to go out alone too often and the guard at the gate always pleasantly inquired where she was going if Buchner was not with her. The atmosphere was becoming stifling.

Today though was a good day. She loved sitting here in the sun lounge when the rain was beating against the windows and glass roof.

And she had guests too. Although neither appeared particularly comfortable in the other's company.

Hauptmann Karl-Heinz Fischer had arrived soon after lunch and left his driver in his *Kubelwagen* at the front of the house. She had not been surprised to see him. He called regularly, always when Buchner was out, and would sit in long silences here or in the large drawing room, where sometimes he would play piano for Claire. She would sit and watch his right hand moving expertly but slowly on the keyboard. When he had finished, he would turn, his empty left sleeve pinned to his jacket, his left eye lifeless, and he would smile, embarrassed, ashamed. She could see it in his face: the awful injuries had robbed him of playing the complete tune and, he felt, robbed him of his chance of holding Fraulein Winter. She knew he was hopelessly in love with her but she let him come to the house because he never came towards her, never said or acted inappropriately, and talked about things other than the war. Buchner knew he came, of course, but he would never consider Fischer a threat or rival of any kind.

Sat on another of the wicker chairs was a different man altogether: Hauptmann Joachim Voss. Voss sat bolt upright in his chair, an athlete. If I were to clap my hands, Claire thought, he would sprint to the foot of the garden, return without losing his breath and then slap my face for daring to make a demand of him. His *Luftwaffe* uniform was pressed and immaculate, the Knight's Cross just completed the perfect appearance: the war machine.

Both men were smoking one of Fischer's cigarettes, Voss having just arrived. He was here to see his uncle, of course. He often made these visits now and Erhard was always delighted to see him.

'Last time we met you were on the Eastern Front, Voss,' said Fischer. 'I understand you have been transferred back to the Fatherland.'

'There is much work to do there,' Voss replied.

'Are you still flying?'

'I'm based at Rechlin, north of Berlin,' Voss responded, neatly sidestepping the question.

'I have a relative near there, near Buchholz, do you know it?'

'No, I'm afraid not.'

'They said there has been a great deal of build up around Rechlin.'

Voss turned and looked squarely at Fischer.

'I really don't know. I only do my duty.'

Claire reached forward for the silver coffee pot. 'More coffee, gentlemen?'

'Allow me, please, *fraulein*,' Voss said, pouring the warm, black liquid into three cups.

'You are here to see, Standartenführer Buchner?' Fischer asked, only mildly perturbed by the other man's coldness.

Voss nodded.

'In that case, I should detain you no longer.' Fischer stood up awkwardly.

He nodded at Claire.

'Thank you once again for your company, *fraulein*.'

'Not at all, Herr Hauptmann.' Claire smiled warmly. 'I am only sorry you did not get to play the piano for me this time. I have been practising a little myself too.'

'Then I look forward with even greater pleasure to next time,' he said.

Voss stood and the two men exchanged salutes.

'I will see you out,' Claire said.

When she returned to the sun lounge, Voss was studying a photograph of Buchner and Claire together. 'I am sure your uncle won't be long,' she told him.

Within ten minutes, Erhard Buchner walked through the door, gave Claire a kiss on each cheek and then led Voss into his study.

Claire brought them both coffee, tapping the door before entering. It had high ceilings like all the rooms in the house but seemed smaller than the others. It was packed with three heavy red leather chairs, two low tables and Buchner's enormous oak desk. Books lined one of the walls from floor to ceiling.

As Claire entered, Buchner was stoking the lowly burning fire and Voss was sat back in one of the leather chairs, studying a cigarette which he had taken out of Buchner's silver box. The Führer looked down on them from a portrait above the mantelpiece.

Claire placed the tray on a low table and Buchner kissed her again. 'We won't be long, my love.'

Claire smiled and left, pulling the door until it gave a loud click.

She moved away now, knowing there was no way of hearing through the solid oak. Besides she had some ideas about what the two men discussed.

The only papers Buchner kept at home where locked in the heavy drawers of his desk. He always carried the key with him in his uniform. But one day, after spilling wine on his tunic, he had left it aside for her to give to an orderly and she had found the key.

She had carefully entered the study and held her breath as the little golden key had turned in the desk drawer lock.

She had gone through everything, knowing he would not be back for sometime. A number of the documents had referred to *Pericles*, which Claire took to be a person's codename at first. He or it had been in France but was now at a location known as Batienoir. There was no indication as to where this was, although Falkenberg's name appeared in some of the documents. She copied sections from them.

Other documents referred to items codenamed *Wenzler*, *Steinhoff* and *Seitz*, three film-makers whom she knew Buchner admired. These too mentioned Falkenberg.

The meetings with Voss and Falkenberg now took place whenever Voss could come from Rechlin. Most meetings were held at Falkenberg's country house and Claire was no longer always invited to stay.

However, she knew there was something in the meetings of importance and, in any case, she passed everything on.

Her system was simple. She had meetings arranged with the same courier – whom she now also got to copy Buchner's key from a mould she had taken - on different days every fortnight at three alternating locations: a street near the town hall, the hat section of a department store and a corner of the busy Place D'Armes.

Claire encoded her message using a special code previously agreed with Eva Heigl and based on a French-language version of *Moby Dick*. The courier took the messages to Eva Heigl in Belgium who decoded and then encoded the message again in her own way ready for transmission. Heigl's code was based on a five-figure group cipher based on key words and sentences from a book known only to her and her contacts in Moscow. She transmitted from three alternating positions in Brussels.

The message featuring Claire's information on *Pericles* was transmitted by Eva Heigl on March 23, 1943. Heigl put out her call sign on 39 metres, received her acknowledgment from Moscow on 43 and transmitted the message on 49. Life had become very difficult for her and her GRU colleagues in Brussels and many had been arrested by a special *Abwehr* network determined to break the Soviet spy ring.

But Heigl had so far stayed one step ahead of the Germans. Her message was intercepted and filed by them but they had no idea what it said.

Having sent the message, Heigl moved to a different location, encoded her message again and transmitted on a very different frequency to someone else.

Again, as she had before, she indicated the source was the Moscow spy codenamed *Capricorn*. This second message was one of which even *Capricorn* herself was completely unaware.

On the day of Fischer's awkward meeting with Voss, Claire stood in the sun lounge smoking cigarette after cigarette. In her mind she was thinking about *Pericles* and the papers in Buchner's desk, and when his office door opened, she stood silently straining to hear.

'A few more weeks and we will talk again,' she heard Buchner say. 'Everything you are doing now at Rechlin is of the utmost value, whatever you decide. Whether you are with us or not. You understand that, don't you?'

She heard Voss' boots squeak on the polished floor.

'I must return to my unit, uncle.'

'Of course, of course. I appreciate these chats, Joachim. I know we are putting you under tremendous pressure, but I am sure you understand why. Next time we meet, next time, we will be able to brief you completely with regard to *Pericles*. Then, then, I will have to push you to decide. For the Fatherland, Joachim. Heil Hitler!'

'Heil Hitler!'

'Goodbye, Joachim.'

Three weeks later Buchner was preparing for another trip to see Max Falkenberg. His Mercedes was out the front, his driver behind the wheel.

Claire had asked again to go with him, without pressing, but by saying she was bored in the house, had given up her friends for him; she had run his lapel between her fingers, kissed his neck, but he had said no. He was agitated, not with her but about the meeting.

Then, as he was about to leave the black telephone echoed through the large, cold hallway.

Claire answered and a brusque voice she recognised as Falkenberg's asked for Buchner.

Buchner took the telephone.

'Hello? Yes, hello, Max.'

Claire shut the front door as he spoke. It was a sunny May day but the air was cold and a breeze rushed through the house.

'Max, I'm very sorry. Very sorry. How is she? I can. I was just leaving. Of course, yes. Yes. Goodbye.'

Buchner replaced the receiver slowly.

Claire went up to him and put a hand on his arm.

'Are you alright, Erhard?'

'It is Kurt, I'm afraid,' he said. 'Liesl's husband. He has been killed in an air-raid.'

'Poor Liesl. She must be devastated.'

'Yes. You must go upstairs and pack,' he added. 'Our meeting must go ahead. Falkenberg wants you to be there, to be of company to Liesl.'

'Okay, Erhard. Of course.'

'And hurry, we can't be late.'

Within 20 minutes Claire had packed and a soldier was putting her case into the trunk of the Mercedes.

Buchner slapped the driver's shoulder with his glove and the car sped out. Coming out of the house it turned right towards the countryside and the old border with Germany.

Had it turned left it would have passed a dirty blue van which had been parked down the road for the last half an hour as the driver ate his sandwiches. The van had been repainted since that day in Grunberg and the letters *ATF* covered over but Jean still risked using it: he could not afford to get rid of it altogether.

As the Mercedes disappeared he slid back the small window and let his cigarette drop onto the pavement.

Then he put the van into gear and turned around in the road in one smooth circle. As he headed back into the city he passed another car which had been parked near Buchner's house for even longer that day. In it sat a German officer who struggled with the gears and who, according to regulations, should not be driving at all. As Fischer watched Buchner and Claire head off, he felt a terrible headache come on which made him weep with pain.

Chapter Thirty-Two

The Falkenbergs' home seemed colder than ever. Max Falkenberg had been riding when they arrived and was leading his horse as they got out of the Mercedes.

'Max,' Buchner said. 'How are you?'

'I am fine, Erhard,' he answered, passing the reins of the tall grey to a stable boy and shaking Buchner's hand.

'Leisl is in a terrible state,' he told them. 'She will not talk to her mother. And I am, well, no use in these situations. I came outside to ride.' Falkenberg turned to Claire. 'Perhaps you can help, dear? If you don't mind.'

'Of course. I'll be glad to help.'

'Good,' Falkenberg said, dismissing his daughter's grief quickly. 'Erhard, we have much to discuss.'

The two men turned towards the house with Claire following a short distance behind. Falkenberg told Buchner that his son, Wilhelm, and Joachim Voss would be arriving later.

The three walked through to a large drawing room at the back of the house. On an ornate settee with long curved back sat Frau Falkenberg and Liesl. There was space for another person between them but Frau Falkenberg was reaching forward to tentatively place a hand on her daughter's knee.

Liesl was rocking gently, her face white and streaming with tears. She had something in her hand which, as she moved closer, Claire could see was a photograph of her husband in uniform.

Frau Falkenberg said quietly: 'Liesl, Herr Buchner and Fraulein Winter are here now. Please present yourself tidily.'

Liesl softly wiped her nose with a white handkerchief and slowly lifted her head. Her mother took her by the elbow and made her stand.

Slowly, Liesl walked forward, put her arms around Claire's shoulders and began weeping again into her neck.

It was hard and tiring work. Liesl only wanted to cry and hold onto Claire. She tried to talk about Kurt but always ended up sobbing and wailing.

Claire could say nothing to console her, just offer cigarettes and listen.

Every now and again she walked to the window of Liesl's bedroom and looked out, combing the drive for headlights.

When they eventually came, she sat on the bed and hoped to coax Liesl to take the sleeping tablet her mother had insisted she use.

'Get some sleep, Liesl,' she told her gently. 'You will be better for rest.'

'It won't bring Kurt back, Claire,' Liesl shot back. 'How can I just *sleep*?'

Claire smoothed her arm and gave a sympathetic smile.

'I know, I know. Nothing will make it better. But Kurt would not want you to make yourself ill.'

Liesl rubbed her eyes and took a sip of water.

Claire softly stroked her hair and moved some strands out of the wet trails of tears on her face.

Liesl took the small sleeping tablet, placed it on her tongue and swallowed so more water.

'You won't go anywhere?'

Claire shook her head. 'I will be here by your side all night. Try to rest.'

Claire tidied the pillows as Liesl slipped off her skirt and then got under the covers still wearing the rest of her clothes.

Claire moved the little chair nearer the bed and sat back.

Liesl lay on the pillow, facing Claire, smiled and reached out her hand. Claire took it and, as Liesl fell asleep, she sighed at her own callousness.

Wilhelm Falkenberg had been drinking more than the others. Claire could hear that in his voice.

It was Buchner, though, not his father who chastised him: 'I know we are friends here, Leutnant, but the business we are about could not be graver.'

'Yes, Willi, tell us again,' Falkenberg told his son. 'But carefully, a great many lives depend on the outcome of this meeting.'

From her position above the great hall, Claire could see the stern look on Falkenberg's face as he held court around the grand table. She imagined he thought of the others as his knights. But he looked more a sorcerer than a king. His wiry body and thin hands and face made her shiver.

'I assure you, father, you, Standartenführer, and you, Hauptmann Voss, that I am quite level-headed, quite in control of what I say,' said Wilhelm Falkenberg. 'I take the drink to steady my nerves for what I am about to tell you. But my thoughts are sober thoughts, which I have considered many times on my way here tonight.' He paused, taking a breath so deep that Claire heard it from her hiding position in the gallery. He was like a diver about to take the plunge into icy water. 'I will make my report,' he said. 'At a recent meeting at the Wolf's Lair two of the items previously discussed here, our codenames *Wenzler* and *Seitz*, inquired after by the Führer. The meeting was attended by Herr Otto Ambrose, of *IG Farben*. The Führer asked him what the British and Americans were doing about poison gas. The Führer said that while he understood they had large quantities of mustard gas he understood we – Germany - had the only stockpiles of what we here call *Seitz*, what our classified documents refer to only as *N-Stoff* and what the Führer called *Tabun*. Ambrose said that while we had patented *Tabun* in 1937 and 1938 it was always certainly known about around the world. With that, the Führer left. I do not think this subject shall be raised with him again.'

There was a brief pause.

'How was our Führer?' asked Buchner.

'He was…disappointed,' said Wilhelm. 'Stalingrad, the Ruhr raids, North Africa, Ukraine.'

'I understand.' There was another pause. 'Seitz?'

'The patents for *Tabun* belong to *IG Farben*,' Max Falkenberg explained. 'But it was known to scientists for many years before the war began. My scientists, also. You have seen my factories, Erhard. So while in military terms it is highly confidential, in reality the information is already in our grasp.'

'Tell me about it.'

'Tests have shown it to be absolutely deadly,' Falkenberg said. 'Before the war it was tested on guinea pigs and white rats, but we did not know how the results would translate if it needed to be used in a time of war. Albert Speer bought in apes. But it needed to be tested on humans. We knew it was deadly – a number of our own workers have died through exposure to *Tabun*. Now, though, in order to save German lives, tests have been carried out on *untermenschen*. The results are astounding. A drop on the skin is all

202

it takes. *Tabun* kills the person in minutes by attacking the nervous system. It is a miracle weapon; it makes the mustard gas of the Western Front look like a smelling salt.' Falkenberg leaned forward. 'Our U-Boats are achieving glorious successes in the North Atlantic. We can choke their armies and empty their stomachs, but we need to break their hearts also, just as they attempt to break hearts in our cities and streets. We sit here at a pivotal moment in the future of our nation. We must speak candidly, each assured in the other's absolute loyalty to the Führer, that goes without saying. It is out of that loyalty that we seek this new way now.'

Claire held her breath as she shifted on the hard chair on the cold gallery and then pulled her green cardigan tighter around her shoulders.

Now Voss spoke for the first time.

'If the Führer has dismissed the use of such a weapon, at least for the moment, then he has his reasons. To doubt it, is treason.'

'Our Führer has aged five years for every twelve months of this war, Herr Hauptmann,' stated Wilhem Falkenberg. 'No-one has sacrificed more for the Fatherland. Perhaps it is time for others to accept some of that burden.'

'The cause is greater than any of us,' said his father. 'If it is through fear of retaliation that we fail to act, that we fail our Fatherland, to whom each of us has pledged everything. We have nothing to lose in this fight, but everything to give. As the Führer himself once said: "There is only one right in the world and that right is one's own strength". The truth is so obvious, so stark and real to us here, that none of us may turn away and ignore it. We will always live with the shame of failing to act when we should have. I understand your hesitancy, Herr Hauptmann. My God, be assured of the agony it has taken to bring us to this point. I have been alive longer than you, if you do not mind me saying. And my life has been defined by the injustice, the betrayal of Versailles. No more will I live with that. I have given my life to make Germany great again. But there is only so much we can do. I am not a military man. My son, despite the uniform, and forgive me, Willi, is a civil servant. You are here because of your exceptional bravery. Because of the very special skills you have acquired, not only in Russia, but now – especially now – at Rechlin. *Tabun* is ready. *Pericles* is ready. Where we go now is down to you.'

There was a shuffling of chairs which startled Claire.

'I just want to take some time with my son,' Falkenberg said. 'You must both be hungry. I will get my cook to prepare something.'

'Allow us a few moments to talk, Max,' Buchner told him and Claire saw him stand too.

There were footsteps as Falkenberg and his son stepped across the great hall, opened a heavy door and left. She saw Buchner come around the large table, the flames from one of the torches on the wall, flickering on his face.

'Do you believe in God, Joachim?' he said at last.

Voss did not move.

'I have seen too many comrades die to worry what God thinks,' the airman said. 'I believe in strength, might, our Führer and our nation.'

'Then you will understand exactly what I am about to say,' Buchner said, leaning forward on the table.

Behind her Claire heard a noise on the stairs. She was in a narrow gap between two concrete pillars and frantically looked for somewhere to hide. Her room was along the corridor and whoever was coming would easily reach the gallery before she got inside her door.

She stood up, stooped to remain out of Buchner's gaze, and moved to the table the other side of the pillar. It was draped with a red silk cloth and had three pieces of silver ware on top. She lifted the silk quickly and slipped under the table.

She heard a piece of silver tip with a dull thud.

In the hall, Buchner carried on speaking: 'Life, creation, God, call it what you will, is a force,' he said. 'An overwhelming force.'

The footsteps changed their sound as they moved from the steps to the carpet which ran the length of the gallery. There was a gap between the bottom of the cloth and the floor and Claire watched as a shadow came nearer.

Two polished black boot caps stopped inches from her face.

She could feel the blood pumping so loudly in her temples she was sure that the other would hear.

She sensed him lean forward and lift the piece of silver to replace it upright.

'It is an unerring force,' said Buchner. 'It hurtles through time and space, consuming without mercy. It eats everything up. Consumes everything in its path. It will consume you and I. That is life. God. Destruction. Consuming and destroying to survive.'

Claire, curled in an uncomfortable ball, let her body relax a moment. Down the corridor, she heard Wilhelm Falkenberg tap quietly at his sister's door. She hoped he would not go inside as she did not want to explain to Liesl in the morning that she had deserted her after promising to stay.

But Falkenberg did not wait long. Claire supposed he felt it his duty to try to speak to her. When she did not respond he turned quickly on his heel and went back to the stairs.

Claire looked through a chink in the silk. From this angle she could see Voss listening in silence to his uncle. Both uniforms appeared dark and menacing in the limited light of the hall.

'Right now, Joachim, we are gods. We are part of that force. The most dynamic energy on earth. We have to consume and destroy to survive. It is not cruelty, but necessity. It is not a question of right or wrong; it is a question of strength and of destiny. What God or creation has set in motion cannot be undone. The earth is hurtling through the universe, life is consuming everything. It is the same with us. This cannot be undone. This cannot be stopped.' Buchner thumped the table with his fist. 'It has to be won. We have to take to go forward, to feed, or we die. That is our life. That is our strength. And our curse.'

Buchner sank down in the chair as if exhausted by his speech. He kept his gaze steady on Voss though.

'You are my nephew, Joachim,' he added, gently now. 'Despite the medals and the uniform you are still my sister's boy. I know what I am asking of you. But I know how very proud she would be...'

There was a long silence in which Claire felt any movement would give her away.

When Voss spoke, there was a steeliness to his voice which surprised his uncle so much that Buchner almost flinched.

'I do not need avuncular persuasion or Falkenberg's scientific lessons,' Voss said. 'I understand more than anyone here the nature of the oath to the Führer, the value of every drop of German blood... Uncle, no-one knows better than I that any soldier who goes into battle is a fool to assume he will come out alive. There is a fatalism in every great soldier, a necessary biological escape valve, which allows him to surrender the fear for his own life... I do not lack the strength, uncle. I do not lack the skill. I only want to know one thing: will it win Germany the war?'

Chapter Thirty-Three

Neville Bachelor sat in his office in Whitehall, his face entirely expressionless, his body unmoving.

Anyone who came in at that moment might think that the small and rotund figure at the brown desk was no more than a corpse propped up in the stiff-backed chair. Closer inspection would reveal that on the red, dark pink face were large drops of sweat.

The sun shone through the window behind him, sparkling off the white sheets of paper which spread right across his desk.

Outside the London traffic moved back and for, but Bachelor was many miles away and so deep in thought it took him a few minutes to stir when the door was knocked.

'Yes,' he grunted.

His assistant, Standish, entered. 'You wanted to see me, sir?'

'Hmm. Sit down, Standish.'

Bachelor reached out his two short arms and adjusted two pieces of paper. Standish recognised them as he had brought both to Bachelor earlier. The first had arrived a few days ago and was from one of Bachelor's agents in Belgium, a Soviet spy he codenamed *Sparrow* who had been turned at the outbreak of war and to whom Bachelor was intensely loyal. The other had arrived that morning and was a report from officers in charge of interrogating prisoners at MI 19.

'This message from *Sparrow*,' Bachelor said. 'Thoughts, Standish?'

'Rather vague, sir,' Standish said, crossing one perfectly pressed trouser-leg over another. 'It refers to a substance called *Tabun*, a nerve agent, and to an industrialist named Max Falkenberg, a rather ghastly fellow and complete and utter Nazi.'

'*Sparrow* has referred to him before?'

'Yes, sir. Would you like to see the file?'

'I think so, Standish, and PDQ. Is it possible this Falkenberg could lead a conspiracy to wage war inside the Reich?'

'I really don't know, sir. There is no suggestion as to the target, although one would assume that if the Nazis were to use a nerve agent the wise tactical spot would be in the east, on the Russians.'

Bachelor looked at the message again. '*Sparrow*'s source. Who is that?'

'GRU agent *Capricorn*, sir,' Standish told him. 'A teacher with a lover in the SS. Standartenführer Buchner, one of those in Falkenberg's circle.'

'What about these others? Falkenberg's son and Voss.'

'Nazis both, sir. Obviously. Young Falkenberg works on Hitler's private staff. Voss has rather gone from the radar, sir. Based at Rechlin.' The pair moved to a map on Bachelor's wall and Standish found Rechlin. 'We understand there may be some sort of testing facility there, sir.'

'Chemicals?'

'We don't know, sir.'

Bachelor had the MI 19 report in his hand.

'You're interested in the North African fellow, sir?' said Standish, tall, thin and embarrassingly long-legged next to his chief.

'Hmm,' Bachelor responded.

'Frightfully strange,' Standish went on. 'A prisoner picked up in Tunisia. German and a chemical weapons expert. Prepared to tell the MI 19 boys everything about this special super gas he says the Germans are developing. I sense a general feeling that it is balderdash. That the Germans simply have nothing like this.'

Bachelor reads out loud from the report: '"Prisoner describes a clear and colourless liquid which has virtually no smell. He says it is a nerve poison which causes the eyes to shrink to a pinhead and induces asthma-like difficulties in breathing".'

Standish notes more sweat on Bachelor's brow as he reads and again marvels at how he gets such a stubby neck to fit inside the tight, white shirt collar.

'"Testing was extremely hazardous. Death occurs within fifteen minutes of exposure… The poison does not lend itself to spraying, but would be suitable for use in shells and ordinance used against fortified positions and areas of population".'

Bachelor looks at the map.

'Balderdash, Standish? Coincidence that these pieces of information land at my desk now?'

'A deception, sir?'

'Perhaps, but not one I wish to ignore right off.' Bachelor is tracing his finger on the map, from Rechlin to the coast of northern France. 'Our minds turn more fully to opening a Second Front in Europe. Is it too much to imagine how this super gas would strengthen Hitler's

Atlantic Wall? A weapon like that would throw our armies back into the sea.'

Standish's eyes flicked nervously at the map. His throat was suddenly too dry to respond.

'*Sparrow* is in Brussels and her source is…where?'

'The city of Luxembourg, sir,' Standish croaked.

'And we have Henri in the area, don't we?'

'Yes, sir,' Standish said. 'He's in the Ardennes.'

'Good. We will have him keep his head down. We need him very soon.'

Chapter Thirty-Four

It was an astonishing feat, Buchner thought, surveying the scene around him, and it was entirely down to his cunning and Falkenberg's wisdom.

The airfield at Batienoir in this secluded southern corner of Belgium, just across the Luxembourg border, had been sequestered by the *Luftwaffe*, of course, but only as a supply depot supporting night-fighter bases in the area.

Using his influence he had secured an area of the base for use in an undisclosed SD counter-intelligence operation. The base itself was ideal. The flat space of short grass had been cut out of the densely wooded forest soon after the invasion and had later been extended by the *Luftwaffe*. A series of buildings had been built, each disguised as local farm buildings with steep roofs sloping almost to the ground.

He reached out and touched the wall of the large building beside him. It had a timber covering but underneath he knew was thick concrete.

He squinted his eyes against the sun and looked around him. It felt isolated, safe. The nearest neighbour was a monastery of nuns four miles away through the forest. *Batie*? he thought. A French fort? If the name somehow came from that it was well chosen.

There was never quite silence, though, he had noted. One could always hear the insects in the trees or as they skimmed over the long grass just beyond the high perimeter fence.

And now the noise of an engine cut through the summer's afternoon and Buchner watched a Mercedes come out of the road between the trees and turn to stop at the main gate. Passes shown, the driver continued on, passed an open hut in which Buchner could see the delicate shape of a Fieseler Stork and across to the second gate which marked the entrance to this restricted area in the southern section of the field.

The SS guard at the gate went to the driver's window, checked some papers and then waved the vehicle through. Within a few seconds, Joachim Voss was stepping out of his car and walking towards his uncle.

Buchner stepped out of the shadow of the disguised hangar and into the sunshine.

'Joachim,' he said.

Voss saluted, his sharp features rigid and without emotion.

'How are you, nephew?'

'Good, uncle.' Voss was wearing a leather flying jacket. 'This is a very special moment for me.'

Buchner nodded: 'Like a master mariner taking control of a fine ship, eh? And she is a fine ship, Joachim – if it is not treasonable for me to say so.'

Voss did not laugh at Buchner's joke but followed him as he unlocked a side door to the hangar and went inside.

All the windows in the building had been painted black and it was quite cold inside that concrete box. In the darkness ahead of him Voss could see a distinctive shape.

Buchner reached behind him and flicked a light switch. Three bulbs came on in turn, lighting the aircraft from tail to nose.

Voss stood silently for a moment and then edged his way forward.

He moved down the side of the fuselage, past the star of the United States Army Air Forces and edged under a wing tip to stand in front of one of the two propellers on the port wing.

'What do you think?' Buchner walked around the outside of the wing.

'Good, very good,' Voss said, running his eyes over the Plexiglas dome at the top of the aircraft, the top turret, from which two guns stuck out, each capable of four hundred rounds a minute, and down over the cockpit windows to the nose cone. 'A B-17F. Almost exactly like the one we have been testing at Rechlin...'

Buchner grinned.

'How are they?'

'Very simple to fly,' said Voss, moving to the nose, reaching up and running his hand along the side of the craft. 'Four Wright Cyclone engines capable of 1,200 horsepower, bristling with Browning .50 calibre machine guns, heavily armoured – I know, of course, where that armour is as we have been testing its weaknesses at Rechlin – and a good strong undercarriage...'

'Well, six months ago this one didn't have an undercarriage left,' Buchner told him. 'This one came down in a field in western France late last year. 'The rudder was shredded,' Buchner went on, nodding towards the tail. 'But the pilot made a remarkable landing. The ball turret underneath, of course, was smashed to pieces, the undercarriage crumpled and the propellers twisted as all four engines were running…But working with a colleague in the *Luftwaffe* we managed to ensure that little by little we brought our *Pericles* back to life…'

'For one last battle,' Voss stated, his jaw tightening.

Buchner nodded silently.

'And with some modifications, of course,' Buchner told him. 'Particularly inside. The rear gunner area remains but anyone looking to move in the middle of the fuselage will have to tread carefully. We have, of course, increased the armour around this mid-section to protect your bomb-load, but you won't have the usual 10-man crew on this mission. Just a navigator, top turret gunner and someone in the ball turret.'

'Then the armour should not have a significant impact on our speed,' Voss said. 'Less men, less equipment.'

'I read your report on your crew,' Buchner stated. 'Excellent. Remarkable men.'

'Thank you. They are. I served with all of them in Russia.'

'If you have such faith in them, Joachim, then so do I.'

'The east breeds remarkable men,' said Voss. 'Each knows his duty. Each understands the nature of the *totaleinsatz*, the absolute effort which is required of us all. Each had already volunteered for training in the event of high command requesting volunteers for a *selbstopfer* unit.'

'They need not all sacrifice themselves, you know, Joachim,' said Buchner. 'If you can be absolutely sure of the target.'

'If we are successful in our mission, uncle,' Voss said sternly, 'then I am sure we would all rather die in an instant than parachute to earth in time to see what horror there is to greet us.'

Claire lay in Buchner's bed with her head on his shoulder.

It was early, about 6am, but the bedroom was already bathed in the yellowy summer sunshine.

Buchner had been in a strange mood the night before. At first, she thought she had done something to upset him – or worse, he suspected her – but he had quickly snapped at her that it was something to do with Joachim Voss and had poured several glasses of schnapps down his throat.

Then he had apologised to her and said, 'It's the war, my love, nothing for you to concern yourself about,' and had started kissing her face and neck.

Somehow she still managed to close herself off when he did that. The kissing, the lovemaking. She shut herself down to what anybody would think of as emotion. She told herself that this was her work face, her front, and his powerful and sometimes rough use of her body had nothing loving in it for either of them. She doubted the truth of that, of course: Buchner, in his own way, loved her, she was sure. He had even talked about moving her to Bavaria, away from the bombs and away from her own people – the ones who whispered now and who, if the war was lost by the Germans, would surely make her suffer in God knows how many ways. Then, she wondered, if Moscow would save her.

Buchner's breath smelt of stale alcohol. He had dragged her to bed last night, leaving the curtains open, and afterwards quickly fallen into a heavy, laboured sleep.

But, yes, she could take the kissing and the touching; it was this - *this intimacy* - that she found repugnant, almost impossible to stomach. Here, now, in his arms, trying to sleep. Knowing that not for one minute could she really relax.

The soft morning breeze picked up the thin curtain and bellowed it upwards like a ghost.

Buchner shifted, but his right arm, remained clasped around her.

'Darling,' he said sleepily.

She sensed a rare vulnerability in him, despite the strong manly smell, the power of his forearm above her.

'Are you alright, Erhard?' she whispered, not wanted to bring him around too much. 'You seemed very worried last night.'

'No, not worried, darling,' he said.

'Is Joachim alright?'

'Something... something is going to happen, darling,' he opened his eyes wide. 'Very soon. I can't say what. But it will be remarkable.'

'What is it?'

'Of course, I can't say,' he held her hand and kissed the palm.

'Joachim is involved?'

'Yes. He may not come back. And I don't know what will happen to me afterwards, do you understand? No, of course, you can't... Claire, it may be safer for you if you moved out for a while.'

'Erhard, are you in danger?'

He laid his head back on the pillow and laughed.

'We are all in danger, Claire,' he said. 'From east, west, south and north. At this particular point in humanity, during this struggle for our civilisation, perhaps only he who risks most danger can prevail. You are not German, my love, and perhaps you do not understand.'

'I want to understand.'

Buchner stroked her hair.

'My love, do you hear what I say? It will be safer if you move out. I can get you a new flat. And some protection.'

'I want to stay with you, Erhard.'

Later, Claire slipped into Buchner's office and went through the slim red file in the drawer. The reports were brief, typed and on single sheets of paper. One was from Buchner to Falkenberg and stated simply: '*Pericles* prepared and in position, Batienoir. Being maintained by special team of groundcrew.' There followed a list of dates, next which Buchner had handwritten: 'Intelligence from England suggests large raids planned on central Germany. Regular raids monitored. Return routes logged and charted by staff. Opportunities for dates early to mid August. Plan and route agreed. Subject to final weather checks with Cherbourg, etc. We will have to trust to luck with regard own fighters.'

Falkenberg's note: '*Pericles*' sword and shield prepared for delivery to Batienoir. Date agreed. Here's hoping for success in August.'

The file contained a photograph on the back of which Buchner had scribbled *Pericles* in pencil. Claire turned it over, recognised the shape of an American Flying Fortress bomber like those that streaked daily across the sky. It was on a hard-standing and there was little to give away its location: the background showed only a thick forest. The men all around it appeared to be preparing the aircraft for flight. All three, she recognised, were in the uniforms and caps of *Luftwaffe* ground-crew.

Chapter Thirty-Five

The Place D'Armes in Luxembourg *ville* was filled with shoppers enjoying the summer sunshine. The terraces of the cafés were busy with small chattering groups: older men smoking, young women laughing and joking, and, of course, the soldiers.

Despite her own circumstances, Claire always found the site of the uniforms – bright green in the sunshine – a little strange. There seemed so many. She looked at the soldiers who were with the local girls and searched in the faces around them for the hatred she knew would also be directed at her.

She was wearing a black skirt and beige blouse with a grey jacket over it. She tried not to wear anything too bright or distinctive when she was meeting the courier, not wanting to make it easy for anyone who might follow either of them. She was always careful and realised that so far she had been lucky. She had put herself in a position of great danger by becoming an SS officer's lover but it was also somehow extremely safe. It was as if she had put her hand so far into the fire that she could not feel the heat anymore. Besides, the Germans knew how much she was despised by her own countryfolk. Why would she put herself in that position? The worst they would think of her was that she was an opportunist, a whore. *The worst...* She smiled at that, and thought of the further irony too: the clattering of coffee cups and the smell of cigarette smoke which surrounded her was a reminder that most people were not doing anything against the occupation. Most were simply getting on with their fairly normal lives.

The courier, a pretty but serious young girl who was no more than 16, arrived at the usual café and took the table neighbouring Claire's. The switch was quick and clean. Claire waited for a few moments, finishing her cigarette, before rising and leaving the apparently empty packet and some money on the table.

She would then walk along the Place D'Armes without looking back. Meanwhile the girl had stood, her faded linen skirt swishing and left in the other direction, the cigarette packet in her hand.

Once around the corner, Claire would dip into a department store and do a circuit to see if she were being followed. After waiting for a few moments, pretending to look along the rather empty rails, she realised there was no-one after her. She then slipped out of another door.

Back in the Place D'Armes, though, Hauptmann Fischer had moved from his spot across the square and was struggling to keep up with the girl. He almost lost her a few times because not only was she walking quite quickly but he also had to stay back: his appearance made him stand out.

He saw her arrive at the train station and watched her slip onto the platform with her ticket for the Brussels train.

Eva Heigl was a red-headed woman with a thin body and a narrow bird-like face. Born in Belgium, she had been recruited by the GRU after a brief love affair with a communist in the 1920s. An agent from Moscow had realised her potential, persuaded her to break off with the man and to work for Moscow – but with no outward allegiances or links to the Comintern.

She attended all the cultural events and societies which met at the library and in the community, and reported back on changing attitudes, trade union activity and local municipal meetings. Colleagues thought she was quiet, diligent, a typical librarian spinster. And she was.

Except for the fact that she was a committed communist and loyal to the concept of an international worker's revolution. However, when Stalin and Hitler signed a non-aggression pact in August 1939, Heigl was wracked with doubt. Having only recently taken a two-week tour of Germany, she had seen the Nazi future for herself and, on the outbreak of war, vowed to do all she could to aid Hitler's defeat. On November 7, 1939, on 22nd anniversary of the Revolution, she made contact with London and offered herself as an agent. From then on everything that she sent to Moscow Centre, also went to London and Neville Bachelor (although she was no traitor and never informed Bachelor what instructions she received from Moscow). She had doubled her workload and also her pay, although she spent the London money so that Moscow would not get suspicious.

All the while Eva Heigl remained exceptionally careful - never mixing with any known members of the Belgian Communist Party, and outwardly showing no interest in politics or in what the Nazis said people should and should not be reading. This way she had escaped two crackdowns on Russian *pianists* – radio operators in Belgium and the Netherlands.

Capricorn's courier arrived in her library that afternoon to return a book on Africa. The messages were under the dust jacket and Heigl carefully slide the sheets of paper out and put them in her bag.

After work she stood in a slow queue at the bakery before heading to a narrow cobbled street in the district of Etterbeek and the dark four-storey building in which she had lived for 10 years. She barely noticed who was in the street but saw the ambulance further down the road and muttered to herself in sadness that some poor person was in trouble.

She climbed to her top floor flat and turned the key in the lock. It was a modest apartment with a small bedroom, toilet and a main room with a table, chairs, rather threadbare couch and a small cooking area.

Once inside, Heigl made coffee and looked at *Capricorn*'s messages. It would take her some time to decipher and then encode them for transmission, but she quickly noted they were marked extremely urgent.

She cut herself a slice of bread and decided she would contact London first. She opened the window and glanced into the street. She had a tiny balcony which was just large enough to stand on and which stretched just a little wider than the window itself.

As she felt the evening breeze come in she glanced down into the street. Again nothing much but the small ambulance.

At the kitchen table she worked for an hour encoding the message for London and shortly after 7pm she fixed up a single wire aerial and screwed her Morse key to the table. At 7.06pm, comfortable at the table and sitting bolt upright in the chair, Heigl began to transmit *Capricorn*'s latest message to London.

For five months, officers from a special *Funkabwehr* squad set up to find Soviet radio operators had been using cross-bearings to pinpoint the *pianist* using the call-sign TCV. They had tracked TCV to Brussels, where three monitoring squads with direction-finding sets had posted themselves at points in the city and waited for each message.

Each time Heigl transmitted the loop aerial of the receiver sets would be turned until her signal sounded loudest. It was a torturous job for the officers: boring, uncomfortable and depressing. TCV did not transmit regularly like some, often leaving almost a week between messages, and took so many precautions - switching call-signs and wavelengths – that the hunters thought they had lost their prey many times. On top of that, it took several months before they realised TCV was also switching locations, however, after a painstaking search they narrowed down the transmission sites to three small areas.

Then, it was out of the vans for the *Abwehr* men. For several weeks four members of the team had been walking the night streets of each area with mobile detectors under their coats or in suitcases.

Now two of them were in Etterbeek, shuffling down the narrow cobbled street. One opened the rear doors of the ambulance and went inside. 'She is in one of these houses here,' he told the uniformed officer in the back of the vehicle. 'Each has about 10 apartments.'

'Take further bearings,' came the reply.

It took some time for Heigl to transmit her message to London. When she had finished she had pains in her right hand which shot up her thin arm. She rubbed it carefully and considered whether to transmit to Moscow from here or to send tomorrow from an alternative location. She would take a break before encoding the message for the GRU.

Taking off her reading glasses, she went to the cooker, struck a long kitchen match and lit the gas before moving the kettle onto the flame.

There was a shout in a street, the kind she often heard on a summer's evening. But something made her walk to the window and look down. Dusk was just beginning to fall.

Nothing much appeared to have changed. Just the one vehicle. There were a couple of men walking in the road now but nothing about them took her attention: they looked like sullen bank clerks walking home.

She turned back to the ambulance. *Why had it not driven off?* There seemed to be no activity at all around it. No driver or nurse.

The two bank clerks were walking up and down the streets. *They must be warm.* Their overcoats were dark and heavy; their collars were turned up. They both wore soft hats which she could see were pulled down low too.

It was then she realised.

She started to turn and as she did was disturbed by another noise, a screech of rough brakes. At the corner of the next street, which she could just see from this vantage point, a large army lorry had pulled up. A door opened and an NCO went around to the back. Within seconds a squad of men had assembled in the street.

Below her, in her street, the two men were looking up and around them now, and she could see the small direction finding units under their coats, the headphones clamped to their ears.

The ambulance door opened and someone got out. He was pulling thick woollen socks over his jackboots and was frantically indicating to the NCO at the far end of the street for the men to be quiet.

Heigl rushed to the small cupboard under the sink and reached inside, her arm straining for something stashed away at the back. She took out a small accounts book and held it over the sink. She lit a match, made sure the flame caught at two corners of the book and put it down on a plate.

Then she gathered the papers from the table and started to burn those too, watching them shrivel to black.

She went to her door, opened it and stood out on the landing. Her heart racing, she peeked over the balcony.

For a minute nothing moved. Then she heard whispered orders which the officer was trying hard to keep quiet but which echoed up the hollow atrium at the centre of the building like cries in a cave.

She saw someone move – a soldier and he was only two floors below. He looked up, his pale, young face bright in the gloom under the dark helmet.

She gasped and turned quickly, locking her door. In her bedroom, she bent down with a grunt and took a pole from under the bed. Using the hook on the end, she opened the attic access and pulled down a ladder.

She lifted her rough, tweed skirt and stepped onto the ladder, climbing carefully to the top and grazing her knee as she pulled herself into the dark space.

As she heaved the ladder up, she heard a harsh rapping at her door. She shut the cover, her hands shaking, and a rifle butt smashed its way into her home.

She stepped gingerly through the darkness towards the skylight. Cobwebs tangled into her face and mouth. She heard herself whimper in fear but clenched her fists and concentrated on what she wanted to do.

She reached up and opened the skylight.

She could hear the Germans in her rooms now. They were banging, shouting, throwing things. My God, she had left her Morse key and aerial out. *Well, it did not matter now, you silly woman. Just hurry, hurry…*

'We must take her alive,' a voice shouted.

She stood on an old box so that she was already almost halfway out the skylight and pulled herself right through.

The roof was steep here and she was about halfway up the slates. It was only now she felt real fear. *Where am I going? Oh, God.*

She could see the tall buildings across the street and more rooftops beyond. The street sounds seemed frighteningly close.

She pulled her legs out, noticing that her stockings were torn and that her skin looked white and wrinkled underneath. The roof was hot under her hands.

She was now lying flat, terrified of sliding towards the edge, but knowing she had to push herself onwards.

Carefully, afraid to move too much, she reached across with one hand to let the skylight drop back into place. It fell with a bang and, for a second, she lost friction with the roof's surface. She began to slide, her hands flailing and slapping against the tiles. She could not stop.

She screamed, waiting to plunge over the edge.

But she stopped suddenly with her feet against a narrow concrete guttering which formed a ledge almost a foot wide.

Her heart was banging in her chest. Her hands and knees were bruised and bleeding.

She imagined the soldiers in the street taking aim at her back with their rifles. But no shots came.

Face down on the black roof, she began to edge her way along the small parapet. *There has to be an escape through next door's roof.* She tried to think logically. Looking under her right arm she could watch her steps without looking back over the edge of the building.

She had gone a few strides when the skylight she had crawled through was pushed open and banged hard against the slate.

Heigl looked across and saw a head appear as someone started pulling themselves up. If she was seen here, she was trapped.

She half-turned to the right, pushed herself up off the tiles and took two quick strides while balancing on the guttering.

She had only a short distance to go before she could jump down onto the lower flat roof of the neighbouring building.

Her head was dizzy and light; her legs so weak they would barely move. Her ankle twisted and she stumbled, seeing the houses across the street swirl and twist, and the summer sky suddenly crash away from her. She cried out as her ankle clipped the side of the roof and she fell into the street below.

Chapter Thirty-Six

Philip Mortain was looking down into a gorge through which a road and wide river wound like lengths of white and light blue ribbon. To the north there was a steep bend at which he got first warning of vehicles arriving in that direction. To the south he could see down into the valley basin.

It was good here, on top of the hill. Easy to see anyone who was approaching, plenty of time to get away if need be, and it smelt good too.

It was early morning, but the same sunshine which made the water and road surface sparkle in the gorge below him was already beating down on the rock against which he lay.

A few feet away Alain Gerard and a radio operator named Paul were stretched out in the grass, the tapping and whining of the set carrying on the air. The insects in the bracken and pink heather were buzzing as if in response.

A shadow broke across Philip as Marc Rameau moved across the small ridge to settle in the long grass at his side.

Philip glanced at Rameau, watching him pick at the holes in his black shoes before laying back in the sunshine and looking into a cloudless sky.

Rameau's presence reminded Philip of that moment in Liège. Many times he had played it out in his mind. If he had taken another coffee in that safe-house room, if he had hesitated a moment longer for any of a dozen reasons, he would have been inside when Rameau and his mother had come in. They would have cried and laughed at each other, hugged and been silent, sat and talked, and talked. He would know more about what happened to her – he knew from Gerard and Rameau about the camp, but only tantalising, heartbreakingly small details – and he could have asked about little Jimmy.

That look in her eyes. He had analysed it over and over. There was sadness and confusion at seeing him, suddenly, in that strange place. And joy. Longing, in wanting to reach out to him. Shame, at her own appearance, her obvious weakness, her inability to offer a mother's help. But there was something else too. Something in her heart was broken.

Soon, soon, he would be with her.

222

Gerard had moved her on a barge to Namur. She was safe there. Young Maurice was looking after her. And soon he would get there too. Gerard had considered sending her on an evasion line through to Spain but there would be no need for that. He would arrange a Lysander from London to fly over and pick them up. Then they would be together again and he would ask not to return here. All he wanted was to be back with his mother, protecting her. The war seemed so unimportant when he looked at her eyes. Only bringing her, James and him back together mattered.

After all, his time here had been one long waiting game, trying to negotiate between different resistance groups, defending London against angry tirades about levels of support, fending off questions about when the invasion was coming and organising drops of weapons and money. He wondered sometimes, when he heard the American bombers going over by day and the RAF droning over by night, whether he would have done more, would have better satisfied the craving he had felt on leaving Jersey, if he had stayed in the RAF to twist his way through the flak over Hamburg or Düsseldorf or Berlin.

'You are thinking about your mother?' Gerard said. 'She is safe. We have taken all the precautions, you said. The Namur house is a new house. She will be safe and comfortable until I can get her away. Henri, I have followed your English orders. The line is safe.'

Philip nodded. Yes, they were more secure now, although he supposed he had broken his own rules by even explaining who Grace was.

The transmission stopped and Paul began to decipher the messages. 'It's a long one,' he stated, a pencil in his mouth, his white shirt open to reveal pinkness to the skin on his chest.

Philip watched a rabbit come from a small crop of rocks, scamper towards them, eat at the dry grass and stare at the men suspiciously.

Eventually, Paul handed Philip a sheet of paper, which the Jerseyman read carefully twice.

'Do you know an Erhard Buchner, SS?' The question was directed at Gerard but it was Rameau who suddenly sat up.

'He's a senior member of counter-intelligence here in Luxembourg,' Gerard said.

'Why?' Rameau asked.

'London would like us to kill him,' Philip said.

There was a silence, and then Gerard scoffed: 'Do they have any idea what they are asking? It is alright in London... This man is an SS Standartenführer. You don't just walk up to him. Besides, who will suffer afterwards? Us, here. Not the people of London.'

'What is this about?' Rameau stated.

'He's involved in a plot which London is concerned about. With a man named Voss. It's not a decision I imagine they make lightly.'

'It's unheard of,' said Gerard dismissively. 'Where will the money come from for an operation like that?'

'More to the point,' said Rameau. 'Where does this information come from?'

'The source is close to Buchner.'

'I know this Buchner,' Rameau told him. 'His lover is Bertrand Gillier's niece.'

'I know that,' Gerard shrugs.

'The information comes from close to Buchner?' Rameau rubbed his chin and took a cigarette from one offered by Paul. 'What is the target of Buchner's operation?'

'They do not know,' Philip responded.

'This is the usual mess we get from London,' Gerard said, facing Philip. 'I see them as suggestions, not orders. They suggest Buchner be stopped but that is a whole different thing from making it happen.'

'Have you heard from Jean?' Rameau said.

Gerard hesitated. 'No. Why do you ask?'

'You've set him off to kill Gillier's niece, Claire Winter.'

Gerard shrugged again: 'So what?'

'Who's Claire Winter?' Philip said, cutting across them both.

'A traitor,' Gerard said. 'She sleeps with Buchner.'

'If your man Jean does anything we will never get near Buchner,' Philip told him angrily. 'The Nazis will have security so tight...'

'He has been watching her, that's all,' Gerard protested. 'I spoke with him yesterday.'

'What did he say?'

'He has his orders.'

'What if this woman is your source, London's source?' Rameau asked.

'You don't know that,' Gerard said, turning on Rameau.

'I don't. But it makes some sense.'

'You are guessing. She's a pretty girl, I understand, but don't forget who you are, Marc.'

'No,' said Rameau. 'But if she is we can get to her, find out what this is about. I mean, if Jean does not get to her first.'

Within half-an-hour, after getting confirmation from London that Claire was the source of information on Buchner, Rameau, Philip and Gerard were heading towards Luxembourg city in Gerard's old wood-gas powered car.

Gerard drove it as if he was at Le Mans, swinging around corners, the vehicle lurching on its high suspension.

'Jean told me he had word that Buchner had gone away, without his girl,' Gerard said. 'He said there was only one guard on the house who changed every four hours. They just stand at the gate and don't enter the house at all, and they go back and for to the barracks at Boulevard Saint Michel. He said there was little protection around the perimeter and it was easy to get in. He used a friend, a telephone engineer, to check the house. The windows and doors are alarmed. But he said on nice days like these the doors into the garden are often left unlocked.'

'Are you saying Jean plans to kill her today?'

Gerard pushed the car into a lower gear as they entered houses on the outskirts of the city. 'He has been planning this a long time, Marc,' he stated.

The report was clear. The United States Eighth Air Force was to attack in a huge formation. The target was deep inside the Reich: factories around Schweinfurt. Further raids were suggested in the north, 'targets unspecified as yet, but more information to follow'. Buchner had written next to this: 'Northern targets unsuitable for our purposes owing to return routes of enemy terror fliers.'

The report added: 'Raiders leaving airfields on the east of England between approximately 0600hrs would arrive over targets in central Germany at approximately 0900 to 1000hrs, before regrouping over Germany/Belgium border for return home.'

Claire shuffled through the rest of the drawer, then stopped suddenly, holding her breath.

The front door of the house opened and clicked shut. Silence.

A boot scrapped on the cold hall floor, and took slow steps forward, inching closer to the open door of the study. She knew it could not be Buchner. He would not be back until tomorrow. She even knew where he was: the place he called *Batienoir*.

She pushed the papers back into the drawer, her eyes all the while on the door.

The steps came to a stop and then a hand gently pushed the door open wide.

'Hello, Claire,' Hauptmann Fischer said. 'Found anything of interest?'

Claire sat open mouthed at Buchner's desk for a moment but quickly recovered her composure.

'Karl!' she said. 'Why didn't you say you were coming? You gave me such a shock.' She stood up and came around the front of the desk,

Fischer stepped forward into the room.

'What did you find in the desk?'

'Oh, I was looking for a list Erhard was meant to leave for me,' she said weakly.

'In his study?'

'What is this, Karl? Why are you asking these questions?'

Fischer gave a smile and looked away from her eyes for a moment.

'Oh, Claire. You're good. You're very good. I have to admire the way you have played Buchner for an absolute fool.' He stepped closer and she instinctively recoiled so that the backs of her thighs were against the desk. 'I'm not going to hurt you, Claire, but I know what you've been doing.'

'I don't know what you mean, Karl.'

He laughed: 'It's ironic. I only found out by accident, I suppose you would say. You see, I didn't suspect anything. No, just the opposite. I followed you out of a schoolboy longing.' His eyes were watering, as she looked at him, he again turned his head away. 'I just liked to be near you. Liked to watch you. Not in a creepy way. Please, no, don't think that. I just liked to be near…'

Now he lifted his eyes and they both held each other's gaze for a moment. Claire had always felt a genuine sadness for Fischer. He was the embodiment of the wounded humanity that she was there deep inside herself, under the pretence.

'Karl.' She tried to smile but it was more difficult now. 'I honestly don't know what you mean.'

'Claire,' he answered more forcefully. 'My God, do you think any of this matters to me? Look at me! I don't care. It's just you I care about.'

Claire let her shoulders drop and at that moment a figure flashed across her vision behind Fischer then stepped swiftly into the room and crashed something hard and black into the side of the German's head. Blood spurted out of Fischer's right eye and he cried out. Unable to break his own fall, he crumpled hard against the foot of a heavy bookshelf.

The attacker, short but violently built, admired his work for a moment, and then turned in Claire's direction.

Claire watched the pistol in his right hand rise towards her stomach.

'Well, well,' he mocked. 'Just how many German lovers have you taken?'

'Who are you?' Claire said, inching back along the side of the desk.

'I come from friends of your uncle, Bertrand Gillier,' Jean said.

Claire's jaw hardened with anger.

'Don't stand there with that gun and talk about my uncle,' she said. 'How dare you let his name cross your lips.'

'You can fight me,' Jean sneered. 'I thought you would. I mean I know whose side you are on.'

'There's a guard outside the front,' Claire told him.

'I know, I know,' Jean replied. 'We'll just have to be quiet, won't we?'

He took a small cylindrical object from his pocket and began to screw it onto the end of the pistol.

In horror, Claire realised what it was.

She looked hurriedly around her. There was no point trying to argue with this man. There was nothing she could say. She had to fight and quick.

She grabbed a letter opener shaped like an Arabian sword off the desk and rushed towards him.

Jean put out his left hand and easily held her off, but as he did so, Fischer grabbed hold of his legs.

Jean began to topple to his right, Claire twisting the hand holding the gun. The elongated barrel of the silencer wavered towards her and then away.

She and Jean fell to the floor.

Jean's eyes turned for a moment to his legs where Fischer's arms were flailing. His good eye was streaming with blood from the earlier blow.

Jean pulled his right boot free and planted a vicious kick into Fischer's nose and mouth.

He then wrenched his hand free from Claire's half grip and turned the gun towards Fischer.

Claire screamed, 'No', and brought the letter opener down into Jean's thigh at the exact moment his finger pulled the trigger.

Gerard drove past Jean's van a few streets away and carried on towards Buchner's house.

Near the back wall, they got out of the vehicle and Gerard kept watch as Rameau hurled a coat over the barbed wire at the top of the wall and dragged himself up.

In an instance, both Rameau and Philip were in the flower bed at the foot of Buchner's large garden. They could see no-one moving in the windows at the back.

'Let's make this quick,' Philip said and ran across the lawn.

As he neared the patio windows at the back of the house he could see one of the doors was slightly open.

Philip looked quickly around him. The tall trees both sides of the garden obscured the neighbouring buildings.

He took a .38 pistol out of his jacket pocket and stepped inside the house. He could feel Rameau behind him.

They walked on the balls of their feet through the sun lounge and a larger room with a piano. The house seemed silent and empty.

It was not until they reached the hall and glanced up the white staircase that they heard it. A gentle sobbing.

Philip stepped across the hallway and turned his body into the open doorway, holding the gun in front of him.

There was a gasp from Claire who, after Jean's scream of agony, was expecting the guard.

Philip and Rameau moved quickly into the room, glancing only briefly at the bloody mess crumpled in the corner.

Claire was sitting back on the floor against the desk. She now had Jean's pistol in her hand. Philip went to her quickly and took it from her before she had the chance to react.

Jean was gasping and breathing painfully, the blade embedded halfway up his thigh. He was bleeding profusely and, as Rameau took his hand, he could feel the strength rushing out of the little man.

'She…' was all he could say before the weight of his head was too much and it fell back against the floor with a thud.

'Is he dead?' Philip said.

'Not yet.'

'What about the other one?'

Rameau looked at the bloody mess of Fischer's face.

'Yes.'

Philip turned to Claire. Her blouse was loose on her shoulder and her hair fell roughly over the side of her face.

She was trying hard not to look at Fischer.

'We don't want to hurt you,' Philip said. 'Do you know why we are here?'

Claire shook her head.

'What do you know about *Pericles*?'

A look of confusion came over her face.

'You're here for that?' she said. 'What about him?' She gestured towards Jean.

Philip turned to see Rameau trying to staunch the flow of blood from the man's thigh. The heavy dark liquid was now covering as much space on the light carpeted floor as Jean himself.

'That was something else,' Philip said. '*Pericles*,' he went on. 'Do we have time?'

'No,' Claire said. 'I don't know. Voss? Do you know of Voss? They are at the airfield. The notes…this is it, I think.'

'The target? What are they after?'

'They talk about raids on central Germany.'

'That doesn't make sense,' Philip said. 'Let me see.'

He helped her up and she went through the file in the drawer.

'No,' he said at last. 'Looks like they are hoping to join up with returning bombers. But for what?'

'I don't know.'

'Okay,' he said, taking hold of her arms. 'Tell me what you do.'

Rameau came back from a front window.

'The guard changed,' he said. 'No interest in the house.'

Philip pulled the door closed, pushing every document from Jean's pockets into his own.

Claire stood silent, still traumatised from watching Jean slowly die in front of her.

'We have someone who can take you to safety,' Philip told her. 'You will have to do everything he says. Go pack a small bag – quickly!'

When Claire had gone upstairs, Rameau said: 'Will London accept this?'

'We'll tell Gerard not to tell her or them,' Philip replied. 'She hides with my mother. When the Lysander comes they both get on it.'

Rameau nodded, and took a sheet of paper from Philip.

'Do you know where this is?'

Rameau studied it. 'I can find it easily enough.'

'Good,' Philip told him, showing him two photographs. 'These are Buchner and Voss; that's where they are. Gerard can take Claire. You and I will take Jean's van and hope we get through.'

Philip locked the study door.

'Buchner is not expected back until tomorrow,' he said. 'With any luck this mess won't be discovered until we have finished all this.'

'That captain in there will be missed,' Rameau told him.

'He will,' Philip said. 'It depends if those guards report visitors or just log them. And if anyone else knows he was coming here.'

'That's a lot of ifs.'

'Maybe, but once we are over that back wall, we know now what we have to do.'

Chapter Thirty-Seven

Hauptmann Joachim Voss looked around the small room without seeing. His mind was focused, not on the route and plan that they had run through last night and were to discuss in a final briefing in a few moments time, but on the target. The final moment, The point of impact. His heart pounded when he thought of the success which lay ahead of him. *Men going into battle cannot assume they will come back alive*, he thought. The simple man goes to war, cowering, hoping to come through, the outcome secondary to their own survival. Not him. Today was about absolute success, nothing else.

His eyes moved sightlessly over the mug of dark untouched coffee to the brand-new US flak-suit which was draped over the chair, the manganese steel plates of the abdominal protector propped up like a person's torso.

His mind stirred and he walked over to the wardrobe and opened the door to take out a leather flying jacket and cap.

He dressed quickly and, shutting the door, caught sight of himself in the full-length mirror.

He wore his *Luftwaffe* trousers and the Knight's Cross still glinted at his throat. But the jacket was US Army Air Force issue and the cap was that worn by American pilot serving abroad. *Enough to fool any 'fellow' stragglers that fly at our side.*

He adjusted the cap with both hands so that he wore it at a tilt with the bars of rank of a US captain appearing over his left eye. It was a gesture anybody else would have made with a smile, but Voss' face remained expressionless.

Like an actor getting under the skin of the character he was about to portray, Voss casually saluted as an American would.

The briefing had taken place as the sun was rising and it was bad news. In the room were Buchner, Voss, Falkenberg, a *Luftwaffe* captain named Graumann, an orderly and three other men. The last of these were Voss' chosen crew: Reichel, his navigator; Pieper, top turret gunner and Thiel who would man the ball turret protecting the aircraft from below.

'Where did you get your information on the raids, Herr Standartenführer?' Graumann asked.

'I have a source, a very good source,' Buchner replied, unwilling to admit he had an agent with contacts in the Air Ministry in London.

'Well, it is good information,' said the *Luftwaffe* man, whose mouth turned down at one side in a permanent smirk. 'American bombers are approaching the Dutch coast already. More than a hundred of them. It is quite a surprise, actually. You see while most of Europe has the weather we have here, fine, clear skies, a high pressure, there is low cloud as dense as fog over England. It's safe above around 3,000 feet but it is dangerous weather into which to launch a large formation of aircraft.'

'So they are heading for Germany?'

'Our fighters will intercept them shortly.'

There was a pause.

'Hauptmann Voss, I am aware of only the briefest details of your mission...'

Buchner cut across the captain: 'That is unavoidable, Herr Hauptmann, as I am sure you will understand.'

'I understand, Herr Standartenführer, but as I am sure you will realise it means I am limited in what information I can give by way of a briefing. I can say this: firstly, there are likely to be heavy casualties among the returning bombers. They will meet heavy flak whatever their target inside the Fatherland. And they must of course return also. This will take them back along this line here. As you will see it runs just south of and almost parallel to the Dutch-Belgian border. In this corridor, the Americans will be in the hunting grounds of *Luftwaffe* fighters from Münster, Mönchen-Gladbach, Woensdrecht, Schipol, Deelen and Leeuwarden. The areas around Eupen – the US fighter rendezvous area - Liège and Maastricht are likely to be deadly and I have suggested to Hauptmann Voss that he link with returning planes to the west of here. Antwerp is also likely to be...unsafe.

'To this end I have provided maps of high-tension wires, low hills and buildings along a route to the Dutch coast agreed with Hauptmann Voss.' He looked directly at Voss. 'Your altimeter will be unreliable at some of the heights at which you shall be flying.

'Later in your flight you will have one distinct advantage. You are flying in a B-17. No radar operator on the ground and hopefully other B-17 crew member in the air will be able to tell your true identity.'

Voss nodded and continued to look at Graumann thoughtfully.

'Can I help further, Herr Standartenführer?'

'Cloud base over south east of England?'

'About 1,000 feet. Intelligence expects the cloud to clear around lunchtime.'

'Thank you, Herr Hauptmann,' Buchner told Graumann, standing as he did so. 'It is imperative you keep us informed of changes in weather here and over England, and of the progress of the Americans.'

'I shall receive a briefing in an hour and every thirty minutes after that.'

'Good. Joachim, take a walk with us.'

Outside, Buchner and Voss lit cigarettes and wandered in the general direction of the hangar in which *Pericles* stood waiting. Some men were moving busily inside the restricted fencing.

'I am having her readied,' Buchner said.

Two men were carrying wooden boxes of ammunition inside the building.

Voss nodded silently.

'You are happy with your route?'

'Yes, uncle. What about the device?'

Falkenberg was staring at the ground-crew, but without seeing them. He was imagining.

'Herr Voss, it is perfect. The central device is nine parts *Tabun* and one part *Chlorobenzene*, a stabilizer. It is surrounded by a casing of high explosive. On impact it will create utter devastation. In the hours following annihilation...'

The two military men looked at him silently.

'Their terror fliers destroy Hamburg,' Falkenberg added. 'They burn German cities which have stood for 500 years and more. The Americans by day, the British by night. A million homeless, tens of thousands dead. And they expect no revenge? This will make the blood run ice cold in their veins.'

Chapter Thirty-Eight

The forest was a patchwork of light and shade. A golden sunshine turned the trees into stark skeletal shapes but rarely penetrated the heavy canopy of leaves except in narrow blinding shafts of yellow. Here and there, small open glades were studded with pink and white flowers but for the most part the forest floor was brown and dark.

Rameau and Philip had covered the van with branches and shrubs and walked for about a mile. They had crossed a stream, the water coming up to just below their knees and waited silently for a few minutes before daring to cross a small roadway.

It was cold under the trees and even the occasional burst of sunlight made them shiver.

Rameau led the way, the Sten gun on a strap over his shoulder, a cap pulled down over his head. Philip followed five paces behind, stepping over the fallen trees, holding back the branches, watching for movement in the endless shadows which stretched away to both sides of them.

They had been walking for half-an-hour when the forest suddenly thinned and the airfield lay out before them. They stalked along the last line of trees and found a place to crouch down a few feet from the wire.

Philip put his hand on the fallen oak behind which they knelt and looked both ways along the wire. He could not see a sentry.

He unbuttoned his coat and reached inside to find a small set of field glasses. With the sun at the back of his neck he was sure there would be no glint from the lens to give him away, so he focused on the buildings which lay at the opposite side of the field. He could see the main gates and a sentry box and about half a dozen small buildings. Two men in *Luftwaffe* uniform crossed from a small building to a larger one which Philip took to be a hangar, although its doors were shut.

There were no aircraft to be seen and Philip realised that a small herd of cows grazing at one corner of the field were fake, not realistic enough to fool anyone at the perimeter fence for long but certainly to persuade anyone flying over and taking pictures. From 1,000 feet this was just a small farming village in the forest with its red-roofed buildings. One hangar even had a small steeple like a church.

Philip's glasses moved to the left, and another hangar, fenced in with a permanent guard.

Something moved nearer to him and Rameau grabbed his arm. A sentry was coming along the fence. They ducked down behind the tree and watched him slowly pass by. He paid little heed to the forest or the fence, concentrating instead on secretly smoking a cigarette.

'It's very quiet,' Philip said. 'This is the place?'

Rameau nodded.

Philip put the glasses to his eyes again and watched a man come from one of the small buildings and cross quickly and smartly to the isolated hangar, and receive the guard's salute.

Philip checked one of the photographs in his pocket.

'Think that's Voss?'

Rameau took the glasses and watched the man as he slipped through the gates.

He nodded.

'What do you think he is doing in there?'

Philip shook his head silently.

'Apart from wearing a United States air force cap, you mean?'

'This place is unreal,' Rameau said. 'A minimal guard on the gate, a couple of men on the perimeter... It's a backwater.'

'I don't know. It makes sense, though,' Philip told him. 'If this is a conspiracy carried out without high command's knowledge. I mean, Buchner would have enough weight to throw around with these chaps, get himself some space, but he wouldn't want to be anywhere he was going to get himself a lot of unwelcome attention.' Philip looked skywards to the deep blue which was spread out above them, an expanse so vast as to make the slight trembling of fear building inside him seem small and inconsequential. To the north he could see the white contrails of aircraft many thousands of feet above them. He said to himself: 'Besides we are virtually on the bomber paths.'

'So what do we do?'

As Rameau spoke Voss reappeared and started to march back to the small buildings from which he had first appeared.

'I'd better take a look in that hangar,' Philip said.

He checked the pistol inside his waist-band and pulled some loose items, including Claire's photographs of Buchner and Voss out of his pockets.

'Take these for me.'

'What do you want me to do?'

Philip took a breath.

'London wants us to get Buchner,' he said. 'But I'm guessing, from what Claire says, Voss is our man. If something happens to me, kill him before he leaves this place.'

Rameau nodded.

'Good luck.'

Philip turned and edged back through the woods in an arc which took him away from the wire. Eventually he was at the rear of the large, guarded building into which Voss had gone.

Checking carefully in both directions, he crawled towards the fence and snipped a hole with a set of wire cutters. The sun was to his right now and it shone brightly into his face as he ran the short distance to the wall. He tried to peer through a corner of the glass where the paint used to blacken the window had peeled off. He could see a feint outline of a shape inside.

He edged his way along the building and took a peek around. The door was about halfway along and would surely be locked. Anyone going towards it could easily be spotted from the other buildings where most of the ground-crew was obviously based.

He returned to the window and taking a penknife from his pocket began to prise it open.

'The American bombers struck at Regensburg,' said Graumann.

'Regensburg? That far south?'

The captain looked from Buchner to Voss and the silent old man who said little, but just fiddled thoughtfully with the Nazi party badge on the lapel of his black jacket.

'Yes,' he went on. 'And I am afraid they are not returning. It appears they are flying on over the Alps towards their bases in North Africa. It's not something we've seen before.'

'Christ!' They were in the base's small operations room. Buchner shot a glance at the floor, and then back to Graumann.

The *Luftwaffe* man addressed him, his face serious. 'However, about an hour ago our coastal monitoring stations picked up another wave leaving England. An even bigger force. Two hundred, maybe more, aircraft. It seems unlikely they will hit a target and fly onwards also.'

Graumann's slightly self-satisfied smirk returned.

'Then we must be prepared,' Buchner stated, his back straightening. He clenched a celebratory fist in front of his face and smiled at Voss. 'Get your crew together, Joachim. You shall wait at your stations.'

Philip's fingers were bleeding as he twisted them under the frame and pulled. There was a splintering of wood and he stopped suddenly, afraid the sound would travel on the still forest air to the guard at the front. He let the window drop back in place for a moment and tiptoed to the side of the building. He could see the guard's back. He was standing to attention.

Figures moved over near the smaller buildings to the left. A group of people appeared to be coming Philip's way.

He stepped back quickly, pulled open the window and hauled himself up. The sound of his landing echoed around the concrete floor and walls of the building. He reached up. The damage was to the outside of the frame. From inside the window appeared closed as normal.

He moved forward towards the huge shape in the darkness and felt his way under a tail fin.

All of a sudden the area around the corner hangar was a hive of activity.

Having moved in the opposite direction to Philip, Rameau was now looking directly at the hangar doors and he watched with mounting concern as they were pulled open, giving him a perfect view of the large nose and four propellers which filled the space inside. He saw Voss and his crew sharing a few words around the aircraft as the ground-crew ran back and for all around them.

He looked for signs of Philip, at the hangar and at the edge of the trees where they had separated.

His hands moved nervously on the Sten gun. He knew the Germans were obviously making the airplane ready for take off. If Philip was to act, it had to be now.

Philip had never set foot inside an American Flying Fortress before but he knew they did not normally look like this.

Pulling himself in through the forward entrance door, he had glanced towards the pilot's position and noted that it seemed as normal. But coming through the bomb bay, he had seen the size of the device which had been fitted to take up the guts of the aircraft. It sat across the passage over the bomb bay so that Philip had to edge his way around it, gripping the thickened armour, new against the original structure of the craft.

He glanced over the large grey bomb, held tightly in place by a serious of metal bars and arms. It looked like the bomb bay doors were sealed.

He squeezed through to the rear, hearing voices outside and lay low in the tail gunner's position. Anyone coming to the rear of the bomb doors might see him. And he knew that in a B-17 crew that meant he would somehow have to deal with a radio operator, two waist gunners, the ball turret man and the tail gunner himself. He took a knife from his pocket and laid it at his side and nervously looked over his pistol.

'Schweinfurt,' Graumann said, indicating a place on the map east of Frankfurt.

'The factories,' Buchner said, taking off his hat and wiping a patch of sweat on his brow.

'There were attacks around the Pas de Calais. But diversionary and by the RAF. The Americans flew on to Schweinfurt.'

At the same moment a cool breeze blew into the hangar.

The cool breeze, Buchner thought, *was Joachim Voss*. His nephew stood immaculate in his flying gear, his jaw strong, the medal ribbon tight at his neck.

Buchner felt his breast swell with pride.

'They are turning?' Voss said.

Graumann showed him the map.

'They hit the target from the west, turned north and must surely soon be turning west for the run home.'

'Then they shall come back over Belgium and fly out over the Dutch coast and over the *Kanal*,' he said.

'Over the Channel, Joachim,' Buchner said, putting a hand on his shoulder, 'is where you shall leave them.'

Voss saluted each of his three-man crew as they climbed inside the plane.

He pulled himself up into the pilot's seat and found himself sitting in a position which had become so familiar to him at Rechlin. The compartment was not big enough to stand up or lay down straight in but he had spent years in the far tighter space of the Stuka.

He looked around him. To the front, sides and on the ceiling were the switches, controls, levers, dials and gauges he had studied for the past months. They were even on part of the floor. No matter how long he had spent working with them, he had never counted them. One hundred? One hundred and fifty?

He struggled to get himself comfortable, his flying boots, gloves and flying suit all restricting his movement. He pulled on his flying helmet, adjusting the earphones, oxygen mask and throat microphone. Then took a deep breath.

Pieper now slipped into the co-pilot's seat to begin checking the fuel and engine gauges. Although he was going to be manning the top turret gun, Pieper, a thin man with pock marked skin, was also an experienced flight engineer. He would be calling out the airspeed as Voss concentrated on getting the aircraft straight off down the grassy runway and clear of the tree tops.

Voss primed and started each engine, warming them up to 1,000 revolutions per minute, checking the prop feathering at 1,500. He then took the engines up further, watching Pieper's face as they made further checks.

Reichel, the navigator, was conducting his own checks too and preparing himself for take-off in the nose of the aircraft.

In the rear, Thiel, who would man the ball turret protecting the aircraft from below, came so near Philip that he could see the look of intense concentration on his face as he inspected the yoke which hung from the ceiling of the B-17 and held the ball turret in its precarious position half out of the bottom of the fuselage. *A suicide job*, some called it.

Philip squeezed into his corner and watched Thiel sit in one of the jump seat near the waist guns.

As the engine tone went higher and higher during Voss' checks, Philip held his breath as his cramped hiding place filling with noise, dust and a rush of cold air.

When the first of the 1,200-horsepower engines roared into life there was a battering of wings as a flock of birds broke from the trees behind Rameau.

Rameau narrowed his eyes at the deep, harsh sound. It was something like a giant motorbike.

He lay flat out, the Sten gun in front of him, and pushed his hand worriedly through his mop of dark hair. Somehow he would have to force himself up. He had to stop the plane.

The perimeter sentry was in the distance to his right, almost at the front gate. Both he and the gate guard had stopped for a moment to witness the sight of the US bomber moving forward out of the hangar.

Rameau ran down through the shallow gully which separated the trees from the fence and dived forward into the dust, his wire cutters already in his hand.

He snipped quickly through as the engines rose again. The olive-drab shape came out in a sharp turn to the right and then a wide half circle.

The B-17 was ready for take-off, its propellers a whir.

Rameau pulled himself through the wire and got up on one knee, releasing the safety catch on the Sten.

Slowly the aircraft started to move forward. Rameau was no more than 300 feet from it and it was slowly coming nearer and nearer, its engines a deep throaty roar. It would pass within 100 feet of him.

He heard a shout to his right: the sentry had seen him. So had those in the hangar but they dare not fire now for fear of hitting the airplane as it crossed between them.

It was coming now and he could not miss.

He aimed for the cockpit, the Sten at chest height, his eyes looking clean down the sights. He could see the pilot's face.

He pulled the trigger, expecting the gun to shudder in his hands. Nothing. Just an empty click.

The bomber's wings shook slightly and the starboard wheel left the ground a fraction before the port.

Rameau dropped the Sten and took the pistol from his belt.

The nose of the airplane lifted, obscuring his sight of the cockpit but he fired three quick shots which pinged into the aluminium between Thiel and Philip.

There was a screech above the drone as the bomber whipped past him.

The perimeter sentry was running towards Rameau, his Schmeisser submachine gun in his hands.

Rameau turned, hearing the machine gun open up.

He pulled himself through the fence, ripping his clothing and the skin on his arm as he did so.

There was more shouting behind him now and the earth at his feet broke up as bullets cracked through the air.

He tumbled into the perimeter ditch and then scrabbled up the other side. As he did so he caught a glimpse of a figure close inside the fence. He half-turned, fired two quick shots and saw the guard throw himself to the floor.

Rameau tore into the woods, hot lead ripping into the branches and disintegrating the leaves around him.

Chapter Thirty-Nine

Reichel first set a course north-west, then north. In a short time Voss spotted the contrails and then the distinct shapes of a number of B-17s flying a couple of thousand feet above them and returning to their base in the south east of England.

Skimming across the rich green Belgian countryside, Voss turned north-west again to run along the same route as the bombers above him.

They were at under a thousand feet and Philip could see the hedges and houses disappearing behind him as if they were toys spread out on a lush green carpet.

Philip crawled forward and could see Thiel's position in the ball turret.

'My God,' Pieper said and Voss craned his neck to see a squadron of Messerschmitt 109s buzzing the bombers like bees.

As the crew watched the sky over their heads it seemed suddenly filled with aircraft. Messerschmitt 110s diving between the Americans. Escorting P-47s chasing the *Luftwaffe* pilots away from the bombers. A fighter went into a dive, fire ripping from its engine. As it ploughed through the blue sky the flames died out but Philip saw no parachute and it smashed into the ground less than a mile away. Philip craned his head upwards. It was strange to watch this terrifying battle in which men were being killed from this distance below. A bomber banked sharply and streaked earthwards like a mighty eagle, mortally wounded.

Another B-17 tried to break free from the mêlée, diving within a couple of thousand feet of *Pericles*. Two fighters went with it, hunter and hunted firing mercilessly on each other. Suddenly, the bomber broke in two, the front half of the fuselage, wings and cockpit, rising up as if in slow motion, before both halves tumbled away.

He wondered how long it would be until they reached the coast and the English Channel beyond.

Back in the small hut, Buchner watched the clock. His hands were clasped firmly together. *Pericles* was in real danger at that moment, he knew. From the *Luftwaffe* itself. Fighters would be scrambled from Woensdrecht and Deelen and Schipol. And there were the American P-47s if something had gone wrong.

If only there were someway he could know what was happening. He wondered how the news would break. What would be the English reaction? How would they describe what had happened? What would be the response in Berlin?

This, this waiting, he thought, it took him back to Gleiwitz and that drab hotel at the outbreak of war. The waiting and the excitement. Knowing that you were a part of something truly momentous, a moment of supreme importance to your nation, to world history. They had not known then, of course, how momentous it would be; what a truly incredible sequence of events it would trigger. It brought the world tumbling down on Poland, on France, Holland, on Luxembourg. Others had known. The Führer. The planners. Not he. But now he was in control.

He looked at his hands. They were damp with sweat. He had to prise them apart as if one belonged to someone else, someone who would not let go. Yes, here he was. On the brink of something again. He had helped start the war. He would help close it. And with victory. His heart raced.

He opened his leather attaché case and took out a bottle of Courvoiser, blew into a glass and poured himself a generous measure of brandy.

Something moved in the corner of the room and he looked up. It was one of the *Luftwaffe* police officers. He wandered how long he had been standing there.

'Herr Standartenführer,' he said. 'I am afraid we have found no trace of the intruder. He appears to have had a vehicle in the forest.'

'Then order the roads closed down,' Buchner told him. 'Tell them there is a known terrorist nearby. When he is found they are to report directly to me.'

'There is something else, sir,' said the man. 'There were two breaches of the perimeter fence.'

Buchner's face turned pink with rage.

'Then have the whole area searched again,' he shouted, banging his fist on the table.

He stood for a moment, the chair legs screeching in the floor, but there was nowhere to go.

He tried to focus his mind on Voss. Voss was in the air. *Pericles* was in the air. The intruder had fled. Nothing could go wrong.

Voss saw Antwerp out of the co-pilot's window and then Brugge off to his left. 'Dutch coast ahead,' he said.

Below him, Philip watched people picnicking and swimming on the Dutch coast. It was another world.

There was some firing from German naval ships below, a cracking in the air outside the aircraft, the stench of a thick black smoke. The plane's starboard wing rose and then levelled.

Thiel cursed.

Philip edged forward, feeling the wind from the waist gunner positions catch his jacket and hair.

He glanced outwards. They had passed the flak of the coastal defences. He watched the jagged coast disappear behind him. The next landmass would be England.

Suddenly a black shape streaked across his vision and there was a deafening explosion. Philip fell flat on his face, hot lumps of metal streaking above his head and bursting against the side of the fuselage.

The B-17 lurched upwards.

'Take him, Pieper.'

Voss manoeuvred to give his top turret man a clear shot at the fighter. Pieper's guns opened up.

Philip clung to the floor as Voss twisted and jinked.

'He's coming again.'

Voss turned the other way as the fighter passed the port wing.

'Strange firing at one of our own, sir,' Pieper called out.

'If he hits our cargo we are all dead and the mission has failed,' shouted Voss. 'Shoot him out of the sky!'

Thiel scrambled out of his position and headed for a waist gun. Holding the side of the fuselage he pulled himself backwards.

He was a well-built man, his bulk exaggerated by his heavy flak jacket.

He had been through the horrors of 100 missions over England and Russia, seen friends ripped apart by English flak and the cannon fire of the Spitfire. *Every mission had seemed a suicide mission so he might as well crew a weapon which he knew would really hurt them.*

He had seen all the horror. But nothing prepared him for seeing Philip lunge at him at the back of the B-17.

He half-caught, half-deflected the flying figure so that they both crumpled against the mounting of the starboard waist gun so that its barrel lifted upwards with the blow.

Philip twisted his body, freeing his right arm and pushing the knife forward. He felt it bury deep inside Thiel. But the German had his hands around his neck and they were squeezing hard with the force of huge arm muscles.

Thiel's face went red as he turned Philip onto his back.

Philip's chest was in agony. The German was choking him and pushing his body into his stomach at the same time.

Philip let go of the knife and brought his right arm up to push his fingers into the other man's mouth. Digging in his nails, he ripped outwards into his cheek.

Thiel screamed and released his grip, lifting his body upwards.

The plane lurched, Voss taking it higher again.

Pieper fired another short burst as the fighter came at them again. This time the Messerschmitt was also greeted by fire from the navigator Reichel who had shifted into the Plexiglass nose to add to the bomber's fire power. They each raked thirteen rounds a second into the attacking aircraft.

As Philip pulled himself from under Thiel he saw the hilt of his knife buried in the other man's chest.

Finally, Thiel saw it too. A look of absolute surprise crossed his face. He looked up at Philip, staggered and fell forwards against the contoured curve of the fuselage.

Philip held the open sill and looked out.

They were climbing fast above the sea. He held his jacket tight around him. He was cold, his breath was short.

He could see a Messerschmitt 110 circling behind their tail, ready to come back at them again. *Shoot us down.*

There was smoke coming from one of the engines on the right wing.

Philip looked above. He was light-headed, dizzy and for a moment he thought he imagined the shapes above him. *No, they were passing below the main bomber fleet.*

Voss levelled out. The German fighter came at them again, an air-to-air rocket screaming alongside the body of the plane.

The B-17's engines groaned and the plane went into a dive so steep that Philip thought they were going straight into the sea. *Voss is dead.* He shut his eyes and gripped the gun mounting. *Thank God, this is it.*

But then Philip was pushed into the floor again and they levelled out.

'He thinks we've had it,' Voss told his crew.

'Turning point approaching,' said Reichel. 'Turning south-west. Should be over target in 20 minutes.'

Philip stood. *Southwest.* As the plane banked left he saw the returning US bomber fleet hold its course thousands of feet above them. They were returning home, continuing on towards somewhere in East Anglia or Lincolnshire. *Pericles*, with its deadly cargo, was turning for London.

They were coming in low. Fishing boats, naval vessels, people and cars on the coast streaked by beneath them.

'Thiel?' Voss said. No response from the man in the ball turret.

Thames Haven. Larger ships. Jetties. Rectangle shapes ahead. Tilbury Docks.

They were flying steady, perfect height. Straight into the heart of London. *No-one would ever forget this moment. German children would re-enact it for generations to come.*

In the nose Reichel thought back three years to his night-time missions here, setting the city ablaze: the bombs creating orange and yellow bursts in the darkness below like burning coals at the base of a giant grate. *They had survived their blitz, but the people below were ignorant now. Totally unaware that today the heart would be ripped out of their city. Forever.*

'Pieper, check on Thiel.'

Pieper had already slipped down from the top turret to look over Voss' shoulder as they came up the Thames. Now he made his way around the edge of the adapted bomb bay.

As he squeezed through the radio room door, Philip stepped out of the curve of the fuselage, pushed his pistol into his stomach and fired. Pieper crumpled to the floor.

Philip rushed forward, edging around the device at the centre of the aircraft and coming through under the pilot's position.

He saw Reichel turning in the nose to investigate, but was already pushing himself into the narrow gap behind and under the pilot and co-pilot's seats.

Voss turned, his blue eyes alight, betraying every thought to Philip in an instance: his bewilderment, then his recognition of the danger and then of his decision to turn the lethal aircraft instantly into the ground, buildings and people below.

Voss turned back in his seat, the city of London a blur in his vision: the dockyards, the houses of the east end beyond...

His hands gripped the controls.

Philip's pistol, curled around the back of the pilot's seat, fired two rapid shots, shattering Voss' spine.

Voss's arms and body went limp, his head lolling in shock, his eyes gazing suddenly lifeless through the cockpit windows.

Philip pulled himself up into the co-pilot's seat on Voss' right and took the controls.

He banked the plane left and began to gain height.

As he did so he felt a movement behind him as Reichel reached up and pulled at his side.

Two shots rang out in the same instance.

Philip's bullet ripped through Reichel's neck, killing him instantly.

Reichel's shot shattered two of Philip's ribs, the bullet exiting his chest and passing though the right hand cockpit window.

Philip grimaced in terrible pain and coughed blood.

His fingers twisted on the controls.

His arms and legs felt strong, rooted to the seat and the controls. But his chest wheezed and begged for air.

In agony at every breath Philip held the B-17 steady, his mind crazed by the pain. He knew he had to head south, somehow get back over the English Channel but he could not read the instruments. His eyes closed and his head pounded. As he tried to turn the controls the left side of his torso appeared to be gripped in a metal vice which was slowly being turned tighter and tighter so that his ribs cracked and his lungs burst.

Buchner had watched the time pass. Wiedler, his aide, was in radio contact with their agent in London. Within minutes the agent would know what happened. Within a short time they should report.

But Wiedler's call had not come. Like Falkenberg, he should have left. Got away and waited for news. But he was a soldier and needed to be here, to await the reports. Until he heard from London he was incapable of doing anything.

The clock had revealed when Voss would be over the target. Buchner had watched it click onwards. He had allowed more time. Still no information. *Something had gone wrong.* From being sure of success he was suddenly as instantly certain of failure.

He tried a number of times to call Wilhelm Falkenberg. Three times he reached someone who said Falkenberg was unavailable. On the third occasion he assumed Wilhelm had been arrested, but then, finally, he rang back. He sounded frightened, broken. 'I cannot talk,' Wilhelm Falkenberg said. 'We have failed.' Then the line went dead.

Buchner left the receiver on the desk in front of him. When an orderly replaced it, it rang again.

The *Luftwaffe* orderly answered it.

'Herr Standartenführer? It is for you.'

Wiedler? Buchner took the telephone quickly.

'Yes?'

'Buchner?' the voice on the end of the line was harsh, accusing.

'Yes. Who is this?'

'Schmidt, Gestapo.'

'How can I help you, Herr Schmidt?'

'We are at your house,' said the voice. 'We require you here urgently. We have some rather urgent questions for you.'

'I don't know what you are talking about, Schmidt,' Buchner responded, straightening his back. 'I do not particularly like the manner in which you are addressing me. Who is your superior officer?'

'Buchner, were you aware that there are two dead men in your house? One of whom is a *Luftwaffe* officer.'

'I didn't know.'

'Then I suppose you also do not know about certain incriminating papers which we have found at your desk?'

'This is outrageous,' Buchner blustered.

'I do not propose to discuss this over the telephone. These are extremely grave matters.'

Buchner sighed, allowing the receiver to drop a little. But he could still hear the shrill voice on the other end as it continued: 'Where are you, please?'

Buchner told him slowly.

'Who is in charge there?'

Buchner handed the telephone to Graumann who answered the Gestapo man curtly a few times and then passed the receiver back to the orderly.

'I am afraid I have been ordered to put you under arrest, Herr Standartenführer,' he said. 'I'm sorry. You are not to leave the base until the Gestapo arrives.'

Buchner nodded and put his hand on the table top to steady himself.

'Perhaps, I could just get some air?' he said.

Graumann nodded and indicated to the orderly that he go with him.

It was a beautiful evening. The forest sparkled in the dying sun. Even the shadows, the dark corners, looked magical.

Buchner buttoned his coat. Not because he was cold, but because it was the neat thing to do. It was time to tidy up. He smiled. *The all-consuming might of Germany would go on. He gave himself to it.*

The orderly never saw the punch that floored him. He crashed to the dusty pathway in front of the building with a single gasp of astonishment.

Then Buchner knelt in the grass, curled in a ball, put the end of the barrel of his Luger pistol into his mouth and screwed his eyes tight shut.

Philip flew onwards. Westwards. Holding a steady height.

Two engines had been damaged in the fighter attacks over the sea. One had long since died. The other went in a belch of black smoke as Philip crossed the Berkshire Downs.

His brow, knotted in pain, was thick with a sweat which burned his eyes. The sound of the aircraft melded into the screaming inside his head. He saw his mother and his father, heard them at his shoulders, holding him upright in the seat. He saw the fields of his farm below him. Heard little Jimmy's voice: *Wait for me!* They were cycling down the country roads towards Gorey, lifting their feet off the pedals, watching the birds dipping in the sky. He held on, felt the soothing breeze in his hair.

Half-an-hour later he crossed into the Bristol Channel south of the city of Bristol itself.

His eyes saw blue and grey, but could not distinguish between the sea and the sky.

Not once now did he think of the awful cargo in the back of the plane. He just wanted to keep the plane alive as long as he could. *Onwards. Onwards. Feet off the pedals. No hands on the handlebars.* It was a feat of determination and endurance rather than courage.

He was not thinking of his own death either. Because he longed for it. Or rather it was sleep he longed for. He did not think of it as death at all. One day he would wake up. But first he had to sleep, shut his eyes and feel the awful agony no more.

The final sighting of the US bomber was by the skipper of a merchant vessel. At 2006hrs, he recorded: 'Spot large aircraft, probably B-17, United States airforce. Flames can be seen from starboard wing. Flying westwards. Out to sea. Much talk among crew of it being a bad omen. It appeared the aircraft was flying itself.'

Chapter Forty

James Mortain's eyes turned from the crumbling brick wall at the foot of his garden and fixed unnervingly on mine.

'They thought I was dead,' he said. 'I was in hospital in Jersey. Under arrest, of course. Under the *Nacht und Nebel* order I was dead, I suppose. No-one had any right to know about me and I had no right to know about my family.'

The last of the sun had gone from the garden and the evening had turned very cold. My arms, a little reddened by the sun, had that chilled blistering of slightly burnt skin. It made me shiver.

'The soldier who shot me actually showed a lot of concern for my welfare. I was in hospital for eight months. I had still not recovered when the Germans finally left. And I was half-starved then, of course. We all were on the island. Even the Germans.'

'What then?'

He put the shoebox down onto the table and pulled the two sides of his cardigan more firmly around him.

'I didn't know what had happened to my brother. I knew my mother had been taken away... She was looked after well and survived. She had thought I was dead, of course. The cruelty of what they had done to her by saying I was dead only really struck her when I found her. Then she dared think Philip was alive too.

'We discovered he wasn't, of course. We were told he had died in Belgium. My mother urged me to find out more but I hesitated: too many twists of fate, too much pain. I knew we had to accept he had died in the war like millions of others and somehow move on.

'We could never settle in Jersey, you see. People were different, they wanted to put the war behind them. I think some of them were embarrassed by what had happened to my mother, felt they could have resisted more. They couldn't, of course. We were only a small island.

'I learned about Alice and thought finding her would help us heal: she was someone he had loved and there was no-one else like that except mother and I. Finding her took time, but it brought us to Wales. We took a small tenant farm for a while. That eventually got to be too much and we moved here.

'I looked after mother but she wasn't the same. Sometimes I couldn't help but think that maybe a tiny part of her was more prepared to have lost me than Philip, who knows. I was ashamed to think it but I couldn't help it.

'Anyway, I left it all well alone until she died.' He swallowed hard. 'But, of course, it nagged at me. I spent years trying to piece together the story. Piece by tiny piece. I met people through RAF and USAAF associations trying to find out what happened to Philip, took forever to find Neville Bachelor, but he told me virtually nothing.

'I found Rameau though and went to see him a few times, but this wasn't until the 1970s. He was a marvellous fellow. He would drive me around places he knew Philip had been. Everywhere. He was very good to me. I found Claire Winter too, and exchanged some letters with her.' He stroked the thick wrinkles on the back of his hand with the tip of a finger. 'You are the first person I have told it all to.'

'Falkenberg?' I asked gently.

'You can find him in history books. Somehow he escaped the wrath of Hitler. Even had his son, who had been sent to the Russian Front, brought back. Falkenberg was going to be prosecuted at the end of the war. But somehow he flourished. Did as well at the end of the second war as he had at the end of the first.'

'How did you cope?'

He shook his head slowly.

'My mother died in her bedroom upstairs here,' he said. 'We were very poor. I was poor then, poor now.'

Mortain was tired but I went on.

'One thing I don't understand. The chemicals. On the plane. What happened to them?'

'Still there, I suppose,' he shrugged. 'I wondered about it myself. But, ironically, it is just how they got rid of most of the Germans' store of the gas after the war. Into the sea. Saddam Hussein used it, you know. *Tabun*. Against the Iranians.'

I shivered.

'We better go inside,' I told him.

I held my hand near his elbow as his stiff limbs lifted his body out of the chair. I did not touch him, just stood there in case he fell. He took his stick and started back into the house. The overweight spaniel followed us slowly.

The corridor through the centre of the stone house had gone cold.

I thanked him for his time and turned down another cup of tea. I said I would let myself out but Mortain insisted on walking me to the door.

When my eyes again met his he looked up at me, defiant and strong. He had sensed there was one more question and he did not seem surprised.

'London?' I said hesitantly. 'The attack... How many would have died?'

Mortain's back straightened. 'I lost my brother. A brother I looked up to and loved very much. That is why that day matters to me.'

Laugharne Castle looked dark and menacing as I walked to my car. I imagined there were knights on its ramparts and emaciated prisoners in its dungeons.

It was late. I felt a long way from home.

Milford Haven was in the wrong direction, but I had to see Tom. This time I would tell him what *I* knew.

I checked my mobile phone. We were in a dip. A communications black-hole. One of the last.

I started the car and drove in silence along the coast through Pendine.

The sun had gone but it was not quite dark. I put on my lights. My eyes ached. *Wasn't this the most dangerous time to be driving?* I suddenly felt frightened, spooked, on edge. Someone walking over my grave.

My lights flashed eerily over the front gate of the MoD research establishment. I wondered about the experiments that had gone on there in the past. A few years ago I'd read they had put a bunker busting bomb through its paces on the famous dunes of Pendine Sands, before using it for real in Iraq.

I carried on where the road runs flat and straight and parallel to the famous beach, once the location of a contest to be the fastest man on land, a contest which ended with a car spinning, and decapitation and death on the hard sand.

I changed down to second and took the tight turn at the foot of Pendine hill.

Then, as I reached the summit of the hill, my mobile phone came to life. The ring chime and the flashing blue screen startled me.

I looked over and saw *Voicemail* lighting up the screen. I pulled over. My eyes were tired.

I called for the message.

It was Tom. He must have called while I was out of the range of a mast in Laugharne. He wanted to talk to me urgently. *Me too. Have I got news for you this time, Tom.*

I checked my watch. It was not too late to call back.

I clicked down to his number and called. Tom answered almost immediately.

'Boy,' he said, without any pleasantries at all. 'We went out again. The plane ain't there.'

I was silent.

'Could they have moved it?' I said at last.

'Might have. There's been time.'

The line crackled between us. It was very quiet in the car. Just the strange buzzing of the mobile phone and my breathing.

'We have nothing,' he went on, an anger in his voice. 'Charlie took no tapes. But I know exactly what I saw.' He spoke as if he had forgotten that I was there too.

My seatbelt was suddenly very tight on my chest. I ran my hand behind it to find relief.

In my rear view mirror I watched the lights of a car coming up the hill towards me. It passed at a crawl and then slowed down further as it turned the corner ahead. Its brake lights blazed a dazzling red which spread in front of my eyes.

'Me too,' I said.

March 2020

21769174R00141

Printed in Great Britain
by Amazon